<u>Nicholas Pells 1967 – 2020</u>

I remember the adventures we planned. I remember well the plots we made and the things we did. I remember fighting monsters in the wilderness in which we camped. I remember we would fall out over girls — and other things, and yet we would always be friends again — soon and long after the girls had gone. Through thick and thin we stuck together, and we fought every challenge which came our way.

Yes, I remember the adventures we planned, on those rainy Saturdays, when we were kids, stuck inside the house, and the make-believe monsters we fought, camping in my parents' back garden. Though we lost touch in the end, I always had you somewhere in my mind and heart.

Now I remember the day I heard you had lost your biggest battle. I am sorry I was not around when the end came. But fear not! For as we planned all those years ago, on that rainy Saturday afternoon, we will meet again and drive those Datsun 240zs' along that highway, while blasting out to the world, the music of the Electric Light Orchestra.

I miss you, my friend.

<u>Acknowledgments:</u>

To everyone who has believed and supported me, thank you.

For Scrappy: My companion and friend of 13 years. I miss you every day, old man. We'll walk together again when we meet on the Rainbow Bridge.

Devolution of a Species

By

M.E. Ellington

www.mess-flicks.com

Produced by Martyn Ellington.
Cover design by Martyn Ellington.
Artwork by Arani Creative.

Paperback ISBN: 978-1-7394162-4-9
E-book ISBN: 978-1-7394162-5-6

www.martynellington.com

Prologue

Abiogenesis: the natural process of life arising from non-living matter.

After the creation of the cosmos, the solar system, and our little insignificant rock. Life began not with a burst of color and the diversity which we see today, but rather, with a trickle of greyness some 3.5 billion years ago. From that moment, life evolved from the most basic of forms to the most complex that has ever walked the face of this planet — The Homo Sapien.
It is our complexity, our absolute mastery of our planet, and our intelligence that keep us at the top. We are the pinnacle of evolution. Nothing, other than our own destructive abilities can remove us from what is ours; the utter dominance of the earth, and all other species upon it.

Or so we thought...

"On that day, the seas will be full, the forests lush and green and the air will be clear. The animals of Earth will live without the memory and fear of man and in harmony with each other. On that same day, mankind will have long been dead."

Joceline Mercier.

1

With an almost silent click and a flash of its small blue light, the flat-screen TV came to life, and Jeff Eastwood was offered more bad news as he ate his breakfast. The two BBC news anchors sat on the ergonomically designed couch looking concerned as they relayed yet more details of suspected terrorist attacks, anarchic public demonstrations, and rioting. It was early, too early for news such as this, the clock on the screen displayed 06:47 a.m., and outside it was still dark. January in England is a long dark and for most a depressing month. After the highs of the Christmas festivities comes the reality of the New Year, and the absolute drudgery of it starting over again like some bad joke. And for many, the credit card bills for the festive period.

He sighed as he took the first sip of his morning tea. Coffee would follow later, but it was always tea first thing. As a special adviser to the UK government on social cohesion, he knew today's news of further rioting, and the increasing, seemingly random violent attacks that are being reported would mean another day of meetings and head-scratching.

In the last six months, there had been an exponential increase in violent behavior around the world and no one anywhere was able to explain why it was happening. These new attacks weren't based on ideals or religious, cultural, or racial differences. This new wave of violence seemed to have no pattern and no predisposition. They were indiscriminate, and sometimes within family groups. And that to the authorities was the worst kind of trend. With no pattern, they could not predict, plan, or even guess where or who would be next. One thing was for sure, it seemed that around the world, human nature was changing. Up to this point, the World Health Organization (WHO) had kept it under wraps. The first reports didn't seem to spark much interest in the general populace who bothered to watch and read the news. But as more attacks were being filmed and uploaded onto social media sites, trends were forming online. Blogs had grown in numbers, and more people were creating, entering, and contributing to online discussions and forums.

As he sat finishing his toast, Jeff recognized the familiar thud of steps on the stairs. He turned away from the TV and smiled at Danny, his seven-year-old son, who'd entered the kitchen with all the usual vigor and exuberance we all have at that age. Wide-eyed and innocent to the world outside Danny smiled at his dad, and Jeff returned it tenfold.

"Hi, son," Jeff said, picking Danny up and sitting him at the table.

"Hi, Daddy."

"Is it Coco Pops? or Cheerio's today?" Jeff asked, already knowing the answer.

"Coco Pops," Danny yelled back excitedly.

"Of course, it is," Jeff replied.

It wasn't often that they did have sugary cereals in the cupboard, but now and again it was a treat, and besides, whenever they bought them, they didn't last long. As he poured the milk, he could hear softer, slower footsteps making their way to the kitchen, and another smile spread across Jeff's face, but this was a different smile, and it was a different love.

He placed the cereal down and lifted his head as Lynne, his wife of twelve years joined them. They had met at a conference when Jeff had worked for the National Health Service, where Lynne still works in the Davidson Ward, at Kings Hospital London.

"Morning, hun," She said, as she took a clean bowl from the cupboard.

"Morning," Jeff replied smiling from behind the mug of his now *only-just warm* tea.

"I see he went with the Coco pops this morning," Lynne said, tussling Danny's hair.

Jeff smiled and then winked at Danny, who tried to wink back but only managed a blink.

"How's the news today?" She asked as she watched the images displayed on the screen.

"Not good, another riot, this time in Los Angeles, and another violent attack in Munich."

"Do you think it's getting worse?" She asked.

Jeff put his tea down and nodded with a look of uneasiness. "We're compiling any information we're getting from the World Health Organization that isn't religious or racial based. Anything that's random or doesn't fit with any known previous patterns."

"We've seen an increase in admissions," Lynne added and continued. "People with savage wounds, like an animal has attacked them, but it never is. It's always another person. Do we need to worry?"

Jeff sighed and shrugged. "To be honest, I don't know, I don't think so. Not yet anyway."

"You don't sound convinced," Lynne said.

"For now, don't worry. We live in a good area. If things become too bad, I'll be the first to know. Just be careful at work."

Lynne smiled and nodded. She was assured for now. "I'm on a late shift tonight so I'll take Danny to school, the sitter will be here when you get in. Don't be too late, will you?"

"No, I'll be in before eight," He replied. Lynne turned back to Danny. "Come on tiger, time to get ready for school."

Lynne led Danny back up the stairs whilst Jeff cleared away the morning pots. He gathered his keys and coat and headed for the door. "See you soon, love you both,"

He shouted as he left the house, pulling the door shut behind him, and checking it. Jeff knew he wouldn't get a reply. They wouldn't hear him. But so long as he'd said it, he felt settled. He got into his Lexus and started the commute to work.

Claire Banks @claire_banks87 – 45mins Just watched @BBCNews. No mention of latest outbreak in African village. Selective news as usual, traveling there to uncover truth.

Forty minutes passed quickly after Jeff had left for work. Lynne was now standing at the bottom of the stairs waiting for Danny, and her patience, as well as time, was running out. Living in central London presented many challenges. But by far the biggest day-to-day problem they faced was the traffic. Journeys that used to take ten minutes only a few years ago now sometimes took over an hour, and if Danny didn't hurry, he'd be late for school again.

"Come on Danny, we'll be late," Lynne shouted from the bottom of the stairs.

"Okay, okay Mom, God!" Danny replied as he stomped down the stairs toward her.

"You know Miss Pickman won't be happy if you're late for school."

Danny didn't answer, he merely tutted pushing past Lynne as he walked through the passageway.

Lynne followed him, closing the link door between the house and the large double garage, to find Danny standing impatiently beside her Toyota SUV as if to make the point that he was now waiting for her, and if he were to be late, it would be his mom's fault. Lynne helped Danny into the car before she sat in the driver's seat. Danny was in the opposite rear seat. This was so she was able to see him in the rearview mirror. She smiled at him, started the engine, and pushed the fob which opened the garage door. Pulling out of the driveway, they started what should be a short two-mile journey to school. In reality, however, it could take forty minutes, but with any luck, not today.

"Have you got your lunch sweetie?" Lynne asked Danny.

"Yes, Mom" came the direct reply.
Lynne looked at him in the rear-view mirror. *He's in an awful mood* she thought to herself. They stopped outside the school gates, and Lynne turned around to face Danny to say goodbye, to tell him to be safe, and to tell him she loved him, as she did every day. But Danny had gone with a slam of the car door. She watched him disappear into the entrance where she noticed Miss Pickman waving at her. Lynne waved back and smiled, and then set off for work.

Jeff pulled into his usual parking spot, and as usual, he arrived at work with only minutes to spare.

Though he had no immediate manager, he was still conscious of his punctuality. He entered the building and made his way to his office, saying the customary hellos to everyone he passed along the way. As he sat behind his desk Colin Moyles knocked on his door holding a large bundle of envelopes. Colin had worked for Jeff for eighteen months. Much younger than Jeff, he'd taken on the role of a personal assistant, though Colin hadn't started with that intention. The role itself kind of evolved that way.

"Morning, Jeff," Colin said.

"Morning," Jeff replied.

"How's the family?"

"Fine thanks, Colin," Jeff answered scanning through the envelopes and memos looking to see if anything jumped out at him.

"How's yours?" Jeff returned the courtesy.

"Yeah, good thanks. Claire Banks has been on again this morning; she still wants an interview." Colin said as he placed the neatly stacked and sorted mail onto Jeff's desk.

"Remind me who she is," Jeff said, not looking up as he thumbed his way through the pile.

"She's that independent reporter, the one that claims there's a link to the increase in violent behavior."

"Is she calling back?" Jeff asked.

"Said she's off to Africa, something about a village attack near Maputo she says is linked to the attack in Montana."

"How the hell did she arrive at that conclusion?" Jeff asked.

"Same witness statements, the same type of injuries. She's flying there to intercept two World Health Organization doctors she says are going there to cover it up," Colin scoffed.

"Bloody conspiracy theorists! Nothing better to do than get in the way. Okay, next time she calls put her through. I'll set her straight." Jeff replied.

"You can read her Twitter feed, goes by the name of *@claire_banks87*."

"Yeah, cos Twitter is something I have *all* the time for," Jeff said.

"Okay, do you want a coffee now?" Colin asked as he began to leave.

Jeff looked up at him and smiled "Do I ever!"

Colin left the office, whilst Jeff continued to thumb through the mail until one envelope caught his attention. Marked *COBRA*, the name used by the UK Government emergency response cabinet, this would require Jeff's immediate attention. With the increasing acts of violence around the world, he'd been expecting this, if not a little sooner.

He slid his letter opener along the sealed edge of the envelope's flap and slid out the contents.

<u>Top Secret</u>

For Authorised Personnel only

MEMORANDUM FOR A COBRA
MEETING ON THE ESCALATING
VIOLENCE IN THE UK AND GLOBALLY

This meeting will take place in the cabinet
office briefing room, Whitehall.

The agenda for the meeting will be confirmed
at the start of the briefing.

Date: January 25th

Registration is at 09:00 hrs. The meeting will
start at 09:30 hrs. Prompt.

Jeff entered the details into his phone's calendar and then filed the memo. Colin brought him a fresh coffee. Jeff nodded and smiled in acknowledgment and then sifted through the rest of the mail before turning his attention to the fifty-four emails that were waiting for him. The day proceeded much like any other, a series of meetings, some of which were to discuss previous meetings or even the next meeting. These irritated him. Too much time is spent considering, thinking, and procrastinating rather than doing. But it was driven by those who had their own political agenda. It seemed by a new breed of career managers that specialized in appearing productive and busy but actually weren't. Jeff felt sure we all know one, or worse, have one.

With the daylight long faded and his office now illuminated by the soft glow of the ergonomically designed lighting, his eyes were becoming weary. He checked the time, 07:26 p.m. Lynne would be at work now, and he remembered his promise to be in for eight o'clock. If he was to keep it, he'd have to leave now. Jeff stretched and yawned; the day had been a testing one. More reports and more violence, and more pleading for the news stations to keep the reporting to a minimum. Like the problems across Europe before this had started, much of the troubles had not made it to air. Either on the radio or TV.

Like all information, it needed to be controlled. Of course, people could find it if they wanted to, but mercifully for those who select what news we see on our screens, most people are too lazy, or scared to find out what's truly happening. And instead, they like to take comfort in the short, yet censored reports the main news channels carried, and believe the soundbites and *fluffy* versions of real life. He stared at the half-empty coffee mug on his desk before locking his computer and leaving. A short time later he was home, though as with many a night after a long tiring day, he couldn't recall the journey home in any detail. He checked the dash clock. 07:58 p.m.

"Home for eight," He said to himself, as he drove the Lexus into the garage, and pushed the button to close the door.
He entered the kitchen where Joanne, their eighteen-year-old sitter was watching the TV.

"Hi, Mr. Eastwood," She said, politely.

"Hi, Joanne," Jeff replied, and continued "Everything ok here?"

"Everything is fine." She answered, hesitantly.

"You don't sound too sure?" Jeff asked her, pulling off his tie, and pouring himself a glass of wine.

"No, no, it's fine. It's just that Danny was a little, well, naughty tonight, it's not like him."

"In what way"? Jeff sounded concerned. She was right, usually, Danny is polite and respectful.

"Well, he wouldn't get ready for bed, and when I tried to make him go to bed, he swore at me and threatened to hit me." She said, obviously a little upset.

"Is he feeling okay?" Jeff asked.

"I think so, I mean, I didn't ask him. He went to bed eventually, he's asleep now, I checked on him just before you came home."

"Okay, Joanne. Thank you, get yourself home." Jeff handed her the customary fee and she left. He made his way up the stairs and to Danny's room. Popping his head around the corner he watched as his little boy slept peacefully. He looked angelic as if he was innocence personified.

How could you be anything but charming? He thought to himself as he turned and headed toward his bedroom. Jeff hadn't intended to fall asleep still dressed and lying on top of the bed, he'd sat on it to get changed, to get out of the suit and tie and into a baggy T-shirt and joggers. But the warmth of the house and the sound of the rain on the window had lulled him into a deep sleep. A sleep he remained in until Lynne had returned home from work in the early hours and woke him after she found him curled up on the bed, half undressed. He remembered her nudging him, the rain still tapping on the windows and the sound of the wind, but he didn't remember getting into bed, or a conversation between them.

At 06:25 a.m. his alarm sounded as it did every weekday, he turned and spooned into the back of Lynne wrapping his arms around her.

"Morning sexy," He said tenderly.

"Morning to you too," She replied giggling. She turned and kissed him before getting out of bed and pulling on her robe. "Another day begins." She said as she left the bedroom.

Jeff could hear the customary laughing and chuckling coming from Danny's bedroom as Lynne woke him. As warm as his bed was, Jeff knew that he too now had to start the day and that as always would begin with a cup of tea, some milk, and two sugars. Lynne entered the kitchen with Danny close behind.

"Morning son," Jeff said smiling.

"Hi Daddy," Was the reply.

"And what's for breakfast this morning?"

"Coco Pops," Danny shouted with a spare amount of enthusiasm.

"I thought as much," Jeff said smiling while pouring the milk on the cereal.

"How was your shift?" Jeff turned the conversation to Lynne.

"It was interesting, to say the least," She replied.

"How so?"

"The police brought in a guy who they thought was drunk, going by his slurred speech and the way he was behaving. But when we finally took some blood his toxicity report showed no alcohol or drugs of any kind, just a highly raised level of lymphocyte activity."

"And that is?" Jeff asked.

"Well, that's just a general term for the white blood cells, but the puzzle was the massive increase in T cell and NK cell activity," Lynne replied.

"Yeah, absolutely, you lost me again," Jeff said.

"I keep forgetting you're a dummy," Lynne said laughing "What it means is that we think his body is fighting some kind of viral or pathogen-type infection. But it's rare to see such an unbalanced level of these types of cells, both do very different jobs in protecting us."

"What's his name?" Jeff asked.

"You know I can't tell you that," Lynne said.

"Go on, just a sir name, not the Christian name," Jeff pushed the question.

"Rawlings — and you don't know that," Lynne said smiling.

"What was it?" Jeff asked.

"That's the thing. As I left early this morning, we still didn't understand what he was fighting against. The path lab was going to run more tests to see if anything can be identified."

"What did the police say?"

"They just put it down to drink or drugs, or both, but it wasn't. In the end, we had to sedate him. As far as I know, he's still under."

"Let's hope so," Jeff said, as he stood to leave the kitchen.

"Hope indeed," Lynne replied, turning her attention back to Danny. "Come on tiger, let's get ready for school."

As he'd done the previous morning, and countless mornings before, Jeff left for work while Lynne dropped Danny at school, and then started her day of grocery shopping and housework before she too headed for work. Whilst this day and all those before had started quite routinely and continued somewhat boringly, the time would soon come when the tedium of everyday life would be longed for and would be nothing but a distant memory.

Claire Banks @claire_banks87 -30mins
Landed in Mozambique. On a bus to
Uamibela, then a lift to the village. Will post
with updates when a signal is available.

2

Claire Banks @claire_banks87 -10mins
Arrived at Uamibela. Hired a ride to the
village. Should get there before @WHO

Doctors Joceline Mercier and Rob Pinkert
arrived in Mozambique and made their way to
the World Health Organization's headquarters
directly from the airport. The trip had been a
long one and they were glad they were at the
journey's end.

Joceline is a tall slim woman and is very
much single and unattached from anyone, other
than her work. Born in France to a French
mother, and Canadian father, she lived her
formative years in Chartres, before moving to
Paris to study *Human Molecular Genetics.*
After moving to Washington DC, she began
working for the World Health Organization,
where she has spent most of her adult life.
Though she still has that slight French
inflection. Graceful, and imaginative, almost to
a point of idiosyncrasy, she was the obvious
choice to head the investigation into the strange
behavioral anomalies that were happening
around the world. As usual, she was a picture
of tranquility and logic, never seeing the need
to be flustered or to lose her composure. She
was calm and calculating and somewhat of a
loose cannon at times.

She would deviate from the required procedures if she felt she could get to the end game quicker.

But she was good at what she did, and though her immediate superiors often found her incredibly frustrating, they needed her on this latest outbreak before it became another pandemic. Something for the news agencies to get a hold of, and give it more life than it should deserve, or have.

Rob Pinkert was very different but having worked with Joceline on other projects she'd requested him without hesitation to be her number two. Rob is married with two grown sons, both of whom serve in the US Navy, aboard the USS Green Bay, a San-Antonio class amphibious transport vessel. He is by any measure very much average and typical in his height, overall stature, and appearance. His wife Helen is used to him being away from home, and she often thought that's why their sons had joined the Navy. The nine-till-five job in some bland office just wasn't in their boys' blood. But this time it was different, Rob was different.

He'd been in the field during some of the worst health threats in recent history, SARS, Bird Flu, Ebola, and most recently, the Coronavirus outbreak. But Helen had never seen him affected in the way he was with this new epidemic. With the other epidemics, he knew what they were dealing with, and they knew how to fix it.

But this was very different, and on the one occasion she had inadvertently interrupted Rob and Joceline, she'd heard in their voices how concerned they are.

Rob had been frustrated by the last Ebola outbreak. He'd been on the ground in Uganda during the 2012 flare-up. When he returned, he made it known that another Ebola outbreak would come again, and keep coming, while monkeys and bats that had been caught in the wild, and then boiled whole, continued to be sold in the makeshift roadside markets. But this *thing,* whatever it is, is unlike anything he'd worked on. And it worried him. So much so he'd put together a bug-out pack complete with a tent and survival gear and told Helen to keep it in the trunk of her SUV and to keep the gas tank full. Just in case.

Joceline and Rob sat in the back of the old *Mango taxicab*, which had once been a top-of-the-range Toyota Camry, as it made its way through the packed streets. They'd been working together since November of the previous year when the World Health Organization had been asked for help by the Federal Emergency Management Agency (FEMA) which included the Centre for Disease Control (CDC) after the first case had been reported and observed in Montana. The World Health Organization had been brought in because what happened in Montana was now being seen worldwide, and FEMA had no jurisdiction outside of the United States.

The taxi pulled up outside the main gates of the headquarters for the World Health Organization.

Rob and Joceline climbed out and retrieved their belongings from the trunk. Rob paid the driver and then watched as the old car left in a cloud of blue smoke.

"You'd think in a country this hot; they'd keep the air-con working," Rob said as he wiped the sweat from his forehead.

Joceline nodded "How about just cleaning it once in a while, it smelt like sour milk and vomit in there," She replied.

They approached the main gate and presented their I. D's to the armed guards who after looking them up and down opened the gates and allowed them access. Cases of this outbreak had been reported in Northern Europe as well as the Mediterranean countries and Russia. So far nothing was being reported in Asia or China, but then they didn't expect China to be too forthcoming with this type of information, or with a cry for help. But it was Africa and the Middle East that had seen the largest explosion of occurrences and that was why their first port of call had been Africa, and last to be visited was Mozambique. From here they would travel to London, and then back to the facility in Washington D.C which was where they had set up the base of operations until this epidemic could be dealt with. Inside they were met by the head of the facility. Doctor Akachi Osei.

"How was your trip?" Akachi asked.

"A long one," Joceline answered.

Akachi smiled and led them through the main reception area and to the back of the facility where the research is being carried out. A large workbench had been set up, and along it sat five lab technicians, all of whom were working on various stages of research. They continued through and to a small meeting room.

"Please sit," Akachi said, as he pointed to the chairs that were placed carefully around the long oval table. Rob sat opposite him with Joceline on his left.

"Are you any closer to finding out what this is? Why people are behaving and acting the way they are?" Rob asked.

"I'm afraid not Doctor Pinkert, we have seen evidence of what is happening. We have one or two reports of it here in Maputo, but at the moment, it seems to be in the outlying villages where most of the incidents have been reported," He answered.

"Have you managed to bring anybody in?" Joceline asked.

"How do you mean?" Akachi replied.

"When they have acted violently, have the police arrested anyone?"

"When this happens in the villages the police take very little notice and are hesitant to get involved. Of the two incidents that we know of, one attacker was shot while strangling a woman at the market, and another fled when the police showed up."

"And the body of the man who was shot?" Rob asked.

"Who said it was a man?" Akachi answered "The woman is currently in the morgue at the Hospital Central de Maputo. It's a short ride from here, I can arrange transport to get there first thing tomorrow."

"Yes, please," Rob said. Akachi stood and left the room.

Rob turned to Joceline "Do you think this body will confirm our thesis?" He asked.

"I don't know, but this is the place we need to be," Joceline answered, quietly.

Akachi re-entered the room "I have arranged transport for tomorrow morning, for now, a taxi will take you to your hotel." He said, smiling warmly at them both.

"Thanks," Rob said.

The following morning, Rob and Joceline found themselves in another old taxi heading for the main hospital of Mozambique's capital city of Maputo. Joceline was looking over the notes and detailed documents they had compiled through witness statements and CCTV footage of the attacks, as well as the battery of tests they had carried out on the first reported case back in Montana. So far, they were at a loss to explain why normally rational people changed their behavior over what seemed to be a relatively short period of time, and why the body's immune system seemed to be unable to respond to the symptoms that all of the victims of this disease showed.

But it was early days, even when the origin of a new outbreak is of a known strain, it can take weeks to understand why on a particular occasion, either it or our body's immune system is acting differently. And so far, all of the samples collected and tested left them at a loss to explain what it was, or where it had come from. This was a new and as yet undiscovered disease, and no one was even sure how to categorize it. Some were calling it a pathogen, and others a virus. The truth was, at this stage, no one knew.

They arrived at the hospital by mid-morning and already the temperature was rising high, and the hustle and bustle of Mozambique's capital were well underway. At the reception, they were met by Akachi.

"Good morning, how did you sleep?" He said shaking their hands in turn.

"Well, thank you," Rob answered

"Okay," Joceline replied.

"Come, I'll take you to the morgue," Akachi said as he turned and held out his arm, pointing toward the staircase that would take them down to the lower floors, where the morgue and chapel of rest were to be found.

The corridors were dark, and the paint that had once been bright cream on the top half of the wall, with a soft green from waist height to the floor was now faded and cracked, and in some places missing completely. Plaster had flaked and peeled away exposing the brick behind it, and only some of the fluorescent lights above shone. Others were out completely, while the remainder hissed and flickered and crackled as the tubes exhausted the last of their gasses.

Eventually, they reached two large wooden doors that were in the same disrepair as the corridor, and above them was a washed-out sign that read: *Mortuary*. Akachi pushed the doors open and gestured for Rob and Joceline to enter. They walked past him and into a square room painted in the same cream and green paint as the corridor and judging by the condition of the walls, it had been painted at the same time. Along the left wall were stainless steel doors with large locking handles and they both knew what was behind them. In the middle of the room, the floor was slightly concaved with a drain positioned exactly in the middle, and above it, a large stainless-steel table. Above that hung three large round lamps with a centrally positioned handle allowing the operator to point the light to wherever it is needed. Akachi took the wooden clipboard from the old rusting hook by the door and scanned down the list of names.

"Ah, here she is," He announced "4-F." He said placing the clipboard back.

Joceline and Rob followed him over to the stainless-steel doors. Akachi placed a hand on the handle labeled 4-F. There was an audible hiss of air as he pulled the heavy door open, followed by the smell of decay, and death. He grabbed the gurney and pulled it out of its dark resting place. On it was a body covered in a white sheet. Blotches of leaking bodily fluids had started to stain the sheet. Akachi checked the tag that was fastened to the big toe of the right foot and then pointed to the corpse.

"This is her," He said.

"Do we know her name?" Joceline asked.

"No, we have no ID for her other than a note from her village saying she's been possessed and banished by the village elder," Akachi replied solemnly.

"Poor woman," Rob said, and then continued "Do they not understand it's an illness?"

"You have to understand Doctor Pinkert, that many villages and people are still very superstitious. To them, the changes we have seen in these people is how they see demonic possession, this is what they believe," Akachi responded quite strongly as if he was defending the villages' treatment of her.

"I didn't mean to offend Akachi," Rob said backing down.

He was a polite man, always looking for a diplomatic way of dealing with cross-cultural conflicts that often occur in these situations. Rob had been instrumental in helping a township during the Ebola outbreak. It was traditional for the family of the deceased to bathe and prepare the dead, but with Ebola, this was one of the primary reasons it spread so rapidly. For Western doctors to enter these homes and deny the families these rituals caused confrontations, some of which became violent.

But Rob put in place a system that respected the traditions and also met with the quarantine procedures which eventually saw the outbreak contained. Joceline moved closer and pulled back the white sheets to reveal the cadaver that lay before them. She was of average height and size for an indigenous black female of this region, and in that respect, there was nothing remarkable about her. Who she was as a person of course they didn't know, and this wasn't why they were here, and why she was of interest to them. Her loves, pet hates, friends, and family were to Joceline and Rob unimportant but not out of their minds completely. They still had to be respectful of who she once was. What they needed to confirm was what they had seen in every other case they had studied since they had been involved with this. And that started with taking blood and DNA swabs. As Rob began that process Joceline carefully turned her head and started to feel along the nape of her neck, down to where the skull joins to the spine. Akachi watched her as she did. Joceline ran her fingers down and just at the base of the skull she stopped and sighed heavily. Rob looked over at her while he took swabs from her groin.

"Is it there?" He asked.

"It is, just like the rest," Joceline answered.

"What is it?" Akachi asked.

Joceline didn't answer, she just looked and shook her head before gently turning the woman's head back and laying it down carefully. But Akachi could tell that whatever she'd found, whatever it was that Rob had asked about was not only expected but also very much dreaded.

"Are you finished here?" Joceline asked Rob.

Rob nodded. "I am, yes,"

"Where is this woman from?" Joceline asked Akachi.

"She's from a small village near Uamibela." He replied.

"How far is that from here by road?" Rob asked.

"I wouldn't advise that you go there, the villages have claimed that people have become possessed by demons, this woman was one of them, and they sent her away, sent her here," Akachi replied.

"How far?" Joceline pushed for an answer.

"It's about three hours by truck, but it is hard going." He answered.

"We need to see the village. Can you get us there today Akachi?" Rob asked.

Akachi sighed heavily but relented. "Yes, I'll arrange for it."

"Thank you," Joceline said.

The single-track road that led from Maputo wasn't as bad as they had expected, but the old truck that had been commandeered didn't smooth out the ruts and potholes. Eventually, they turned off the tarmac road and started along the rougher tracks which would take them to the small village where F-4, as they now referred to her, was originally from.

Joceline sat in the rear seat with Rob, while Akachi sat up front next to the driver who had agreed to take them. As they bounced over the hardened mud tracks, the truck left a wake of dust which made its way into the cab through the gaps in the doors and windows. The old diesel engine droned loudly, and with the windows closed in an effort to stop some of the dust, and air-con long since operational, the heat inside the cab was unbearable.

"Back there, back at the hospital, you are sure you could feel it?" Rob asked Joceline again raising his voice above the droning diesel.

"Yes, it was small, but it was there, I could feel it. It was in the same place as the others." She answered.

"Then there's no doubt," Rob said, despairingly.

"It would seem not. Whatever is causing this mutation has crossed not only the Atlantic, and into Europe, but it's also now in Africa. It's jumped continents and if it can do that in such a small amount of time, I'm not sure there's anything we can do to stop it," Joceline said.

"But that's why we're here, humanity walked out of Africa, this could be the source," Rob said.

"But the first reported case was in Montana, and he hadn't left the States," Joceline said.

"No, but someone could have traveled from Africa to the States, passing it on," Rob argued, politely as always.

"But you know we carried out a full track of his movements, his associations, and friends, those physical and on social media. He simply had no contact with anyone from Africa, either directly or indirectly." Joceline insisted.

"How long until we reach the village?" Rob asked Akachi, changing the conversation.

"About an hour," Akachi replied.

Claire Banks @claire_banks87 -1hr
Arrived in the village: No sign of @WHO. Looks deserted. Set up a live link for updates.

Rob turned and looked out of the side window and across the expanse of grasslands that stretched out before him.

He knew Joceline was right, but he'd pinned his hopes on traveling back to the CDC facility in Washington with some news on where this originated. Anything that would give them the break they needed. And whilst some had concluded and even insisted that Africa would yield results, they had been on the continent for a month chasing up every lead that came in. At first, the majority of them were misidentified illnesses that could be easily treated. But as the days passed, more and more reports turned out to be accurate. Whilst here, they had kept in contact with the World Health Organization's offices in Munich, Germany, where they had been collating and organizing Europe's response to this crisis. And like Africa and the United States, at first, the cases were sketchy, one or two here and there, but as the weeks passed, they became more and more prevalent. And it seemed now, that no country would be clear, or as Joceline had said — *Uninfected.*

Claire Banks @claire_banks87 -40mins
We were chased from the village! Driver Killed by monsters. Think they've gone. I & the guide are going back tomorrow. Need water & food!

A little over an hour later the truck heaved to a stop and Rob was rocked forward by the unexpected halt which brought his mind back to where he was. Wiping the sweat from his forehead he climbed out of the truck and found himself in what appeared to be an abandoned village. He moved closer to Akachi and Joceline who had stepped in front of the truck to gain a clearer view.

The driver, in accordance with Akachi's instructions, had remained in the cab with the diesel engine running. Slowly they moved forward past the first hut. In the middle of the village, they could see that the fire pit had not been used for a day or two. And next to it was an old, beaten-up Land Cruiser. Akachi walked to it.

A laptop was on the roof of the Land Cruiser, which was connected to an uplink antenna. On its screen, the laptop displayed the connectivity of the satellites it was locked onto. Someone was running a live link when they left. On the back seat were bottles of water, and various power bars. The keys were in the ignition, and around the driver's door was a pool of drying blood, and a trail that led away. Something or someone had been dragged away from the truck and into the bush behind the village. He moved to the front. The hood was open. Akachi placed his hands on the engine. It was still warm, but a large wooden post had been driven through the radiator, penetrating it. The post had gone clean through and had become wedged between the crank pulley, and the chassis leg cracking the sump. Under the Land Cruiser lay a large pool of old engine oil and coolant.

Akachi knew that however this had happened, a great deal of force had been involved.

"What is it?" Rob asked.

"This truck hasn't been here long. Something's not right," He answered.

"Why would they let the fire burn out?" Joceline asked Akachi

"I'm not sure, but it is unusual to see a fire like this out," Akachi said as they walked past it.

"Why?" Rob asked.

"This fire pit serves the village. It is used for cooking, protection and is where the villages congregate. Much like a water cooler in your office," He said smiling.

Joceline smiled and Rob nodded, lifting his eyebrows as he did. They continued into the center of the village. It was quiet and Joceline could see that Akachi was feeling uncomfortable, something was troubling him.

"What is it?" She asked.

"I do not understand why the village is empty, why it has been abandoned." He answered.

"Maybe because of F-4?" Rob asked.

"I do not think so, she had been sent away in an attempt to clear the village of whatever spirit they thought had possessed her. Look, over there." Akachi stopped and pointed to a small enclosure — The paddock which held the village livestock.

Akachi led them over to it. As they approached, they got a clear view of what was inside it. Rob and Joceline stopped. Rob put his hand to his mouth. The smell had hit him only seconds after the sight had.

"What is this?" Akachi whispered to himself.

Inside the small, fenced area was the livestock, and they lay slaughtered. Every animal had been brutally attacked and butchered, the cows, goats, and even the dogs that had scavenged around the village. Some of the smaller animals had their heads pulled off and tossed across the paddock, while others had been disemboweled, and Joceline could tell it had happened when they were still alive. They had all seen dead animals and humans before, and even carried out examinations and autopsies on them, but this was different. It wasn't the clinical, medical exactness of such an autopsy. This was savage, it was primal, and it was terrifying. As they stood in disbelief the silence was shattered by a howl. It vibrated and echoed around the silent village.

"What was that?" Rob asked.

"I do not know, that is not a sound I've heard before," Akachi replied.

It came again and this time it was joined by another which seemed to emanate from the other side of the village.

"I don't like this," Rob said, backing away.

"Just a minute, we have to document this," Joceline said as she started taking photographs of the carnage inside the paddock.

"We must go now!" Akachi insisted.

The howls came again and this time they were accompanied by a hail of stones and rocks. A large rock landed by Rob's feet, and it was soon followed by another hail of smaller stones. The three of them turned and ran for the truck. As they rounded the huts, they could see the truck turning around.

"Stop! Stop!" Akachi shouted.

But the driver ignored him, it was under attack, stones, and rocks rained down on it, and with each hit, they could hear whoops and cries of delight. The truck spun its wheels and left the village leaving them standing beside the fire pit. For now, the stones had stopped coming and the howls and cries had stopped too. The silence that had met them when they'd arrived now returned. But this time it wasn't so comforting.

"Why do you think they've stopped?" Rob asked.

"It may be because they think we left with the truck; they may not see us where we're stood," Joceline whispered.

They stood rooted to the spot, turning slowly around them, trying to see what had attacked them.

"What do we do now? We have no water or food?" Rob asked.

"There is some in that abandoned Land Cruiser," Akachi said.

"Can we use that to leave?" Joceline asked.

"I'm afraid not, the engine has been destroyed. But it's worse than that." Akachi said.

"How?" Rob asked.

"It will be dark in an hour." He answered.

As the silence continued, they felt like they were being watched, being studied by someone or something that was deciding whether or not to attack again. Maybe Joceline's theory about being out of the line of sight was correct. Maybe whatever had launched a salvo of rocks and stones could no longer see them and thought they had left with the truck. But dare they take that chance? Whatever it was that had taken so badly to them being here, it seemed obvious to them was also responsible for the massacre of the animals they had come across. But another question stirred around their minds. What happened to the people that arrived in the Land Cruiser? Why abandon the truck so quickly that you would leave expensive equipment in it, and more importantly, out here at least, food and water?

Rob squatted down next to a large rock that had hit the cab of the truck, cracking its windshield. He placed his hand over it.

"Jesus, look at the size of this rock! I can't cover it with my hand." He said trying to move it.

"Can you lift it?" Joceline asked.

Rob placed both hands around it and cradled it, then leaning back he pulled it upward and stood "Just about."

"How far can you throw it?" She asked.
Rob lifted the rock up and onto his chest and then using both arms he pushed it away as hard as he was able to. It landed inches away from him.

"That's it," He said panting.

"Whatever it was that threw that, is much bigger and stronger than a man," Joceline said.

"What is the biggest predator that's indigenous here?" Rob asked Akachi.

"Take your pick, lions and spotted hyenas are common, but around these parts, nothing can throw that," Akachi answered.

"No, a lion cannot throw a rock," Joceline said.

"We have primates, the chacma baboon is quite large, and though smaller than a man, it is stronger." He said.

"You ever heard them howl like that? Or slaughter a paddock of animals? And I doubt they would be able to throw rocks that size, that distance." Joceline snapped back.
They became silent again, still looking around to try and see something. But there was nothing.

"We must start walking or go into one of the huts and barricade the door until morning," Akachi said.

"How long before it's dark?" Joceline asked.

"Maybe an hour, not much more," Akachi answered.

"Then we walk to the main road. If we stay here, we're vulnerable, especially once night comes." Rob said.

The three of them started the walk back along the dusty track that they had come in on. As the sun began its slow descent, the shadows became longer along the ground and though the surrounding area was for the most part wide open, each of them felt like a thousand eyes were burning into the back of their heads. After half an hour of walking, Akachi, who was leading them, spotted something in the distance. He stopped and pointed to it.

"Look, the truck. He must have stopped to wait for us!" He said excitedly.

The truck was stationary in the middle of the track. As they got closer, they could hear the old diesel engine ticking over, and they could see the small red tail lamps in the dying light. In front of it, the ground was lit by a warm soft light from its old and dirtied headlamps. Rob patted its side as they walked to the cab. Akachi opened the door, ready and willing to thank his driver for waiting for them. Any anger at him for driving off had long left him. If he was honest with himself, when the attack came, he wasn't so sure he wouldn't have done the same thing. He pulled the driver's door open, only to find an empty seat.

As he did Joceline pulled open the passenger side door.

"Where's the driver?" She asked Akachi as they looked at each other across the vacant bench seat.

"I have no idea." He replied.

"What's wrong? Why aren't you getting in?" Rob asked as he approached the front of the truck.

Joceline closed the door and turned back to Rob "The driver is not here," She said.

"He's what?" Rob asked.

"Not in the truck," She confirmed.

"Well, where the hell is he?" Rob asked, looking inside the cab for himself.

Akachi was already standing in front of the truck looking around. Had the driver gone to relieve himself in the bushes which skirted the dust road? Akachi thought as he scoured the surrounding landscape as best he could in the fading light. He moved back to the truck and sat in the cab checking the glove box and door pockets. He pulled out the driver's walkie-talkie and cell phone.

"Why would he leave the truck and not take these with him?" He asked himself out loud.

From the driver's seat and in the soft glare of the headlamps he was able to make out a figure moving, and though it was some distance away it seemed to be walking toward them. *This must be him,* Akachi thought to himself with some relief. He turned and shouted at the others.

"Joceline, Rob get in, the driver is here, he's coming back," He said.

"Bout damn time!" Rob said as he followed Joceline into the cab. Akachi flashed the high beams at the approaching figure to welcome him, and to hurry him. But as the glare of the increased light hit the figure, they all noticed something. It was walking upright, and it was bipedal, but whatever was approaching them wasn't walking like a human adult male. It was lumbering, and as it got closer and became more defined in the lights of the truck they could all tell it was much bigger. Joceline squinted and moved forward in the seat.

"What is that?" She whispered.

Rob didn't move, he sat perfectly still, shaking his head. "I don't know."
Akachi put the truck into first gear and revved the large diesel engine, as he did the approaching figure stopped. Akachi revved again and popped the clutch. The truck jumped a few feet forward, but the figure didn't move. He revved the truck again and this time it reacted. Squatting, it bent forward, and then with speed, it raised itself to full height and howled. It was the same bloodcurdling howl they'd heard back in the village.

"Go!" Rob screamed at Akachi.
He didn't need a second request. Akachi floored the gas pedal and released the clutch. The truck jolted heavily and heaved itself forward.

As the engine revved, Akachi pushed it into second gear and then third but the figure didn't move out of the way. Instead, it charged the truck.

"Oh my God," Joceline cried as she braced herself for the coming impact.

At the last possible second, Akachi pulled the truck to the left. As he did, they heard a loud thud on the right side, and the truck shuddered. Whatever it was that had faced them was surely now dead. Akachi removed his foot from the gas pedal and the truck started to slow.

"What are you doing?" Rob asked.

"I have to stop, hit and run is an offense, my friend." He said as the truck slowed to a crawl.

"Fuck that Akachi! Whatever that thing was, is dead, and is probably responsible for your missing driver. Keep going, get back to Maputo, we can report the whole fucking thing then."

Akachi planted his foot hard on the gas pedal and the truck picked up speed. As the taillights disappeared in the dark, howls filled the night air. But these howls weren't in pain, and they weren't mournful for their fallen friend. They were angry. Back at the facility in Maputo, the damage to the truck was clear for them to see. Whatever it was they'd hit on that track had caused more damage than even the largest human male could have and there are no other known bipedal animals that stand as high as the creature they saw.

Even the largest of all apes, the gorilla, does not stand over six feet when on its hind legs. Not modern apes anyway. And whatever this thing was, it was large, tall, and by the evidence of the rocks that were thrown at them, very strong. Joceline and Rob had come to Africa to find answers but as the time approached for them to leave all they had found were more questions. The bodies of the people they had managed to examine like F-4 all exhibited the same symptoms as the specimens they had looked at in America and Europe. It didn't seem to matter what ethnicity or race they were. This infection had the same effect. But this wasn't the greatest problem. All but one of the specimens were dead, only Brad, the very first case reported was still alive, sedated, and held at the facility in Washington D.C. If they were to progress any further with this, then for now at least that's where they needed to head back to. Sample the DNA and blood from F-4, and the other victims they had examined, and try to establish what their next course of action was because right at this moment no one knew.

As the taxi pulled up outside the facility, Joceline and Rob thanked Akachi for his help.

"Are you going back to the village?" Rob asked as he loaded his bags into the car.

"Yes, but in force. I won't be caught out quite so easily the next time, and of course, I'll inform you of any relevant data I collect." Akachi said.

"Take care," Joceline said smiling as she climbed into the taxi next to Rob.

Akachi watched as the taxi merged with the traffic and then disappeared into a sea of car roofs and trunk lids. He smiled and waved, but he knew they weren't looking back.

The journey to the airport and even the process and time it took to board the Boeing Dreamliner for the flight back to the US passed without any conscious thoughts by both Rob or Joceline. What they had seen and experienced had left them both baffled and without any answers as to what it could have been. Rob had estimated that the creature in the headlamps had stood nearly seven-foot tall. What was that thing? That monstrous creature that had chased them from the village and then charged their truck head-on. Was it connected to the random and escalating violence that was sweeping through every town, city, country, and continent?

As the flight continued without incident, and they were both finally able to relax before their work would continue in Washington, Joceline and Rob were unaware that they would soon have their answer. And it wouldn't be what they or anybody had expected.

3

Claire Banks @claire_banks87 -45mins
Been hiding in a hut for two days. Guide
asleep. Water almost gone; food has. Battery
about to die.

Two heavily protected police riot vans came
to a halt in a cloud of dust in the center of the
village, just south of Uamibela. The lead van
pulled alongside the abandoned Land Cruiser.
Akachi climbed out, along with the eight police
officers in full riot gear that had joined him. The
second van pulled up behind them. Another
three police officers climbed out, followed by
four forensic experts from the World Health
Organization.

Akachi walked to the Land Cruiser, the
laptop and uplink antenna were missing, as
were the water bottles and food that had been
there only two days earlier. He could imagine
wild animals taking the food and water, but
what a monkey or hyena would need a laptop
for he couldn't figure. Someone had been back
but looking at the village it wasn't any of the
villagers themselves. This place was still
uninhabited.

Akachi turned to the police sergeant, Oliver
Tambew. "Take four men and look around.
Check each hut and the animal pen behind the
village. I'll keep two here with me, send the
other four with the forensic team."

The sergeant nodded his understanding of Akachi's instructions and went about organizing his team. Though it was early morning, Akachi was eager that they wouldn't be driving back to Maputo at night. He'd set a four-hour time limit once they were in the village, and whether he found anything to explain what had happened to them two days ago, or not, he was leaving. He checked his watch. 11:48 a.m.

"It's eleven forty-eight, we leave at fifteen forty-eight, no exceptions," Akachi announced to the group as they began to head out on their assignments. "And keep a sharp lookout," He finished.

As the two teams dispersed Akachi went back to the Land Cruiser. Something troubled him about this truck. It had when he'd first seen it, but he'd not had the chance to consider it much following the events that had taken place. Why was this beaten-up old truck in the middle of the village? It wasn't from Maputo, it must be from one of the outlying towns, and no one in a village this small would own and run a truck. Someone had come here looking for something, and they had beaten Joceline and Rob to the village. He'd figured by the tech that was with the truck that it must have been hired, and though he hadn't found what the pool of blood by the driver's door had come from, it would be fair enough to assume it was the driver.

That would explain why the keys were and still are in the ignition. Akachi moved to the front again and looked under the truck. There was no dust piled up in front of the tires, it hadn't stopped heavily and skidded, pushing the locked wheels through the dirt. Whatever had taken place here, it had happened after the occupants of the Land Cruiser had stopped without any threat or panic, set up the tech, and began looking around.

Oliver Tambew had been told very little about why they were here. All he knew was this. A village had been attacked, its livestock decimated, and the villagers had fled. He'd also been told to be armed with live ammo and be ready to shoot to kill, anything, or any animal, that didn't quite seem *human.* Though he had no real idea of what that was supposed to mean. He and the four men were now at the last few huts. They'd searched each hut in turn, in a pattern that saw them start at the center and move to the outlying reaches of the village. They had found nothing. Since Akachi had last been here a strong wind had whipped up the dirt, any *odd footprints,* as Akachi had called them, had been covered now with a fresh layer of dirt. Oliver stood back and waved two of his officers to the last hut. Taking a packet of cigarettes from his pocket he placed one in his mouth and shielding it from the wind, he lit the end with a small lighter. He drew back a deep breath and felt the frustration of this assignment drain away while he watched the officers enter the hut. Gazing up to the deep blue sky he breathed out a cloud of smoke and watched it disperse quickly in the breeze. As he drew back again, one of the officers that had entered the hut called him.

"Sergeant, sergeant over here, we have found someone,"
He threw his cigarette down and made his way over to the hut. Walking out of the glare of the mid-day, and into the darkened hut he could see two figures kneeling in front of his officers.
As his eyes adjusted, he could see that one of the figures was a male, mid-twenties, and local. But the other was different. She was in her thirties, Caucasian, and with blonde hair.

"Who are you? What are you doing here?" Oliver asked.

The Caucasian woman answered with a dry throat and a weak voice. "My name is Claire Banks, and this is Johnathan, my guide."

Oliver turned to the officers. "Go and get Akachi. It seems we have found the owners of the truck."

**

Six months earlier: The offices of the independent online blog: *Verum Indicium.* New York. Claire Banks had started her blog out of frustration at what she called the selectiveness and obvious bias of the mainstream news channels. Depending on what you watched you either got the liberal view or the alt-right view. But either way, it was, without exception, not what was happening. In her early days running the blog, she assumed this kind of self-interest by the news corporations, or the ruling political bodies of the day were restricted to the U.S. But after traveling across Europe to report on the aftershock of the UK referendum, she found it wasn't. And it was when a contact in England had referred to the BBC as the *Belgium Broadcasting Company*, that she took notice of events in Europe.

Although the Brexit fallout was still being debated and argued over now that the withdrawal from the EU had been completed, and the Coronavirus pandemic was finally under control, the rising reports of violence across the globe were now what fascinated her. The main news channels had initially reported the then sporadic outbreaks. But as it became more common, and the patterns changed, there seemed to be an unwillingness by the major networks to continue reporting the events as they took place. Claire had seen this before during the refugee crisis in Europe. The news agencies had initially flooded the TV screens with images of people fleeing war.

But when the mood across Europe began to change, and sympathy began to wane, so did the reporting frequency and content.

She knew her blog was no threat to the major networks, and that even if they knew she was there, they would pay her no mind. Most people watch the major networks because it's easier that way. They don't need to go looking for the news, it's beamed directly to them while they eat their Cornflakes.

As Claire would often tell anyone that would listen, "Anybody lazy enough to just let the big news decide what you hear, deserves to remain stupid."

Claire had followed the story and had latched on to Joceline and Rob when they had visited Germany. She, like them, had trailed a lead to the Isar hospital in Munich. It was shortly after Brad had been found in Montana, and the symptoms were identical. Since then, she'd been one step behind them. But when she learned of the case in a small village in Mozambique, Claire seized the opportunity to get a jump ahead. She knew the red tape would slow them down, but as an independent journalist, she was only responsible to herself and so she was able to react quickly. And she did. Even with her limited financial resources, she'd arrived at the village an hour before the truck carrying Joceline and Rob.

**

Akachi arrived at the hut where Oliver had discovered Claire hiding with her guide. He walked in slowly and sat next to her. He could tell she was a mixture of terrified and relieved. Handing her a bottle of water, he knelt beside her.

"What happened here?" He asked gently. Claire took a deep breath, and a bigger swig of the water before explaining the events that had unfolded.

**

2 days earlier: The village.

Claire was sat in the back of the old Land Cruiser as it heaved its way along the seemingly unending dusty road that led to the village. After landing in Maputo and making her way to the small town of Uamibela, where she rendezvoused with her driver, Thomas, and guide Johnathan. Like most people in the local area, they had heard of the possessions that had taken over the village. They had been reluctant at first to take her, fearing that they too would become possessed by the evil spirits said to inhabit the village. But with a few more U.S. dollars, they had been convinced. And so, at first light, the next day, they had set off. It had taken a little over two hours to reach the village. The Land Cruiser slowed to a gentle halt.

Thomas switched off the diesel engine and the village became silent, except for a soft breeze that whipped up the dirt the old truck had disturbed.

"I do not like it here. It feels evil!" Thomas protested.

"We're fine, just a few minutes," Claire replied, reassuring him.

"I will stay with the car," Thomas said.

Claire stepped out of the Land Cruiser and made her way to the fire pit they had parked close to. It was clear that the fire that once provided protection, a means of cooking, and heat during the cold nights had been out for a few days. She returned to the Land Cruiser and pulled out her tech bag. Placing an uplink antenna on the roof, she connected her laptop to it, and acquired a satellite, before syncing her phone to it. Johnathan stood by her, keeping sentry while she completed the technical, and in this isolation, frustrating task.

"Are you ready to look around?" Johnathan asked.

"Yes, let's go," Claire replied.

No-one had heard the fence post as it flew through the air. It wasn't until Thomas screamed, and they simultaneously heard the sound of the post penetrating the radiator, followed by the hiss of boiling water as it escaped, that they knew they were under attack.

"What the fuck!" Thomas shouted as he climbed out of the truck.
Johnathan scoured the horizon and between the huts, desperately trying to see who had thrown the post at them. But he could see no-one. Thomas lifted the hood. Claire and Johnathan joined him at the front.

"Fuck man! The engine is dead," Thomas said.
Claire saw the engine oil and coolant spilling out, gathering around Thomas's feet.

"What do we do now?" Claire asked Johnathan.

"We walk back before another attack comes," He answered.

"It's a long way. I know the World Health Organization staff are on their way. We should stay and wait for them," Claire said.

"How do you know this?" Johnathan asked.

"It's my job to."

"But that still doesn't explain where this post came from," Thomas protested.

"I think we should take cover until they get here," Claire said.

"I think you are right," confirmed Johnathan.

"I'm staying here with my truck. If the bastard that threw this post shows himself, I will kill him!" Thomas shouted in the general direction that the post came from. As a warning to whomever to stay away.

It was then they heard the first howl. Claire had heard nothing like it before. Even on wildlife documentaries. This howl was primeval, blood-curdling, and terrifying. Claire, Thomas, and Johnathan looked around them, trying to get a fix on which direction the howl had come from. Another came, this time behind them, then another at the front, and another to their left. Claire began to fill with the warm realization that whatever was making this sound had them surrounded. And with the truck dead, there was no way out. All she could do now was hope that Joceline and Rob would arrive quickly, and with numbers.

"We need to hide," Johnathan said.

"I told you I'm not leaving my truck!"
Claire saw something in her left peripheral vision. It was a huge dark shape. And it was fast. She spun around but it had gone. As she did Johnathan spun around trying to focus on another large dark blur passing close to him. Thomas ran back to the driver's seat, he sat in and pulled the door shut, locking it. Fumbling with the keys he turned them in some futile hope that his trusted Land Cruiser would fire. But it didn't. With the post tightly wedged by the crank pulley, the engine didn't turn over. Another shape passed close by Claire.

"Johnathan, what do we do?" She asked. Frightened and panicking.
Johnathan grabbed her arm and began running for the closest huts.

She followed him looking back at the Land Cruiser and Thomas who was sat motionless in the driver's seat. They darted between the three huts that had been built close to each other and on the periphery of the village.

Johnathan knew the lay of the land, and he knew where in this vast expanse they may just find some cover. He pulled Claire down into the recess that led to the village well-head. Lying flat they could see back into the village. Around the Land Cruiser were four large shapes. Claire struggled to comprehend what her eyes were telling her. They were bipedal, around seven feet tall, with a massive frame. She took out her camera and zoomed in on them.

Adrenaline now coursed around her body and she shook. The four figures began howling at the truck as they circled it. Thomas blew the horn, and that was when they attacked. The largest animal ripped off the driver's door, pulling Thomas from the truck, throwing him to the ground with the ease a child discards a rag doll. Shaking, with tears running freely from her eyes, Claire continued to film.

The four creatures now circled Thomas, whooping, and howling as they did. Thomas stood and struck out with a right hook, catching the smaller one on the jaw. It was knocked back, but it didn't go down. The other three then attacked. As they surrounded him Claire couldn't see past the dust and large dark shapes that now covered Thomas.

But she could hear his cries of pain, though they only seemed to last a few seconds. The attack ended, and as they separated, and the dust settled, it was clear to see that Thomas had been torn apart. She fell back into the recess crying. She could feel the warmth of urine run down her leg, as her bladder emptied — her body's response to the fright and horror she'd witnessed. Johnathan lay next to her. They had nowhere else to run. If they moved now, they would be seen. They had no choice but to hope that whatever these things were, their hunger, or blood lust, or whatever had driven them to that barbarity had been satisfied and that they would forget about Claire and Johnathan.

Claire must have fallen asleep. Exhausted by what she had seen. She was woken by shouting and the sound of a large diesel engine. She came around to full consciousness quickly, waking Johnathan as she did. By the time they had turned and looked out from their hiding place the truck was already leaving the village under a bombardment of rocks and stones, and the whooping that had preceded their encounter. What Claire and Johnathan couldn't see from their vantage point was Joceline, Rob, and Akachi who had been left behind by the truck. Believing that she wouldn't make it through this night, Claire sent out a tweet, hoping that the uplink was still active.

The night was cold and long. Neither dared to allow sleep to come, but neither was able to keep it away. And so, the night was spent in terror while awake, and blissful ignorance while asleep. As the sun came up Johnathan woke Claire.

"Claire, I think we should make for the truck. We won't survive the day without water."

"Do you think they've gone?" Claire asked.

"I can't hear them, and I can't see them. It's early they may still be asleep." He tried to reassure her.

"Okay then."
Claire and Johnathan climbed out of their makeshift hideaway. Sore and stiff from a cold night on the floor they carefully walked back to the Land Cruiser. Around the driver's door, Thomas's blood was now dry. Johnathan took the water and food from the back seat while Claire dismantled, and took down the laptop and antenna.

"Do we need that?" Johnathan asked as he pushed the supplies into a small bag.

"Yes, when we hunker down, I can relay the footage I got."

"That footage is of my friend being killed!" Johnathan protested.

"Yes, and his death will mean something."

"What do you mean?"

"The World Health Organization has known something is happening. This started in the U.S. Then there was a case in Germany, and now it's here. But this is the first time a civilian has seen it, never-mind captured evidence," Claire explained.

"We should move," Johnathan said.

"Where?" Claire shrugged as she asked.

"When I was watching them, they paid no interest to that part of the village." He pointed to the last hut at the back of the village by the animal pen. "It is as if they are frightened or worried about something in that hut."

"If they're frightened, shouldn't we be?" Claire asked.

"No, we can use it. It may be the only safe place here."

Claire followed Johnathan to the outer edges of the village and to the hut he felt would be safe. They entered and Johnathan closed the wooden door behind them. Claire sat on the edge of one of the single beds set out around the edge of the hut. Johnathan handed her a bottle of water. "There are only two small bottles, we must drink sparingly." He said.

During the day, the howls and whooping came and went.

From behind the closed door, Claire and Johnathan could hear them walking around the village. Sometimes they would tap against the metal of the Land Cruiser as if they were curious as to what this strange metal object was. Other times they would attack it with branches and burnt wood from the fire. But Johnathan had been correct. Of all of the places they moved around in the village, this hut was the one place they kept away from. At one point, Claire had been able to slide her phone under the door and take more footage of a large individual as it wandered close by. As the sun set and they retreated to wherever they go at night, Claire and Johnathan studied the footage. They could see the basic similarities between these *things* and the great apes and even a human. They were bipedal, but unlike the great apes, their legs and arms were proportioned much more like a human. And their stride and gate too were much closer to a human than an ape. But their facial features were not close to a human's. The skull was smaller, longer, and not as high. Its eyes were deep-set, and its jaw was much thicker. Its neck too was shorter, and the shoulders that supported the strange-looking head and neck were massive and muscular.

It was also heavy. The indents it left in the ground were much deeper than even a large heavy man would leave, and by the way, the Land Cruiser rocked when they pushed it, she could see they were *super-human* strong.

Claire plugged the antenna into the laptop and then slowly and carefully slid it out from under the door. Moving back into the center of the hut, she remotely moved the antenna until she found a satellite lock.

"What are you doing now?" Johnathan asked.

"I'm going to tweet out our predicament, and then I'm going to upload the video footage to YouTube, let the public see what WHO has been hiding." She answered.

"Do you think that is wise?"

"Why would you ask that?" Surely people should see it. Shouldn't they?" Claire asked.

"Yes, but when we're back in Maputo, safe and sound."

"And if we don't make it back?" Claire asked.

"Just thinking out loud," Johnathan answered, before getting into bed and pulling the blankets over himself. "Goodnight." He said.

Claire smiled to herself and sent the first tweet.

Claire Banks @claire_banks87 -45mins
Been hiding in the hut for two days. Guide asleep. Water almost gone; food has. Battery about to die.

She began transferring the footage of the attack, and the large *"thing"* as she had decided to call them, to her laptop.

But as the transfer began her laptop died, its battery exhausted.

"Fuck!" She whispered to herself.

Frustrated, exhausted, and hungry, Claire climbed into the other bed and fell asleep.

As light broke the following morning, it was Claire who was woken by the sound of human voices. By the time she'd mustered herself and thought about waking Johnathan, two Maputo police officers had entered the hut. When they'd seen her, they had excitedly called back to their sergeant. Who in turn had sent for a man called, Akachi.

**

When Claire had finished telling Akachi what had happened he turned to his sergeant and told him to gather his men and the forensic teams and to meet him back at the vans. Then he turned to Claire and Johnathan.

"Come with us now, back to Maputo. I'd like for you to talk to Dr. Mercier," Akachi said.

"You mean Joceline Mercier?" Claire asked.

"You know her?"

"No, I don't know her, but I know of her. I've tried to contact her on numerous occasions about this epidemic. But all I get is static."

"Well, Miss Banks. I think she'll talk to you now," Akachi said, smiling.

Claire and Johnathan gathered their things and followed Akachi to the waiting vans.

As they walked by the Land Cruiser one last time, Johnathan said a silent goodbye to his friend. Claire watched out of the window, and through the riot bars as the village disappeared in the distance. She had come here hoping to find evidence of something that had the World Health Organization mobilizing its resources more than it had in any other pandemic. And that included Coronavirus. She knew whatever was causing such a response deserved her attention too. But she'd never in her wildest dreams thought that what was behind it, was what she now believed to be some sort of new species or some long-lost legend that had resurfaced.

The drive back to Maputo was — once the vans were on tarmac — smooth and quite comfortable, and Claire found herself falling asleep. She woke when the van jolted, and she found herself in an underground parking lot. On the wall, she saw a sign. World Health Organization: Parking Level C. For the first time, in what seemed to be an eternity, Claire felt safe and relaxed. She and Johnathan were taken up to Akachi's office and offered coffee and food, which they both readily accepted. As they were finishing the coffee Akachi entered and sat behind his large desk.

"Should we see this footage?" He asked.

Claire pulled out her camera. "I'll need to plug it into your PC." She said.

"Of course," Akachi spun his PC around, allowing them all to see.

Claire plugged the USB lead into the PC and pressed play on the camera. The three of them sat in silence as they watched the attack on Thomas, and then the footage Claire had taken of the individual that had wandered around outside the hut.

"Has anybody else seen this?" Akachi asked.

"No, my laptop battery died, I was unable to upload it," Claire answered.

Akachi sighed and sat back. "I'm going to call Joceline, she needs to see this footage. May I have a copy?"

"No. She wants to see it; I'll show her it." Claire answered, defiantly.

Akachi looked over to Johnathan. "And you? Do you want to meet her?"

"I just want to go back to my home and forget this whole thing," Johnathan answered.

"I'll arrange that. Give me five minutes." Akachi smiled at Johnathan as he spoke. Then he left the office.

"Are you sure you want to go home? Wouldn't you be safer here, in Maputo?" Claire asked Johnathan.

"No, home is where I need to be."

Akachi entered the office along with Oliver. "Johnathan, this is Sergeant Tambew, he's going to get you home."

"If you'll come with me," Oliver gestured to Johnathan.

"Goodbye, Claire. Good luck," Johnathan said as he left.

Claire smiled at him but didn't answer verbally. She really couldn't think of anything to say. Ultimately it was her fault that his friend, Thomas was dead. And for that, there were no words.

Akachi picked up his phone and dialed. "Yes, Joceline, hi, I have someone here I think you need to meet. She has witnessed them. And she has video footage. Yes, I will. She is an American national, so that will not be a problem." Akachi put his phone down and smiled. "You see. I said she will see you now."

"What does my nationality have to do with this?"

"She wants you to fly to the center in Washington. It is where they are heading up their efforts against this. It is highly secure and safe."

"How? My ticket isn't transferable, and the flight is taking me to London." Claire answered.

"A private jet will take you, Miss Banks."

Claire sat back in her chair and wondered just what the fuck she was mixed up in. The blog she ran was small-time. She moaned and complained about the political elite, the bankers, the way the news was sliced and diced to fit the narrative needed, and not what the facts were.

But that's all it was. Like so many others on the web. But this was big. Whatever she'd stumbled on, right now, at this moment she wished with all her heart she was one of the stupid sheep, with their iPhones and German cars, going blissfully about their existence following other people's trends, and not thinking larger than their own preprogrammed ideas of life and world events. The office door opened bringing Claire back to now.

"This is my assistant. He will take you to the airport, Miss Banks." Akachi said.

Claire stood, and shook Akachi's hand. "Thank you for coming when you did."

Akachi smiled and nodded. "You're welcome."

Claire Banks @claire_banks87
Stumbled onto something BIG in Africa. Off to D.C. Have a meeting with @WHO. Will update!

4

It was late afternoon when Joceline entered the office where she'd been working since the World Health Organization had taken residency at a CDC facility, on the grounds of Washington University. Their division of emergency medicine covered not only Washington but also Montana, where the first case of this new and disturbing outbreak had first been reported. The trip to Africa had been a relatively quick one, as all these fact-finding trips were. In and out, gather the facts, interview as many relevant people as possible, as well as the patient if there is one, or examine any deceased victims and then return to base and study the evidence to look for any similarities and patterns. And right now, they were trying and failing to find what it was that was infecting people of all ages, ethnicities, backgrounds, and states of health.

Normally, nature has a rule. She can be a callous cold-blooded bitch that will strike without warning, but even then, she has a type. It could be the young or the old, the infirm, or those with pre-existing conditions. But not with this outbreak, this took the same amount of time for the symptoms to reach the defined stages regardless of age, or how physically fit or poorly the victim was.

This time Mother Nature was striking indiscriminately, there was no pattern, no way of predicting where or who could be next. With all of our medical advances, we were still a poor second, meaning we could only be reactive, and that put us on the losing side before this game had even begun. After returning from Africa, they had compared the information they had gathered with the advancing symptoms of their initial patient, Brad. They had also compared this information with the information they had collated with Munich, and now they knew what was happening to the victims, even if they still had no idea what was causing it.

Joceline sat at her desk, tired, and frustrated by their lack of progress. As she turned on her laptop Doctor Rob Pinkert entered the small room and sat opposite at his desk. He took a large gulp of his coffee and lifted the lid on his laptop. Both of them stared at the screen, trolling through the seemingly endless list of new emails, trying to filter them out, reading only the ones they were either expecting or seemed relevant.

"One hundred and fifty-eight today," Rob said softly without lifting his eyes from the screen.

"Pardon?" Joceline asked, looking up at him.

"One hundred and fifty-eight emails, and most of them pointless shit." He replied, finally lifting his gaze to meet hers.

"One hundred and seventy-three, I beat you," She said smiling. "But like you, most of them are worthless."

"Have you had anything yet that may point to a cause?" He asked, already knowing the answer.

"No," came the short decisive reply.
Rob nodded and turned his attention back to his laptop screen, minimizing outlook, he opened the last file he was working on and started to type. As he did the phone they shared began to ring. Joceline looked at Rob and then answered it.

"Hello, this is Doctor Mercier." She said.

"Yes, Joceline hi, it's Akachi. I have someone here I think you need to meet. She has witnessed them. And has video footage."

"Can you say that again?" Joceline said. Looking up at Rob and switching the conference calling on.

"I have one of the occupants from that abandoned Land Cruiser we found in the Village. She has video footage of them, and she witnessed them." Akachi repeated slowly.

"Can you get her here, use the private jet asset?" Joceline asked.

"Yes, I will."

"What nationality is she; does she have a passport?" Rob asked.

"She is an American national, so that will not be a problem," Akachi confirmed.

"Get her here as soon as you can Akachi. And thank you, my friend."

Joceline hung up the call and turned to Rob. The relief on her face was obvious. "At last, a break."

"When we meet with the CDC and FEMA, we'll have video evidence and a witness statement," Rob said.

The following morning, Joceline and Rob met the small private jet that was registered to the World Health Organization in Mozambique. The aircraft taxied into the hangar which had been cleared for their arrival, and where Joceline and Rob were waiting.
With the aircraft parked, the door opened, and the small ladders were lowered. Joceline moved toward it. As she did Claire appeared in the doorway.

"Miss. Banks, thank you for joining us. My name is Dr. Joceline Mercier, and over there, by the car, is my colleague, Dr. Rob Pinkert." Joceline said.

Claire met Joceline at the bottom of the ladders and shook her hand. "I know who you both are, I've been following you on this outbreak, and I've been trying to talk to you for the last six months. I guess now, I have some information you want."

"Yes, you do. Why don't we head back to the facility, and talk?" Joceline said.

Claire smiled at her, "after you."

Joceline led Claire to the waiting car where they were joined by Rob, who for now had kept himself somewhat in the background, not wanting to overwhelm Claire. As the car left the airport and began making its way to the facility, Claire was the first to speak.

"Do you have any idea what's happening around the world?"

"We have a working theory, but your video and testimony will either prove it beyond all doubt or send us back to the drawing board," Rob Answered.

"Well let's hope it proves it because what happened in that village needs to be stopped," Claire said.

Rob looked at Claire, and then at Joceline. An uneasy silence fell over the car as they traveled to the facility. After what seemed longer than it usually takes, the car pulled into the underground parking lot at the facility and parked in its designated bay. Joceline exited the car and opened the door for Claire.

"It's this way," Joceline said, pointing to the elevator.

As they walked toward the heavy steel doors of the elevator, which Claire thought looked much thicker and stronger than anyone would expect, she saw the electric gate which they had driven through closing, sealing the parking lot off from the outside world. At this point, Claire realized for the first time that this was no ordinary facility.

It was a high-security building. And her feeling of *What the fuck am I involved with,* came flooding back to her. But it was too late. By the time she'd tried to convince herself that she could walk away at any time, the heavy elevator doors opened and Joceline ushered her inside. No one spoke on the ride up from the sub-parking level.

When the elevator doors opened, Joceline led Claire to her office. Inside the office were two desks located centrally in the room. Around the edges were three more desks, each with their individual PC and landline phone.

"Please sit," Joceline said, as she pointed to the central desks.

Claire sat at the desk closest to the door, Rob and Joceline sat opposite her.

"In your own words, please explain what happened in the village," Rob said.

Claire began telling the story of what happened, and how she escaped, hid, and was found by Akachi. She could tell by their expressions and the way Joceline and Rob kept looking between them that what Claire was telling them was a revelation to them.

"You have a video?" Joceline asked.

"Actually, I have two," Claire replied.

"May we see them?" Rob asked.

Claire removed the USB chip from her bag and handed it over to them. Joceline plugged it into the closest PC and clicked on the icon which appeared on the desktop.

As the video played Joceline and Rob watched, mesmerized by what they were seeing.

"You see this proves our theory. The low, long cranium, the deep-set eyes, and a short muscular neck. It is beyond doubt now Joceline." Rob said as they watched the footage.

"There is one more way to confirm this," Joceline said.

"What's that?" asked Rob.

Joceline turned to Claire. "Please, follow me."

Claire looked between Rob and Joceline before standing and signaling to Joceline she would follow her. They left the office and Claire was led down a series of corridors until they reached a security door.

Joceline turned to her. "What you're about to see is confidential. Do you understand?"

Claire nodded a nervous confirmation. Joceline keyed in a series of numbers, and the door opened. They entered a darkened room. Opposite them lay Brad. Claire drew her hand up to her mouth and gasped. "You have one here?" She whispered.

"It's okay, you're safe, and he's heavily sedated," Joceline assured her. Then continued, "Is this what you saw in Mozambique?"

"Yes, it is," Claire answered.

"It's settled then. This is what's happening around the world." Rob said.

Rob's tone was one of surrender. Whilst the evidence was piling up, confirming their worst fears at what was happening around the world, he'd always hoped that they were wrong, that something would come along that took them in a different direction. But after listening to Claire, watching the footage, and now with her visual confirmation, he knew that now there would be no new directions to follow. He sighed and left the room.

Claire turned to Joceline. "I'm guessing by his reaction this is worse than you thought?"

"No, it's exactly what we thought. And that is the worst outcome it could have been." Joceline answered.

"What now?" Claire said.

"We'd like to keep the video, but you can go. However, I would ask that you drop this story. Focus on something else."

"You're kidding, right?" Claire replied.

Joceline shook her head. "No, this is something you don't want to be involved with, it's something you shouldn't have become involved with."

"Yeah, well I am, and it's too late now to turn around and walk away," Claire answered defiantly.

"It is your choice, of course, Miss Banks. In that case, you may leave."

"What that's it? You're just going to let me walk, no warnings about keeping quiet?"

"This isn't the KGB Miss Banks, and I can't stop you from posting your blog, or whatever it is you do. I can only warn you that there are bigger players involved than the World Health Organization or the CDC. And they won't allow this type of information to be leaked, especially when they have the source name and details." Joceline replied.

Claire stood and picked up her bags. "You can keep the chip. I have other copies."

"I'll have someone escort you out of the building. Thank you for your cooperation." Joceline picked up the phone closest to her and asked for security. As she did Rob entered the room.

"Miss Banks is leaving us," Joceline said.

"Thank you for your contribution," Rob said shaking her hand.

"It's fine, thanks for, well flying me back I guess," Claire said. Still feeling a little bemused with the ease at which she was able to leave. Though it came with the heavy threat that if she was to post the videos, she may not be quite so free. And Claire knew that they didn't need to park a car or some obscure van, outside of her office or home to keep an eye on her. It could be done from anywhere in the world. Even on a smartphone.

As she waited for the last-minute warnings or threats, two security officers entered the room.

"Please escort Miss Banks to the exit," Joceline said.

With nothing more said between them, Claire was escorted to the main entrance, and shown through the doors. She stood outside and listened to the hustle of the city around her. Still unsettled, and still convinced that as she walked away a heavy hand would clamp down on her shoulder, and some blank government goon would warn her to keep quiet. But as she flagged down a passing cab, the hand never came. As the cab pulled away and the building disappeared behind her Claire finally sighed, and relaxed. Back in the office Joceline and Rob watched the footage again. As they did her phone rang.

"Hello, Joceline Mercier."

"Miss Mercier. This is Colin Moyles, personal assistant to Jeff Eastwood from the UK government's COBRA committee, can you hold for Mr. Eastwood please?"

"Yes," Joceline confirmed.

The line clicked and then Jeff came on the phone "Hello, Doctor Mercier, we don't know each other but I'm working in conjunction with the World Health Organization on this growing epidemic, and I've been tasked with alerting yourself or Doctor Pinkert with any developments within the UK." He paused, waiting for her to respond.

"Yes, I know of COBRA and the UK's role in this crisis." She replied.

"We have had what I believe is the first live admission to a UK hospital and I thought you should be aware of it. The hospital is Kings Hospital London, the name of the patient is a Mr. David G Rawlings. I'll email the file to you." Jeff continued.

"Thank you, Mr. Eastwood," Joceline said, and then she hung up.

"Who's that?" Rob asked.

"It was a liaison from the UK's COBRA committee. He called to say the UK has admitted its first live case. I think we should go and take a look." She said.

Rob smiled. "We can go tomorrow, it's almost time for our meeting."

Joceline checked her watch against the clock on the wall. She and Rob had been asked to update the World Health Organization, as well as the U.S. Department of Health, and Homeland Security, which included FEMA. In only a few minutes they were expected to give some sort of definitive supposition as to what was causing this, and when they would be able to start fighting back.

"Are you ready?" She asked Rob, nervously. Joceline was a confident individual, competent at her job, and she would stand her ground with anyone on a one-to-one basis but standing out in front of a panel of people — whether they were her peers or not, made her uncomfortable.

"I am. You still want me to take the stand?" Rob asked, knowing full well what the answer was going to be.

"Yes please, that is if you don't mind?"

"No, I don't mind, it's fine. But I will need help with the Q and A."

"If I must," She answered, with a sense of inescapability.

"You must," He playfully said and continued. "Let's get it over with."

Rob and Joceline entered the large conference room. At its center was a large horseshoe-shaped table, the open end being where the stage and the lectern are. Rob climbed the stage and stood at the lectern, holding onto either side, Joceline sat next to it, looking down at her notes, trying to avoid eye contact with the delegates that sat around the table. Rob picked up the small remote control and pressed the *start* button, and the ceiling-mounted projector instantly displayed a large image of a typical caveman scene on the large screen behind him, and he knew by the reaction of the delegates, that it'd had the effect they wanted. He turned slightly and pointed to the screen.

"Good afternoon, ladies and gentlemen. This is what we all think of when we mention early man or Neanderthals," He turned slightly and smiled at Joceline, then with another click and an image change, he continued.

"The fact is these kinds of images could not be farther from the truth as we now understand it. We know that Neanderthals had a complex social structure, much the same as early modern man, and it is possible that without the appearance of the Homo Sapien, Neanderthals could have become the dominant species on the planet." As Rob pressed for the next image, he was interrupted by a rough gravely sounding voice, he recognized as Doug MacAskill, an Emergency Management Specialist with FEMA.

"Excuse me Doctor Pinkert, but we're not here for a history lesson, and why we Homo sapiens are here, and those things aren't."

"Hello Doug, nice to hear you," Rob said trying to keep a sense of levity "Actually, the term Homo simply refers to the human genus, and so all of our ancestors including Neanderthals are classed using the Homo or Hominid term. It is only Sapiens, us, which survive today. But this is not a history lesson, I am giving you this information so you can better understand what we think or believe is happening."

"By that, you still don't know for sure?" Doug asked.

"If I may continue, then I'll answer your questions," Rob said, this time without the light-heartedness.

"Please do," Doug replied, shifting uncomfortably in his seat.

"Thank you," Rob nodded to him and continued. "You have all had the report and in there it explained that we all carry an amount of Neanderthal DNA, some social and racial groups more than others, but it is there. We now know that when the two groups, that is Neanderthals and Sapiens lived side by side they interbred, resulting in a dormant gene pool that is still present today, in fact, we all carry dormant DNA from almost every step of evolution."

"Really?" Doug interrupted.

"Yes, in fact, some are found in all areas across the world, and others are much more localized," Rob answered.

"Explain what you mean, please Rob," Doug asked.

"Well, one example would be the Denisovans. A race of hominids that we believe died out around forty-thousand years ago. But some evidence points to interbreeding between Humans and Denisovans as little as seven-thousand years ago. When we analyzed their DNA, we found a genetic mutation only found in people today with Tibetan ancestry. This gene is crucial for life at high altitude. At high altitude, our bodies produce more red blood cells to compensate for the low oxygen levels, but this thickens the blood, which can and does eventually kill. But the Tibetans' blood doesn't thicken. The mutation is called the EPAS-1 gene, and the only other known species to have had it is the Denisovan's. It simply isn't found anywhere else on earth. In fact, given what we think the Denisovans looked like, they could be the foundation of the Yeti myth."

Doctor Elizabeth Shaw, from the U.S. Department of Health, spoke next "But what is causing these outbreaks?"

Rob cleared his throat, aware that he'd strayed a little off track "What is causing the physical, and physiological changes we are seeing around the world is the reawakening of a dormant gene, the Sapien DNA is being overwritten, and changed into a hybrid of Sapien and Neanderthal DNA. What's causing it to happen is something we still haven't figured out."

The room became silent. The candidates looked among each other in disbelief.

It was Doug who broke the uneasy silence "Excuse me, you're asking us to believe that the cause of the violent behavior, and unexplained events in human conduct around the world, is down to us becoming, *cavemen*?"

Rob looked back at Joceline, and then back to the room. "You've all read the report on Mozambique, and that has been corroborated by Akachi who was with us at the time," Rob said.

"Yeah, and it was dark, your driver had abandoned the truck, and Akachi couldn't confirm what the figure was you saw in front of the truck," Doug said.

Rob shook his head "Things have changed significantly since then."

"How so?" Elizabeth asked.

"We received a call from Akachi. He went back to the village with armed police and found a witness. A survivor from the truck we found abandoned."

"What did this witness tell you?" asked Doug.

"It isn't what she told us, so much as what she showed us. For the first time, we have video evidence of this happening outside of the facility. We can now confirm what is happening." Rob said.

"And do you have a copy of this video?" Elizabeth asked.

"Yes, we do," Rob answered.
Joceline pressed the play button. The projector began replaying the images captured by Claire. When it had finished and the lights came back up, all of them, without exception, looked horrified at what they had just seen.

"You can see now, the animals that attacked that driver, and us, were, in fact, Neanderthal-Sapien hybrids," Rob announced.

"Are there any other new reports?" Elizabeth asked.

Joceline spoke next "Earlier I had a call from my liaison in the UK government, they have had such a victim admitted to a hospital in London, we're flying out tomorrow to interview him and collect more data."

"Why are you referring to them as victims?" Doug asked.

"Because it's more sympathetic than saying the infected," Joceline said, firmly.

"Rob, do you have a working theory of why this is happening, even if it's just a guess?" Elizabeth asked.

"We think it's some kind of viral or pathogen infection by the way the body is responding to it. But once it takes hold, we have no natural defense against the effects of the infection, because the dormant DNA is a part of us, therefore the body doesn't see it as a threat. As far as our immune systems are concerned, once the DNA starts its changes, our body is working completely as it should be."

"But you have no idea where the infection is coming from?" She asked again.

"Bluntly, no we don't, but we strongly believe it could be airborne."

"Jesus!" Doug said.

"Why do you think this?" asked Elizabeth.

"Because of the pattern of outbreaks. We don't believe it is a contaminant, something spread by touching, shaking hands, or sharing a towel or bathroom door handle. The outbreaks seem to follow the jet streams. We know that the strongest jet streams are the polar streams. While the southern polar jet stream mainly circulates Antarctica, the northern hemisphere polar jet circulates from the middle to northern latitudes of North America, Europe, and Asia, and has a subtropical jet stream. If we follow the patterns of the Northern jet stream since the first reported case in Montana, we can clearly see a correlation between the airflow patterns and the outbreaks."

"If this is true, how the hell do we stop it?" Elizabeth asked.

"We can't." Joceline now stood and stepped up to the lectern "We cannot stop the spread of it, what we have to do is stop its effects."

"But if our immune systems don't see it as a threat, how do we do that?" Doug asked.

"By teaching our immune systems that it is a threat and that it should be destroyed," Joceline answered.

"And if you can't?" Elizabeth asked.

"Then we fool our bodies, make them believe that the DNA which seeks to overwrite our Sapien genetic material is no longer there, we mask it, hide it," Joceline answered.

"And can you do that?" Doug asked.

Joceline looked at Rob, then back to the room and shrugged "I do not know at this time."

The next person to speak up was Sean Macleod from the Federal Protective Service, the Department of Homeland Security tasked with protecting the U.S. from internal threats. "Now we have an understanding of what this is, and how it may be spreading, how do we identify it in individuals? In other words, doctors, how do we spot anyone who has been affected before they go psycho and attack, or kill?"

"That's a good question. The early stages are not easy to see. The patient often complains of a fever and a headache but not in every case, and less so in younger victims. The one constant thing is the mood change. Mood swings if you will. They become much more regular and aggressive. After that blood pressure and heart rate increase, and there is obvious sweating. Much, much more than would be expected of even an athlete running in a warm climate, and then there are the physical changes." Joceline explained.

Joceline picked up the remote and pressed the *next* button. The projected restarted, and on the screen behind them was a side-by-side picture of a recreated Neanderthal face and a human face. The differences were now obvious to everyone in the room.

"You're telling me that changes in our genetic code can change our appearance and personality traits to that extent?" Sean asked,

"It is a bit more complicated than that but put simply yes. By changing the genetic code, I could give you webbed hands, or even grow a third nostril." Joceline answered.

She pressed the button again and the side-by-side was replaced with a time-lapse video showing the changes in an accelerated time frame that had taken place with Brad, the first known victim.

They watched as his facial features, bone structure, skin tone, and eye color changed.

"Why did his eye color change?" asked Sean.

"Most descendants of European ancestry have light eye color, that is to say, blue, or even light grey. It is only when melanin is produced after a year or so that eye color can change. The Neanderthal's eye color was brown." answered Rob.

"We all came from Africa," Elizabeth said.

"Yes, indeed we did, but sapiens have lived long enough to have individual traits depending on where their ancestors came from – Swedish people being more likely to have blonde hair, Mediterranean people having a slightly darker complexion than people from more northern parts of Europe, and so on. But Neanderthal's didn't exist long enough for these environmental and geographical evolutionary characteristics to make an appearance." Joceline said.

The room fell quiet as they watched the transformation of Brad complete. Joceline was the first to speak once the video sequence had finished. "This is Brad as he is now, the transformation within his genes and DNA is complete. By all modern measures and rules, he can no longer be classed as Homo Sapien."

"So, what's next?" Elizabeth asked.

"We keep working to find a way to stop the virus from taking hold," Rob answered.

"You still have no idea where it started, or what caused Brad to become this?" Doug asked.

"No, we know it started in Montana. Brad was case one, patient zero. But what released it, where it came from, whether it's a mutated strain of avian flu or some other as yet undiscovered organism, we simply do not know." Rob answered.

"What do you know?" Sean asked.

"We know it's not extra-terrestrial," Rob answered.

"Alien? Really?" Elizabeth said sarcastically.

"Meteors crash to earth constantly, and it is a well-accepted theory that life was brought to this planet on a meteor or other space body that collided with the earth. To correct you Elizabeth, we are not all from Africa, we are, in fact, all from outer space. But we know this is not the case with this virus, there have been no significant earth strikes leading up to or since case one. Whatever is causing this has been here all along. But for some reason, it has lain dormant until now." Rob said.

"We're looking for some kind of environmental event, something significantly different." Joceline began and continued.

"But we also have to consider the economic effects as well."

"In what way?" Asked Elizabeth.

"If this does become a pandemic and more people start to turn and become ill, the markets will eventually cease trading, food supplies will run out and power stations will shut down. The economic and infrastructure catastrophe that will follow will probably cause more destruction to our way of life and imminent survival, than the condition itself." Joceline said.

"Okay, keep on it, and keep the media out, for now, God only knows what the public would do if they thought their neighbor was going to turn into a caveman, and the power was going to turn off," Doug said.

"There is one other thing I want to discuss," Joceline added.

"More?" Sean said despairingly.

"We've been looking on the proposition that this is a virus, but it may not be, and I'd like to use the mainframe to look at other possible theories." She asked.

Elizabeth thought for a moment and then answered "No, I think the evidence you have is conclusive enough, any distractions could delay treatment, and we don't have that luxury."

Joceline sighed "We have nothing conclusive, it's all theory and I'm not convinced that our current line of thinking is the best or only way forward."

"You have my answer, Doctor Mercier," Elizabeth answered as she stood and closed her folders.

Sean and Elizabeth said their goodbyes and left, as they did Rob turned off the projector and looked across at Joceline who was packing up her notes.

"See, that wasn't so bad." He said smiling at her.

"She's wrong Rob, something else is in play here, I'm going to partition the mainframe and run some scenarios off the radar." She replied as she picked up her briefcase.

"Look, you research any other ideas or theories you have, just keep me in the loop. I'm going home, spend a night with my gorgeous wife, and I'll see you at the airport tomorrow. And Joceline, get some rest." Rob said as he headed out toward the exit.

Joceline smiled and nodded at him, she was tired and the trip to London would be another quick stopover. She rubbed her eyes and sighed heavily. Perhaps Rob was right and a good night's sleep would see her feeling much better. But rest didn't come easily for her. The events of Mozambique had haunted her since the incident. The absolute violence that had been brought down on the animals only added to her nightmares, and now they knew beyond doubt what was happening, she could no longer pass the figure in the trucks' headlamps as mistaken identity.

Now she knew what it was that had chased them out of the village and had probably killed the driver.

Rob's house was a real slice of Americana. A white picket fence skirted the neatly trimmed garden and the long driveway that ran alongside it led to a two-story brick-built house. It was home and had been for a long time. They had raised their two boys in the house and the kitchen door frame still bore the pencil marks that detailed their growth. It was the one part of the house that hadn't been painted over, and over again, and as far as Rob and Helen were concerned it never would be. As always, he parked behind Helen's minivan and entered through the rear door, and as always, the first thing that hit him was the smell of fresh homemade food. Tonight, it was one of his favorites, Lasagna. He found Helen in the kitchen preparing his meal and setting two places for dinner, which given the time he spends away was a change for her and one she wasn't going to miss out on.

"How was your day?" She asked as Rob entered, hanging his jacket up.

"Oh, you know, full of meetings and research and boring stuff. And yours?"

"Oh, you know, full of cleaning and laundry and cooking and boring stuff," She said smiling.

Helen placed the meals down and they ate with light conversation while the wall-mounted TV quietly played out the day's events. As he always did, he helped her clean the pots, and then they retired to the family room. Rob switched on the TV and sat back in the large chair, while Helen sat across the room and picked up her book.

"I'm going to London tomorrow." He announced softly and almost in passing, hoping it wouldn't meet with too much objection.

"You've just got back," Helen replied rather more sharply than she would normally.

"I'm sorry dear, it's just that we have to get on top of this thing." He said, not wanting to start any kind of confrontation.

"Can't they send anyone else?" She asked.

"You know they can't, I'm in the field on this one, you know that." Rob kept a passive tone to his voice.

Their conversation was interrupted by a breaking news story. Rob picked up the remote and turned up the volume on the large flat-screen TV.

"An airliner, a British Airways Boeing 767 has crashed en-route to New York, over the Atlantic. Everybody on board is expected to have been killed," The news anchor read the headline in her most somber voice. She continued. "Phone calls made to relatives by the passengers seem to suggest that the pilot became aggressive, and may have put the aircraft into a dive, deliberately ditching it into the Atlantic Ocean."

Rob pressed the mute button and looked over to Helen who looked shocked and saddened.

"Do you think it's related to what you're working on?" She asked in a soft voice.

"It would appear so. Aggression is a precursor to the condition." Rob answered.

"Then you should go tomorrow Rob. Do what it takes so no one has to suffer that way again." She said smiling.

Rob's phone rang as the last of the words left Helen's mouth. He reached down and answered it. It was Joceline.

"Have you seen the news?" She asked.

"Yes, just now. Those poor people" He said.

"I've had a call from FEMA, they want us to go to London tonight. They have a private jet standing by, and a car on its way to me and then to you. I guess we'll be thirty minutes, or so." Joceline hung up and Rob placed his phone back down and then looked over to Helen.
"That was Joceline, they've moved the flight forward. We have to go tonight." He said.

"Yes, I heard. Just be careful." She replied.
"I will."

Thirty-five minutes later Rob heard the car pull up outside. He was ready and waiting for them. He picked up his bag and turned to kiss Helen goodbye. "I'll be home in a day or two." He said.

"I know, you always are" She replied.

"I love you." He said.

Helen nodded and kissed him one more time as Rob left. The journey to the airstrip was a quiet one. Both Rob and Joceline were exhausted and neither of them was expecting or wanting yet another long-haul flight to contend with. But even with the speed that the commandeered VIP air force jet would travel at, they would have time to sleep. And that was exactly what they intended to do.

Claire Banks @claire_banks87 -8mins
Had a meeting with @WHO head researchers into this outbreak! They didn't tell me what's happening but have ideas. Read my blog: www.cbanks87.com/thetruth

5

Lynne arrived at work and followed her usual routine. She changed into the standard NHS uniform and checked her messages before catching up on the status of the patients she would have charge of for the duration of her shift. For the first few hours, the shift passed without any real incident, other than the usual routine of dispensing drugs and responding to every press of the call button, which would mean that this shift would meld into all the others. As she stood and watched the timer count down on the microwave oven in the staff restroom, Lynne's mind began to wonder. The news that morning had brought more reports of violence, though now it seemed to be spreading faster. But it was more than that. Supermarket shelves didn't seem as full as they once had, and the roads seemed to be quieter. But at this stage, like most of us, she was ignoring these things, refusing to let her mind wander too far and think too much about what that could all point to, and what it could mean. She was brought back to the reality of the small dull magnolia room with a *ding,* indicating that her pot of rice, with sweet and sour chicken, was ready. She sat and pushed her fork through the uninspiring mulch that had to pass as her meal, sighing as she took a mouthful and flicked through the pages of the out-of-date magazine she imagined had been here as long as she had. As Lynne read again, why we should feel sorry for this particular celebrity, because she couldn't spend as much time with her children as she wanted while she made millions and jetted around the world, she heard a knock at the door. Lynne turned and saw two official-looking people accompanied by her own boss, Doctor Stevens, one of the lead consultants. The man and woman he ushered into the restroom both looked out of place. Dressed in almost identical suits except for the knee-length skirt of the woman, they both smiled and held out a friendly hand as Mr. Stevens introduced them.

"Lynne, I'd like to introduce Doctors Mercier and Pinkert." Lynne guessed correctly that Mercier was the female.

"Hello," Lynne said shaking their hands in turn.

"They're here about the man that was admitted two nights ago. The one brought in by the police." Doctor Stevens explained.

"Oh, okay, and where are you from?" Lynne asked, not sure why they were here, or why it would be of any interest. It was quite routine for the police to bring violent and often drunk members of the public in for treatment.

"We are with the World Health Organization. We're tracking cases of unusual violence." Doctor Mercier answered.

Lynne looked at Doctor Stevens, shrugging. "There wasn't anything unusual as far as I know. We often have the police bringing in violent and disruptive patients."

Doctor Stevens responded to Lynne's dismissal quickly. "Well, it's not that often, but can you just take them to see him anyway." He nodded.

Lynne knew that was a silent *I'm not asking.* "Sure." Lynne smiled and stood, dispensing what was left of her snack into the overflowing trash container. "He's on the ward, follow me." Before Lynne had a chance to take a step, Doctor Stevens interrupted her once more.

"Have you not been told, Lynne?" He asked.

"Told what?"

"He was moved to neuroscience last night and placed in isolation."

"Neuroscience? Why was he moved there?" Lynne asked, concerned.

"It was felt that his condition was more than just a violent tendency, or disposition."

Lynne smiled and turned back to her visitors. "This way then,"

She led them through the hospital, and into the east wing. As they approached the double doors Lynne pulled her staff card from her pocket and swiped the panel on the wall, the doors opened, and Lynne gestured for them to enter. Taking the lead again she walked them up to the large reception desk which was centered in the middle of the ward.

Around that, were the private rooms, and on the east wall hung a large plasma display which showed who each patient was — the room they were in, and the reason for their being there. Lynne leaned on the desk and smiled at the slim nurse who was manning it.

"Hi, this is Doctor Mercier and Doctor Pinkert from the World Health Organization. We've come to see the patient that was transferred here from the EAU."

"EAU?" The young nurse looked puzzled.

"Emergency Assessment Unit," Lynne replied, slightly frustrated and embarrassed that a member of the hospital staff didn't know that particular acronym, especially as that was where most of the hospital's long-term admissions came from.

"Yes, yes," It seemed the nurse too was embarrassed. "He's in room ten, he's heavily sedated. We couldn't keep him calm."

"Have there been any relatives to see him?" Doctor Pinkert asked.

"No, no one, we only have his name because the police searched him and found his driving license."

"What is his full name?" Joceline asked.

"Rawlings, Mr. David Geoffrey Rawlings." She replied, pointing to the plasma screen.

"Can we see him now?" Doctor Mercier asked.

Lynne nodded and turned toward room ten which was directly opposite the desk.

As they entered the energy-saving lights switched on, illuminating the room in a cold but clinical harsh light. Mr. Rawlings lay with a single sheet over him. Connected to him were the usual wiring harnesses that kept a watchful eye on his blood pressure, heart rate, and oxygen saturation levels. Lynne noticed his heart rate was high, as was his blood pressure, and she could see beads of sweat covering his head and his uncovered chest.

She picked up a thermometer and placed it into his ear, thirty-nine degrees, no wonder he was sweating. She turned and called back to the reception desk.

"Are you aware of his stats?" Lynne asked.

"I've been checking him every hour, as Doctor Stevens requested." She replied.

"And is his heart rate and blood pressure normally this high?"

"Yes, in fact, Doctor Stevens reset the alarm levels on the monitor."

Lynne shrugged and turned back into the room. The two doctors were now standing over the patient, examining him. It was obvious neither of them was interested in the stats that she had pointed out. Rather, they seemed to be examining his jawline, and skull dimensions, and in particular the thickness of the brow and forehead. Lynne moved a little closer. From her bag, Doctor, Mercier pulled out a small device which she clipped to each index finger.

She pressed a small blue button and then watched the LCD display with interest. Following a soft *beep,* she showed the display to her colleague. They looked back at each other with an acknowledgment of resignation.

"What is it?" Lynne moved closer, she didn't know what they were looking for, but she knew that look.

Doctor Mercier first looked at Doctor Pinkert before she turned to Lynne and held up the display for her to see. Lynne looked closely at it. She'd seen these types of devices before at her local gym and even at the hospital's diet and weight club, but she didn't think for a moment that the World Health Organization used them. It was a simple basic device for measuring the body's fat and muscle density. It sent a small electrical pulse around the body and measured the time it took to complete its journey. From that, it could tell your fat and muscle concentration. But what Lynne read on the screen didn't seem to make sense. The readings looked wrong to her. The fat density was low, very low for a man this size, and his muscle density was high. Normally these readings were reserved for professional weightlifters and bodybuilders, and even for that standard, it was still high. Lynne looked at Doctor Mercier then back to the screen, it was obvious she was puzzled.

"Doesn't read quite right, does it?" Doctor Pinkert asked.

Lynne shook her head. "No, surely it's wrong."

"It's not," Doctor Mercier replied softly, before continuing. "We need a CT scan of this man's head, and then depending on those results we may need a full-body scan."

"What are you looking for?" Lynne asked.

"At this stage, we cannot say."

"Look, without knowing I can't authorize a scan. I need to complete the paperwork, justify why it's done, the cost, it's just not that easy."

"Not only can I not tell you, but I need it done now." Doctor Mercier insisted.

"Call your boss." Doctor Pinkert said.

Lynne left the room and headed for the reception. She picked up the phone and rang Doctor Steven's extension, hoping he would be at his desk.

"Hello?" He answered.

"Richard," Lynne called him by his first name, something she only did when it was a private conversation, or when she was agitated, and right now she was. "I'm here with the two doctors from the World Health Organization, and they're demanding a CT scan now, they won't tell me why, or what they're looking for."

"Authorize it, Lynne." Was the short reply, and it wasn't what Lynne expected?

"What?"

"Authorize it. Give them access to whatever they need. I'm not sure what they're looking for but they're here on the behest of COBRA, we have to do what they want. That's all I know."

"Will do," Lynne hung up before the customary goodbyes.

She turned and re-joined the doctors who were still examining their patient. Reluctantly, Lynne agreed to the scan. In the control room of the CT scanner, they watched as the images came on the screen. Looking between the bank of screens and the two doctors, Lynne was watching for their reactions and anything she could pick up on the image. Anything that could give her a clue as to what it was they were looking for. She didn't have to wait long. As the image formed, she could tell by their reactions, that whatever this scan was looking for, had been found. Doctor Mercier leaned in toward Doctor Pinkert. She whispered to him, and as she did, they both began to nod. Lynne put a soft hand on the scanner technician's shoulder.

"Give me a minute alone with our guests please." The technician nodded and left the room.

"Okay, you've had your scan, what is it you've seen?" Lynne insisted.

Doctor Mercier sighed and then turned to face Lynne. "Look at the scan, do you see how the cranium is thicker than normal, how the shape is different, it has a longer flatter braincase, a defined occipital bun, and the supraorbital torus is much more distinct."

Lynne moved closer to the screen, she'd seen scans of skulls before and even their contents in medical school, but this wasn't her area of expertise. She didn't have one. She looked back at Doctor Mercier.

"What does that mean for Mr. Rawlings?"

"It's the same pattern we've seen globally," Doctor Pinkert answered, then continued "At first it wasn't many, a few isolated cases, but then we started to see a pattern, a change in people's behavior, they became violent, indifferent, confused easily. People who had lived happily for years in the normal social construct suddenly became unable to function in a family unit."

"Sadly, it seems Mr. Rawlings here is going the same way." Doctor Mercier said.

"But what is doing this? Why are you looking for abnormalities in his skull?" Lynne asked.

"These aren't abnormalities, they're features. The Projecting bones at the side of the nasal opening, the larger projecting nose, these are things we would expect to see." Joceline explained.

"What do you mean by, expect to see? I'm sorry, I'm not following this, why aren't you surprised to see these features? It's almost as if you were expecting them. If I didn't know better, I'd say you're happy you have seen them."

"In a perverse way, I guess we are. We are looking for a pattern, a verification pattern, and with the case of this gentleman, it is certain now." Rob said.

"What's certain?" Lynne asked.

"That this is now world-wide. The UK was until now, the last country to confirm a case. This is now officially a global pandemic." Rob answered.

"You're going to have to explain this to me," Lynne asked, becoming more frustrated.

"Are you familiar with the interbreeding hypothesis?" Doctor Mercier asked.

"No, what is it?" Lynne asked,

"It is thought that around three-hundred thousand years ago Neanderthals left Africa and made their way into Europe and Asia. Then around sixty thousand years ago modern humans made the same journey and lived alongside them. It's believed that during this time, modern humans and Neanderthals bred and that now modern humans contain between one to four percent Neanderthal DNA," Rob said.

Lynne didn't answer, she looked between them.

Joceline continued with their impromptu lecture. "Somehow, and as yet we don't know, the dormant DNA is becoming active, but more than that it is integrating with the Homo-Sapiens DNA, regressing the host back to a Sapien-Neanderthal hybrid."

"Hence the elongated skull and other prominent features," Rob added.

"You are kidding me?" Lynne laughed, nervously. "If this was happening it would be all over the news channels, like the Covid-19 crisis."

"Covid-19 is nothing compared to this. The world knows of Coronavirus, if it was to get out that humans were, if you will, de-evolving, there would be chaos everywhere." Joceline said.

Lynne sat in the operator's chair, stunned. She looked at the screen in front of her. She could see the features that they were describing. But surely, she couldn't conceive of some kind of mutation that was turning people back into *cavemen*. She looked back at the screen and then back to Joceline "What are the first symptoms?" She asked.

"Mostly it starts with severe headaches, followed by irrational behavior and being irritated, aggressive, and violent. People report behavior that is out of character" Rob answered.

"What then?" Asked Lynne.

"We've only seen a few early cases, but the first physical feature after the behavior change is the bun at the back and base of the skull," Joceline said.

"The bun?" Lynne asked for clarification.

"It is called the Occipital Bun. We believe because of the low skull profile, it developed to accommodate an enlarged cerebellum, the part of the brain used for motor actions, and special reasoning."

"If you run your fingers to the base of the spine you can feel a lump, just like a small stale bun," Rob said.

"What's next, what happens to Mr. Rawlings?" Lynne asked.

"He comes with us to a secure and isolated facility in the U.S.," Joceline said.

"America? You can't just take someone from their own country." Lynne protested.

"We can, and we have too. You don't understand what happens to these people. They become animal-like, extremely violent. In the early days' people were killing their families, neighbors, work colleagues. Some families were even reporting them as being zombie-like." Joceline replied.

"Why weren't these crimes on the news?" Lynne asked.

"Do you know how many people are murdered in the world every day? There wouldn't be time for any other TV shows if every case was reported, and besides any acts of violence attributed to this condition have been concealed." Joceline replied.

"Are there any other cases in this hospital?" Doctor Pinkert asked.

"No, I'm not aware of any other admissions, not like this," Lynne replied.

"For now, you can't tell anyone what you've seen here, or what we've told you. By extension, you are bound by your official secrets act." Joceline said, sternly.

Lynne didn't say anything, she didn't need to, and she didn't question it. If what she'd been told was true, she understood completely that this couldn't become public knowledge, as her father had often said. Generally, people are stupid, and it would take almost nothing for society to collapse. Take away the bread off the shelves, and fuel from the filling stations, and you'd soon have a riot. As Lynne grew a little older and wiser, she understood what he meant by it. "Do you have a cure?" Lynne asked them both.

"A cure? No, not yet we are working on a theory that may reverse the process by using the NK and T cells. It's the best hope we have." Joceline replied.

"It's the only hope we have!" Rob added.

"If that doesn't work, then what?" Lynne asked.

"Then we could be facing a genuine threat to mankind's dominance of the planet, and our species' existence," Joceline replied.

Lynne slumped in the chair. She couldn't believe what she was being told. How had today turned into this, she wondered.

It seemed only a few hours ago she was complaining to herself about how routine things seemed to be these days, but Christ she would give anything for mundane now. The vibration from her cell phone soon brought her back to now. She pointed to it and excused herself from the control room.

"Hello," Lynne answered.

"Hello, is this Mrs. Eastwood?" A polite voice asked.

Lynne hoped this wasn't some kind of sales call or one of those irritating calls about claiming compensation. It wasn't, it was worse. "Yes, this is Mrs. Eastwood, who is this?"

"Mrs. Eastwood, this is Sarah Pickman, Miss Pickman, I'm Danny's form teacher."

Lynne became cold, already on high alert from today's events, now she had the school calling her. A million thoughts rushed through her head. Had Danny fallen, been run down, or choked on his lunch? "Yes, Miss Pickman, is Danny okay?"

"Yes, he's fine, it's just," Lynne could tell Sarah was being hesitant. "Danny hit a child, quite hard, a few times actually."

"He what?" Lynne asked, stunned.

"It's so out of character for him, he seems to have been a little distracted the last few days, is everything ok at home?"

"Yes, we're fine, was he being bullied, did he start it?" Lynne asked, still shocked.

"We're not sure, it seemed to happen so quickly. We've isolated Danny for now, he's with the headmaster but you need to come and collect him. He can't stay in school in light of today's events." Miss Pickman said.

Today's events? Lynne thought to herself. "I'll be there as soon as I can." Lynne cleared the call and re-entered the room.

"Everything okay?" Doctor Pinkert asked.

"Yes, kinda, but I have to go, that was the school my son isn't feeling well," Lynne saw no reason to tell them what the call was actually about. She continued. "Speak to Doctor Stevens about removing Mr. Rawlings."

"Yes, thank you, and remember what we told you. You can't discuss this with anyone." Joceline said as she handed Lynne her business card. "Keep my card, if you get any more cases that fit, or you think of anything else call me."

"Yes, I mean no, I won't. And I'll call you if anything develops. But I have to go."

Lynne left the room and headed for the staff car park, located at the rear of the hospital. Once inside the relative safety of her car, she could feel herself starting to shake. Her mind struggling to comprehend what she'd just seen on the scanner and been told by Joceline, and Rob. But Danny had to come first now. Taking a deep breath, she started her car and set off for the school.

She pulled into a parking space outside the main doors and made her way to the school entrance, and waited to be buzzed in. Inside, Sarah Pickman was waiting for her with a repentant-looking Danny, who was staring at the floor.

"I'm sorry about this," Lynne said. "I'm so embarrassed, how is the other boy?" She asked.

"Boy? It was a girl he hit — she has a split lip and bloodied nose." Miss Pickman replied.

Lynne felt warm with shame, how could her son have done such a thing?

"I promise he will be suitably punished," Lynne said, taking hold of Danny's hand.

"The head has expelled him for two weeks. Hopefully by then whatever this behavior is related to will be sorted." Miss Pickman said.

Lynne didn't answer, she just nodded and marched Danny back to the car. He sat quiet and motionless in his booster seat on the drive home. Lynne was confused about how to handle this. She was seething, they had always stood by the fact that smacking or hitting children for discipline was counter intuitive. But right at this moment, that's what she felt like doing, but she wouldn't, she couldn't, she would never forgive herself if she did. she would send him to his room, take away his phone and iPad, and wait until Jeff returned from work. Later and together, they would formulate a suitable punishment. Until then she would hold her tongue.

She wanted to yell at him, God knows she did, but that would only serve to make herself feel better. Eventually, after what seemed like the longest school run, she'd ever undertaken, Lynne pulled her SUV onto their drive, stopping sharply, still enraged by Danny. She opened his door for him and stood like a guard while he solemnly climbed out, his head still bowed. Slamming the car door Lynne marched her son to the house, and once inside to his bedroom. She held out her hand.

"Phone and iPad!" She demanded.

Danny handed them to her, still silent, and still avoiding eye contact with his mother. Lynne snatched them from him.

"Stay in this room until your father gets home, I'll bring your dinner up later, and no TV!" With that, Lynne slammed his bedroom door and made her way to the kitchen. She checked the clock on the wall, the large replica station clock read 2:46 p.m. her shift had all but finished when she'd had to leave. Lynne busied herself with the day-to-day chores of housework. Once in a while, she would hear some noise from Danny's room, but in general, he was being quiet. The hands-on the large clock moved slowly around until they reached seven o'clock, and outside it was night.

The light from Jeff's car swept through the hall as he pulled onto the drive. *Finally,* she thought, now I can tell him about the shit day I've had.

She heard the clunk of the car door shut and the squeak of the large oak door as he entered the house. In the kitchen, she pulled the freshly made cottage pie from the oven.

"Something smells good," Jeff said as he entered.

"Hi, how are you?" Lynne's usual evening greeting didn't give him any clue what he was about to be told.

"I'm better for being home, seeing you, and smelling that." He answered, smiling.
Lynne set two places at the table and plated up Danny's meal on a tray.

"Is Danny not joining us?" Jeff asked, "Is he unwell?"

"No, he's fine, I've sent him to his room as a punishment." She answered.

"For what?"

"He hit a girl at school today. I was called to the office. I had to go and pick him up. They've expelled him for two weeks, Jeff." Lynne's voice wobbled a little, upset by what she was telling him.

"He did what?" Jeff raised his voice.

"He hit a girl, hard! Let's have dinner then we can discuss it. After all, he's not going anywhere." Lynne needed to calm him. It seemed to work.

"Okay."
As nine o'clock approached, Jeff and Lynne sat in the family room.

The open fire illuminated the large room, as shadows danced around the walls. Softly lit lamps made general conversation and navigation possible, but the atmosphere they created was designed for tranquility and peace, and not for overwhelming the dark. Lynne loved this time of the day. The house was settled and warm, the cleaning and cooking were now a distant memory, and she was curled up on one of the two large sofas. Outside the winters cold wind could be heard whistling around the large bay window, and the soft tapping of the evening's rain made them feel even more secure and comfortable. In the background, Diana Krall played softly through Jeff's father's thirty-six-year-old Technics hi-fi. He took the last sip of his wine and placed the empty glass down.

"What happened at school?" He asked.

"I haven't had the full story, Miss Pickman told me he'd hit a girl and split her lip."

"Did she say why?"

"I asked if Danny was being bullied, but she said he wasn't."

"Bullied? By a girl?"

"Jeff, girls can be just as bad, if not worse than boys at that age."

Jeff shrugged "I guess, so what now?"

"Well, the headmaster has expelled him, and I was told in no uncertain terms that his behavior has to be improved before he goes back to school."

"Behavior? You mean this wasn't isolated?" Jeff asked.

"She said he'd been distant and rude. It didn't click at first but yesterday morning when I took him to school he was in a foul mood." Lynne said.

"What do we do?"

"Well, I've taken his phone and iPad off him as a start. I guess we could ground him for the two weeks." Lynne answered shrugging.

"I'll talk to him too, see if anything is troubling him. He's normally laid back. If anything, too laid back." Jeff said.

"I think that's why I was so shocked, it's so out of character for him."

Jeff decided to change the subject. Lynne had punished him by cutting him off from his friends, and once he'd had a word with his son. he felt confident this situation would be resolved.

"Apart from that, how was your day?" He asked smiling.

"Just as strange," Lynne said, smiling back.

"How so?"

"We had a visit from the World Health Organization, two doctors, a woman called Mercier, she had a French accent, and a man called Pink, or Picker, or something like that. He sounded American."

"Doctor Rob Pinkert?" Jeff asked.

"Yes. Wait, you know him?"

Jeff nodded. "Yes, he's with Doctor Mercier, they're liaising with our department."

"For what?" Lynne asked.

"You know I can't talk about things like that."

"You mean things like people turning into cavemen, and becoming violent murdering monsters, like some plot from a bad sci-fi movie," Lynne said.

Jeff sat back. "How do you have that information?"

"Remember the guy that came in with the police, turns out your two friends, Mulder and Scully, they came to see him. I spent most of the day with them. Well until I got called away."

"What did they tell you?"

"I think everything. They told me about the infection somehow altering our DNA, and the effects it has, and that it is worldwide."

"Did they tell you where the first case was reported?" Jeff asked.

"No, does it matter?"

"We don't know if it matters yet, but the first reported case was in Montana, at the University of Montana to be exact."

"A student?"

"Yup, a nineteen-year-old kid called Brad. Seems they found him leaning over another student he'd beaten almost to death. Witnesses said he seemed distant, almost backward, he was struggling to speak, and he was scruffy and dirty. His friends had reported him missing a few days earlier. Anyway, after they locked him up, they found what the local police called a nest where it seems he'd been living." Jeff explained.

"This was in daylight, the attack?" Lynne asked.

"Yeah, on memorial row on the north side of the campus."

"Jesus!" Lynne said.

"Jesus, indeed."

"Why might it be important, where the first attack was, I mean?"

"Well because of local environmental factors."

"True, but he could have come into contact with it anywhere," Lynne argued.

"Seemingly not. This particular kid, Brad, had never left town, born and raised there. No, whatever had caused this change was a local phenomenon."

"How is he now?"

"Who? The kid he beat up?" Jeff asked, pouring some more wine.

"No, Brad."

"Well, the last report said Brad had regressed to a state where he couldn't talk, read or write. He couldn't understand simple instructions or fathom what a radio, MP3 player, or even what a TV is. When he's shown pictures of these items, he became violent and destroys them, even suffering injuries in the process."

"He's still alive, it hasn't killed him?" Lynne asked.

"No, whatever is doing this is keeping the host, him, alive, it's just changing him. Any dormant DNA or genes leftover from interbreeding thousands of years ago are coming out of hibernation and altering the hosts, or victims' genetic code. They're holding him at the division of emergency medicine, Washington University."

"So, it is a plot from a bad sci-fi movie," Lynne said, gravely.

Jeff sighed and sipped his wine, "I wish it was a plot from a movie or a book. But I'm afraid this is happening, and what's more, we're seeing a rise in the reported cases, and further afield than we thought we would."

Lynne had heard enough, she was hoping her visitors at work were just over-complicating things but hearing it from Jeff she knew this was serious, and the world, the public, and probably even most of the people in charge knew nothing of it.

Jeff interrupted her thoughts "Look, I have a few days due, why not call work, we'll make a week of it, go up to the cabin on Lake Windermere. No TV or internet, just the three of us."

Lynne smiled. It did sound a good idea, to get away from everything, even if it was just a few days. "Sounds good, I'll ask tomorrow." She smiled and finished her wine. "I'm off to bed, goodnight darling, don't stay up too late."

"I won't," Jeff said smiling back at her.

She climbed the wide stairs and made her way into Danny's room. The soft orange nightlight gently illuminated his room. Lynne sat on his bed and kissed him delicately on his cheek, rubbing her hands over his head as she did. "Goodnight Danny, Mommy loves you."

6

In the quarantine department of the CDC facility in Washington D.C, Mr. Rawlings had been placed in an isolation bed after arriving from the UK earlier that day. His symptoms, like all previous victims they had managed to catch alive and sedate, had advanced with every hour that passed. And no antibiotics or steroids had any effect. Like the rest of the victims in their growing collection, Mr. Rawlings' fate was sealed. The term victim was now the official rhetoric, rather than patient or *the infected*. Their only course of action now was to use the spinal fluids and DNA swabs to try and stop its advance. But at this point, everything seemed futile. It was like throwing sticks and rocks against an advancing army of giant robots, or at least that's how one of the lab techs had described their efforts thus far. The isolation beds were placed side by side like cots in a hospital nursery. Each of them had a large clear tent made of incredibly strong vinyl, designed to resist tearing should one of the occupants try to leave. Monitors continuously displayed the vital signs, all of which displayed the same high temperatures and high heart rates. The physical changes of each victim were at different stages, depending on how long it had been since exposure.

The first victim picked up on the university campus, was now almost unrecognizable when compared to his ID picture which hung next to his bed. In line with Joceline's procedures, all eighteen victims that had been brought to this facility had a recent picture hanging next to them, taken from social media sites, or their most recent identification photo. In Brad's case, it was his university ID card, which allowed him access to the various areas he needed. Every aspect of this photo was absolutely unremarkable. Brad was of average height and build. He had short, side-parted light brown hair, blue eyes, and a clear healthy complexion. At least that was what his picture showed. The victim that lay in the isolation bed now bore no resemblance to his former image. His blue eyes had now become a dark brown, the short light brown hair was now much thicker, darker, and longer, and it had the appearance of a feral child. His skin tone too was much darker, and his skeletal and muscle density had increased. Body hair now grew freely and thickly, and the shape of his skull was now visibly different.

The jawline was now thinner, and ridges had formed around the cheekbones and his eye sockets were much deeper. The top of the skull was lower and longer, and the bony bun at the base of the skull was now completely formed. For all intents and purposes, what lay in the isolation beds were no longer modern humans.

By anybody's description, they were now a new hybrid of human and Neanderthal. They were prehistoric remnants of a time in evolution that we thought we had left behind an eon ago. As with all of these days, this one had been a long and frustrating one. But at least now the time had come to go home and try to forget about the day that had passed, and what the coming one would bring. Joceline packed her laptop and tablet in her bag and tidied her desk.

"Goodnight Rob, I'll see you bright-eyed and ready to go in the morning." She said, smiling.

Rob didn't answer, not verbally anyway, he simply gave her a nod and continued his packing as he watched her leave. He wasn't sure if it was the fluorescent light of the office that had been glaring down on him all day or just the severity of what they were dealing with, but he felt tired and in need of rest and painkillers. He could feel the start of a headache. He sighed and decided he would just push through it. After all, he'd soon be home with Helen, and then he could relax and sleep it off.

After finishing the last of his emails, and notes, he left the facility and arrived home after what seemed to be one of the longest commutes he'd taken. It wasn't because there was a lot of traffic, in fact, it was light, very light as the traffic had become recently, it was just because he was exhausted.

He entered through the kitchen door, and as always found Helen sat at the small oval kitchen table holding her head. Rob placed his case down on the floor and hung up his coat.

"Hi, sweetheart." He said, hoping she would perk up.

"Hi." That was all she answered.

"What's up?" He asked, dreading the answer.

"Oh nothing, I think I'm coming down with one of my migraines again." She said.

Rob sighed. She did suffer from migraines and had been taking Sumatriptan for as many years as he could remember. He needed to convince himself that this was all it was and that she wasn't starting with the earlier symptoms. He went to the medicine cupboard and took her tablets from the top shelf and poured her a glass of water.

"Here you are, honey." He said.

She reached up and took them off him and swallowed a tablet. "Thanks, I think I'll head to bed, sorry but I haven't cooked dinner. Order take-out if you want."

Helen stood and slowly made her way out of the kitchen while Rob watched her leave. She looked slovenly in the way she walked, her shoulders were hunched, and she was dragging her feet with each step.

"I'll be up in a minute." He shouted after her, but she didn't respond.

Rob gave her an hour before he made his way up the stairs. The migraine tablets worked well and always knocked her out, and he knew by now she'd be in a deep sleep. He entered the bedroom and smiled. She was asleep and she looked peaceful. He watched her for a short while, but he hadn't just come upstairs to watch her sleep, Rob came up to check something he knew he needed to, but he wanted to delay it for as long as he could.

After what must have been ten minutes but only seemed like thirty seconds, Rob moved from the small chair that was in the corner of the large bedroom and sat next to Helen on the bed. He smiled as he stroked her hair and listened to her soft breathing. Slowly, and with dread rising in him, he gently rubbed his hand around her head and to the back of her neck. He felt a cold apprehension travel through his bones as he moved his fingers to the nape of her neck and then stopped. He could feel the occipital bun forming, and as he did, he could feel an overwhelming sadness replace the apprehension. He lifted his hand away, undressed, and climbed into the bed behind her, cuddling up to her.

"I love you." He whispered as he kissed her gently on her cheek.

Joceline fumbled for the light switch in the dark. On finding it she turned her attention to the phone which had woken her from her sleep. *03:47 a.m. this had better be important,* she thought to herself.

"Joceline, I am sorry to wake you, but we have a problem at the facility." It was one of the night staff, brought in as watchers of the victims during the graveyard shift, she recognized his voice but had no idea what his name was.

"What is it?" She asked, rubbing her eyes while trying to bring herself to at least some level of consciousness.

"It's Brad — he broke free of his restraints. He attacked two of the male victims, and then broke out of the secure room."

"Where is he now?" Joceline was now fully awake, and with thoughts of what could happen if Brad had escaped.

"He's dead."

The reply caught her off guard. She hesitated for a moment and checked the clock. 03:51 a.m. Within four minutes she'd gone from being asleep to this. Her mind scrambled the information together. "How was he killed?"

"The guards, they shot him after he broke loose, it took six chest shots and a head shot to bring him down, but he bit one of the guards before they could kill him."

"And how are the two males he attacked?"

"One is dead, the other is being prepped for surgery."

"No, you must stop them until I get there, he cannot be moved, we have no idea how any anesthetic will react, go now and stop it, I'll be there as quickly as I can." She said urgently.

"Okay, will do."

The call ended with a click and then a single dull tone. Joceline placed the receiver down and climbed out of her warm bed and headed for the shower. She arrived at Washington University forty minutes later and made her way to the secured area where the victims were being held. She entered through the electronically locked doors and made her way to the viewing window which was inside the laboratory.

The glass was bullet and attack resistant, it was similar to the glass that could be found in post offices and banks. It was designed to withstand repeated blows from blunt objects and small arms fire, but Brad had managed to crack the glass with nothing but his bare hands, and this worried Joceline. She knew the muscle and bone masses of Neanderthals were much denser than modern humans, but their strength had never been accurately measured. How could it have been? But now she knew, it was at least equal too, if not greater than a fully-grown man wielding a baseball bat or iron bar. It was completely reasonable to surmise that had the guards not entered the room and killed him, Brad would have easily smashed the building's exterior glass façade and escaped.

"Doctor Mercier." It was the voice that had woken her less than an hour ago. She turned her attention away from the window and recognized instantly the face that the voice belonged to, it was Mark, an intern with Doctor Pinkert.

"Hello Mark," She said smiling. "Where are they?"

"Who?" Mark asked.

"The dead victim and Brad," She replied.

Mark was disappointed that Joceline didn't ask after the guard that had been attacked first. "Andrew, the guard that was attacked, he's being treated now, thankfully he managed to shield his face."

"Face?" Joceline asked.

"When Brad attacked Andrew, he went for his face, and when he shielded it, he attacked his arms and then genitals. He managed to break Andrew's right hand and,"

"And what?" Joceline pushed him to finish.

"He mutilated his genitals, the surgeons are working on him now, but it's a mess. Why would he do that?"

"Primates, especially Chimpanzees target the face, extremities, and genitals when they attack because they're the most vulnerable areas. Who killed him?"

"It was Neill, the other guard who was with him," Mark answered, still shaking from the brutality of what he'd witnessed.

"I need to speak to him," Joceline said.

"He's in here." Mark pointed along the corridor to a security office.

He led Joceline into the security office, where Neill sat drinking coffee. Like Mark, she could see he was still shaking. He half-smiled at her when she entered the room and took another gulp before placing the large cardboard cup down.

"This is Neill," Mark said.

"Hello, I'm Doctor Joceline Mercier." She introduced herself.

"Yes, I know who you are Doctor." He said quietly.

"Can you tell me what happened?" She asked him.

"It's on tape." He said, staring at the floor.

"Yes, I know, but I would like you to tell me in your own words."

He sighed and looked at her, rubbed his hands, and smiled politely. "We heard a crash, then an almighty *kinda* shout, almost a growl, so we entered the room. By then Brad had escaped the restraints and crushed the skull of the guy in the next bed, and was hitting the chest of the next one," Neill explained.

"Hitting the chest?" She asked.

"Yeah, like some kind of fucking Gorilla you see on the discovery channel."

She nodded. "Please, continue."

"When he saw us, he flew at me and Andrew in a rage. I served in Iraq and Afghanistan. I've seen some fucking nut jobs, but nothing like this. He knocked me over like I was nothing and attacked Andrew,"

"Then what happened?" She pushed him to continue.

"By the time I got back to my feet and drew my sidearm Andrew was a mess, he was screaming, I mean really screaming, it was brutal. I fired a round into his back, but he stood and charged me like I'd just tapped him on the shoulder. I emptied six rounds into his chest before he went down. Even then he was still trying to get to me, so I put one in his head. That put the fucker down!"

"Eight rounds in total?" Joceline asked.

"What?" Neill looked at her, confused by the question.

"You said one in the back, six in the chest, and a head shot. That's eight."

"I guess so. Why?" He asked.

"How many bullets does your weapon hold?"

"Nine in total, eight in the magazine and one in the chamber." Neill realized what he'd just said. It hadn't even dawned on him that he was only one round away from being out of ammunition, and even though they all carried two spare clips, he knew he would never have had the time to reload his gun before Brad had gotten to him.

"Call for a relief crew and get yourself home Neill, take the time you need," Joceline said, placing her hand on his shoulder and smiling warmly at him.

Neill nodded his acknowledgment and appreciation of her sentiment. Joceline turned back to Mark.

"Can you take me to the surviving victim please?"

Mark nodded "This way, security insisted we put him in a cell."

She followed Mark back out of the security office and along to the smallholding cells. Inside the first cell lay the victim that Brad had been attacking when the guards had disturbed him. Still unconscious and strapped to the bed with the medical apparatus still attached, Joceline could clearly see the wounds on his chest.

"Can you open the door?" Joceline asked Mark.

"No, they don't want anybody in without an armed guard." He replied.

Joceline nodded, privately relieved she wasn't allowed in. On the evidence of what she'd seen and heard, she knew the straps that were tied across him were not strong enough to hold him, but on this side of the metal cell door, she also knew that didn't matter. She turned back to Mark. "I'll call Doctor Pinkert, I want to perform an autopsy on Brad as soon as I can, prep his body for me."

"Okay," Mark said.

"Oh, and Mark," She said in a softer tone. "Let me know how Andrew is."

Mark smiled. "Will do."

Rob had raced to the University when he'd taken Jocelyne's call, as shocked as she was initially, and then as horrified when he saw the video footage and learned of the details. Joceline looked at the large wall clock before she made the first incision of the autopsy. 06:36 a.m. Brad's body had been placed on the stainless-steel slanted table used for autopsies, and under it was placed a body block. This was used to push the cadaver's chest outward, forcing the neck and arms back. Joceline picked up the scalpel and cut Brad's body from shoulder to shoulder, and then down the center of his chest until she reached the pubic bone. The skin was thick, almost leathery in texture, and far thicker than human skin. And the stench was almost unbearable. She peeled back the skin, muscle wall, and soft tissues, cutting them away gently with the scalpel before pulling the chest flap over the head to reveal the chest wall. She placed the scalpel down and looked at Rob.

"The ribcage is much denser than I thought it would be." She said pushing down on it with her index finger.

Rob swallowed deeply. "Look here, and here. The bullets from Neill's weapon." He pointed to four small, squashed metal slugs that were embedded in the rib cage.

"They can stop a 9-mm slug!" He said.

Joceline looked back at him.

"Let's carry on." She said.

Joceline picked up the Stryker saw. A large vibrating saw designed to cut through human bones with ease while leaving no fragments. The high-pitched sound of the saw's electric motor filled the room until it was replaced by the sound of cracking bones as they were being cut. Joceline and Rob lifted the rib cage out of the body.

"That was tough." She said. Sweat now ran freely down her forehead and into the mask covering her face.

She cut through the larynx and esophagus, as well as various ligaments before detaching the organs from the spinal cord. With the bladder and rectum cut loose Joceline and Rob lifted the internal organs out and placed them onto an adjacent table.

"There." Rob pointed to the right lung.

Joceline could see what he was pointing to — another bullet from Neill's gun had pierced the lung, that was five of the six accounted for. She moved the organs out, spreading them over the table.

"I've found the last bullet," She said. Then continuing, "There, lodged in the liver, it looks like it ricocheted off a rib and lodged here."

"If those two bullets hadn't found their way through the ribcage, Neill might not be here," Rob said.

"But it doesn't make sense. This bone structure is much denser than the skeletons and fossils we have found," Joceline added.

"Maybe during the mutation process, the fusion of Sapien and Neanderthal DNA is causing an abnormally denser bone and muscle structuring. It would also be why they're taller than the fossil record suggested. This is some kind of hybrid mutation." Rob said.

Joceline nodded in agreement. It certainly is correct that Brad was much stronger than Neanderthals had been thought to be judging by their fossil record, and this kind of bone structure was only seen in much larger animals. It's widely known that you can't bring down a large mammal or reptile with a 9-mm bullet, but Neanderthals weren't any larger than modern humans, at least in stance.

"We should inspect the braincase," Rob said. They turned back to the body and lowered the chest flap back over the torso. Picking up the Stryker saw, Joceline cut around the skull, creating a cap that she pried off, exposing the brain.

"Look at this!" She urged Rob around to her side of the table, pointing at the exposed brain. "That brain looks almost human, it's too big for the brain casing. This isn't what we expected, I thought the brain would have transformed too." Joceline sounded concerned.

She knew that this could explain the symptoms that were posing the biggest questions. The violent behavior, high temperatures, and severe migraines the victims had complained of.

"The pain that this type of pressure on the brain would cause must be unbearable."

She severed the connection to the spinal cord and tentorium membrane before pulling the brain free and placing it next to the body. They could now clearly see where the seventh and final fatal bullet had entered the frontal lobe at an angle and had made its way through the brain, coming to rest in the brain stem. They knew this was the kill shot, nothing could survive this.

"This is weird," Rob said. "It's not Neanderthal, but it's not completely human either, some changes have happened, but not to the extent we thought, or assumed they would."

"Could it be that the brain is the last thing to mutate? It may be that the transformation just hasn't happened yet?" Joceline said.

"Brad is, was the first victim we know of. If he regained consciousness from the sedation and was strong enough, and aware enough, to break free of his restraints, attack the others and try to escape, then I would postulate that his transformation was indeed complete. And that he was being driven by an overwhelming instinct to escape and kill any-and-all perceived threats." Rob answered.

"If this is the case, then it is much worse than we thought. We need to finish up here and call another meeting." Joceline said.

Before Joceline left the examination room and scrubbed herself down, she turned back to Rob.

"Are you okay?" She asked.

Rob placed the blooded tools down and hung his head shaking it.

"What is it?" She asked.

"It's Helen. When I got home earlier, she was complaining of a headache. I thought, hoped it would be a migraine, she suffers from them. I waited until she was asleep and then I checked. She's infected Joceline, my Helen will become one of these, these fucking things!" He said, pointing down at the cadaver.

Joceline moved back to where Rob stood and placed a hand on his shoulder and squeezed it "She'll be fine, we'll work out what this is and beat it, you see." She said, trying to reassure him. But as the words left her, she didn't believe any of them.

"I'll finish up," Rob said. "You get cleaned up and arrange the meeting, we need to report our findings."

Joceline smiled at him and exited the lab. She entered the decontamination room where she cleaned herself from the examination and changed.

From there she entered the lab where she found Mark still watching the sleeping victims through the cracked glass. She stood beside him.

"Are they really that strong?" Mark asked in a whisper.

"It seems so," She replied in kind.

He sighed "Then God help us all if this gets out of control."

7

Jeff and Lynne had returned from their impromptu break. A week without any technology except an old CB radio had seemed idyllic, and it was. But now they were back home, and this morning had started much like any other. Lynne came into the kitchen to find Jeff eating his toast, sipping his tea, and watching the morning news. Though the routine hadn't changed much since they had moved in together, what had changed was the news that was beamed into their home, and as a result, the mood it created. She poured her tea and watched as the reporter explained how the violence that had started so slowly only a few months ago had now spread to almost every city and town across the U.K. and the speed at which it was spreading had increased. Every major city around the world now reported acts of seemingly random and unbelievably brutal acts of violence. The normal routine of society had changed. Train companies had started reducing services, not only because the passenger numbers had fallen, but also staff shortages had made it necessary for the safe running of the railways. Airlines too had the same problems, and many airports now had commercial airliners parked with no staff to run them, no pilots to fly them, and no passengers needing them.

As always, when society has a major shift, it was the poorer in that society that felt it first and felt it the hardest. With public transport systems slowly grinding to a halt, and food deliveries slowing, those who had only just managed to keep their heads above water, financially and figuratively speaking, were now unable to get to work or buy food at the cheaper supermarkets. Gasoline and diesel were becoming harder to find, and the gas stations began to profiteer from the demand. As always what you can't have, you want, or think you need, even more. Jeff sighed and put the half-eaten toast down. He knew this was only the beginning, and things would become much worse. Like a domino effect, he knew that once society reached a tipping point, it would collapse very quickly. Thankfully, that time had not yet been reached. For the most part, people bury their heads, the majority of those don't want to see what is coming, or what may come.

As long as they can buy gas, food, and the TV switches on when they want it, they remain in a false sense of security, comforting themselves that the press and media always over-react. They liked the security of the soundbites that politicians would spout on TV political shows and in the political newspapers, especially the more liberal tabloids. For now, the *sheepeoples,* as Jeff called them would go about their daily business in ignorance while denying that a storm is on the horizon.

And for Jeff, and everybody else in government, that was just how they wanted it. He turned and smiled at Lynne, but she knew the smile was only an attempt to mask what his thoughts were. She sipped her tea and picked up his uneaten toast, taking a bite from it.

"Hey, I haven't finished." He said.

"Well, ya' have now," Lynne said as she laughed stuffing the remaining slice into her mouth.

But his smile didn't last long, and Lynne knew her attempt at a distraction had failed. She put a hand on his shoulder and squeezed it as she walked past him, picking up the remote she switched the TV off and sat next to him at the long dining table. Learning what was happening was no doubt an advantage. She had prior knowledge of what may come, but then sometimes ignorance of fate can be an advantage too. She was brought back from her thoughts by Jeff.

"Has Susan mentioned anything?" He asked. Susan, Lynne's mom, lived in the market town of Northallerton, in North Yorkshire, in the north of England, which is where Lynne is originally from. She'd moved down to London after graduating.

"She said some of the larger towns and cities were experiencing problems, Middlesbrough and Newcastle seemed to be in the news a lot, but she just puts it down to the chaffs and scuffers, as she calls them."

"Chaffs and what?" Jeff asked, smiling as he did.

"That's what she calls them, it's a colloquial thing. You know she's a snob," Lynne giggled.

"Yes, she is," He chuckled.

Lynne checked the wall clock "Christ, I'd better get Danny ready or he'll be late for school, it's his first day back." Lynne moved from the kitchen to the bottom of the stairs, at the end of the hall.

"Danny, Danny, are you up?" She half shouted in the rough direction of his bedroom. There was no response. "Danny?" This time it was a full shout.

"Yes mom, God, give me a chance, I'm coming now."

Lynne turned back toward the kitchen. Danny hadn't acted violently since his expulsion from school, but his demeanor and general attitude worried them both. As Lynne entered the kitchen, Jeff smiled and shrugged.

"At least you got an answer," He said.

Lynne just smiled and started to prepare his breakfast, *at least this morning there are no chocolate-covered cereals, so he won't be hyper from the sugar,* she thought to herself.

"I'll see you tonight?" Jeff asked as he picked up his briefcase and phone.

"Yes, I'm on a day shift, so I'll be home when you get in, or I should be," Lynne said as he kissed her on her forehead before leaving the kitchen.

A few seconds later she heard the door close behind him. She turned to find Danny standing behind her, and Lynne jumped a little, surprised by his sudden presence.

"You startled me, sweetie." She said.

Danny didn't answer, he moved quietly to where Lynne had placed his cereal and sat. She watched him, while without saying anything, and with no facial expression he ate his cereal. Once Danny had finished, Lynne cleared the dirty breakfast pots into the dishwasher and switched it on. As with breakfast, Danny said nothing as he left the house and climbed into the car. Lynne watched him as much as she could while driving to school. The slim view through the rear-view mirror reflected the image of a boy that looked distant and gaunt, and the harsh morning sun of a winter's day wasn't kind to his complexion, and Lynne could now clearly see how much paler his skin had become. The youthful full pink complexion expected of a healthy and happy child had become ghostly white, and it seemed to her that it had happened very quickly. Lynne stopped the car outside the school and turned to her son.

"Are you feeling ok sweetie?" She asked.

"I'm fine," Was the sullen, expressionless response that came.

Without any acknowledgment from his mom, Danny left the car and headed in to school. Lynne paused before she drove away.

Should she go after him? Get him checked out, or keep him at home for a while longer? A multitude of thoughts raced through her mind and they all came back to the obvious and most frightening one. Was Danny infected? Lynne had wondered this since the school incident, and she and Jeff had spoken at length about it, but aside from the fact he seemed to suffer no headaches and didn't appear to be displaying any changes in his physical appearance, they both knew that if they raised the question outside of their home, there was a risk that Danny would be taken away to be studied. No, Lynne decided she would wait and see if any of the known symptoms would begin to develop before she admitted him to run tests. With that argument in her mind settled, at least for now, she began her journey to work.

Jeff arrived at his office hoping that the day would continue much as the previous days had, but while they had been away things had become worse, and his morning briefing had changed significantly. Gone were the thoughts of how to implement the army to help the ailing police forces around the country. Now it was happening, and the plan that had remained dormant since World War Two, evacuation of the immediate members of the Royal Family, and the Prime Minister to Balmoral castle in Scotland, was now also being put into effect. The Royal Navy and Royal Air Force had taken up patrolling the coastlines.

All ships, aircraft, and personnel deployed abroad were being brought home to protect the UK from those that would use this crisis for their ends. It was obvious to all of them that the country had started to slow down. Car production had begun to stall, as well as the production of steel, and production in other areas had slowed or stopped completely, and it wasn't just the UK. Across the U.S. Asia, China, and Europe, production that had begun slowing only a few weeks ago was now almost at a dead stop.

In food and clothing factories around the world production too had come to a complete standstill. And the coal, recycled wood, and discarded trash that fueled civilization's mighty power stations, now lay uncollected as the mines and the recycling centers lost their workforces to this epidemic.

The UK's nuclear power stations were at the point of shutting down as the demand for power had started to fall off, and the staff needed to maintain them weren't turning out for work. At the docks of every nation cargo ships, oil tankers, and even cruise ships now remained docked and abandoned, and those ships that had been waiting out at sea for port entry now had no crew on board. Once members of the crew displayed early-onset symptoms, the ships were abandoned. Those that had begun turning into hybrids were left wondering the empty hulks.

The mighty leviathans that once transported goods around the world were now forsaken.

The cheap clothes and toys amongst other things they once delivered to the west in huge quantities were no longer wanted or needed. Some ships had been en route when their crews had succumbed to those that had become violent and were now drifting, or were powering their way to their destination on autopilot. They were now ghost ships. Crewed only by hybrids who had no idea how to operate them.

Most air traffic had now been forcibly grounded by governments after the rising incidences of airliners being brought down by passengers opening the doors at altitude, or by the crew themselves becoming violent mid-flight. Only crews that underwent the strictest medical examinations before each flight was allowed to fly, and only then with the passengers protected by air marshals, with standing orders to Taser anyone who threatened the flight.

Africa and the Middle East had become virtually wastelands, and oil production had stopped. The infected victims roamed the streets attacking those that had yet to succumb, and as each day passed the human world was coming apart at the seams. Some religions believed it was a sign from their God and took advantage of peoples' fears whilst other religions seized the opportunity and started on a path of violence and destruction, blaming other religions and societies for bringing about what they believed to be the end of the world through their God's wrath.

Across the world, mankind was facing a fight for its very survival, but rather than working together and putting our past differences behind us, we did what we always do when things fall apart. We turned on each other and blamed each other. For those that had the correct information, it was clear that this was the beginning of the end. The only unknown was how long it would take, and if there would be any coming back from it. What surprised everyone was just how quickly things fell apart. The civilizations and societies which had taken a millennium to create were now collapsing in a fraction of the time.

Lynne arrived at work just after 10:12 a.m. and what she was met with alarmed her. Her ward was full beyond its capacity. The accident and emergency department were also passed breaking point. The admission to the hospital of people displaying the symptoms was now at pandemic proportions — even surpassing the worst days of the Covid-19 pandemic.

"Hell, of a night we had." Staff Nurse Kelly Coulter said as she walked toward Lynne.

"What the hell happened here?" Lynne asked, still somewhat shocked.

"It seems whatever this is, it's exploded. I'm surprised you didn't see the reports on the news." Kelly continued as she readied the handover documents Lynne needed to be briefed on the newly arrived patients.

Lynne played dumb; she couldn't possibly let anyone know what she'd been told. "Still no diagnoses yet?" She asked Kelly.

"Nothing, one of the virologists in the path lab thinks it may be some sort of muted strain of bird flu, at least it would explain how it spread so quickly. All the fucking pigeons in London!" Kelly replied, becoming ever-more agitated.

It was obvious to Lynne she'd had enough, and now the end of her shift was here she wanted to go home, and as quickly as she could. "Here are the handovers, I suggest you have a look through them, but to be honest every case is the same." Kelly handed her a large pile of brown folders and smiled at Lynne. As she left, she whispered. "Good luck."

Lynne smiled back at her and watched as Kelly picked up her shoulder bag and hurried out of the ward. She flicked through the large pile of files and took one out from the center and opened it. Kelly was right, the similarities between this patient, Mr. Paul Dovecot, and Mr. Rawlings were remarkable. It is the case, as with all outbreaks, each patient bears similar or indeed the exact same symptoms eventually, but it is almost certainly never the case that they happen so uniformly and within the same time scales and the same exact order of appearance. As Lynne closed the file the blue phone on the reception desk rang.

"Hello, Davidson Ward, Lynne Eastwood speaking."

"Hi, it's accident and emergency, do you have any beds available?" came the short and to-the-point question.

"We haven't, we're already overcapacity. You may have to send the ambulances to another hospital." Lynne answered.

"We've tried, they're the same as you. Full!" A dull click came almost immediately, and Lynne knew the caller had hung up.

She replaced the handset. "This is going to be a long day." She said to herself as she began her rounds. The Davidson ward — Lynne is in charge of — is made up of thirteen single bedrooms, and two double bedrooms, and every bed was taken.

In addition, the larger single bedrooms had additional beds squeezed in, making a total of twenty-one patients in a ward designed and staffed for seventeen. And in almost every other ward but the most specialized, it was becoming the same story. The hospital was reaching a point where it simply couldn't take any more patients, or indeed, victims. Lynne recognized the symptoms of each patient, or as Doctor Pinkert had called them, victims, and it was obvious to her that some were in a much further advanced state than others. She also knew that the hospital security was simply not up to the task of keeping other patients, and the staff safe, should one or more of these victims become violent, and with the police forces across the country at breaking point trying to deal with the escalating violence, they had no officers available to help. As she continued to review the files, she came across one in particular which had a pale blue border around the name. This was used to indicate that the patient was under the age of sixteen.

Lynne paused before opening it. Since this had started, she had not seen or heard of any child victims. Even when Doctors Pinkert and Mercier had visited, there had been no conversations about adolescent victims, and that apart from the lack of physical changes had been Lynne's rationale why Danny was not infected and was in fact just being a *moody boy*. She opened the file and looked to see which bed this young victim was in. Room four - bed two. She closed the file, left her office, and headed for the room.

Lynne pushed open the door to the private room and entered. As with all of the rooms that held victims, the lights were dimmed, but she could clearly make out the young girl who lay before her. The Dinamap machine attached to her showed the usual high heart rate and blood pressure, and Lynne could easily see beads of sweat clustered on her forehead.

Her breathing was rapid, and her chest heaved as she panted. Lynne noticed that her complexion was ghostly, the same as Danny's, and that she too looked gaunt. Lynne began to feel sick, a wave of nausea washing over her. There was no doubt this girl was infected, but there were no clear physical changes. She slowly moved her hand over the top of the young girl's head until she reached the base of her skull. Lynne hesitated before she felt for the occipital bun that Doctor Mercier had shown her on Mr. Rawlings. It was there and Lynne now knew the rationale she had used to dismiss Danny being infected was no longer valid. She pulled her shaking hand away not knowing what she should do with this information. She knew Danny would become dangerous. She knew as a loving mother that she should at least check Danny's vital signs and feel for the bun, but if it was there, she knew she would have to bring him in and sedate him. Lynne pushed her hand into her uniform pockets to reach for her handkerchief. The sudden rush of emotions, fear, rage, and guilt had overtaken her, and she needed to clear her mind and her eyes. But as she pulled out the paper handkerchief, she noticed a small white business card. She turned it over and realized it was the card Doctor Joceline Mercier had given her, and it had her cell phone number on it. Lynne grasped the card tightly and left the girl's room.

She entered her office, shutting the door behind her. Closing the grey plastic window blinds, she sat at her desk, staring at the phone. She placed the card in front of her, picked up the receiver, and dialed the number. It rang.

"C'mon, answer," Lynne whispered to herself.

"Hello, Joceline Mercier."

"Doctor Mercier, it's Lynne Eastwood from Kings, London. We met when you visited, do you remember? Mr. Rawlings."

"Ah yes, I do remember. What can I help you with?"

"Doctor Mercier, things here are getting bad, very bad, our wards are full and we're turning new cases away. But I'm afraid my son, Danny, you remember him? I think he's become infected," Lynne tried to string a coherent sentence together, but she was struggling.

"Why do you say *you think*, Lynne? You know the symptoms."

Lynne shrugged before answering, she was feeling vulnerable, upset, and what she needed more than anything was for Joceline to reassure Lynne that Danny was fine. "He's been acting strange, he was violent at school and his complexion is gaunt, almost ghostly, but he hasn't had any headaches."

"In the few cases we've seen in young children, there have not been any headaches reported.

We think because even though the Coronal and Metopic Sutures of the skull have closed, they are not fully fused on children in your son's age group, also the brain itself is still developing, and it can swell without producing enough pressure to cause the severe headaches we see in adults."

Lynne's heart sunk, this confirmation wasn't what she wanted, but it was what she'd feared, and even expected. "What should I do? We don't have the facilities here. We have nothing like you. Can you help me? Please." Lynne pleaded.

"The pandemic is spreading at a rate we did not envisage. Every country is now reporting it and it's no longer confined to the cities and towns. Outlying villages and smaller communities are now being affected, I'm not sure there is anything we can do here you can't do there."

"Please Doctor Mercier, for my son, please let me bring him to you, if there are going to be any breakthroughs they'll be where you are. I can't just sedate him and watch him change into one of those things," Lynne couldn't hold back her tears any longer and she sobbed.

There were a few seconds of silence before Lynne heard Joceline's voice. "Get him here as quickly as you can, I'll seconder you officially. If anyone asks, you're bringing your son with you because you have no one to look after him."

"Thank you, we'll be on the next flight."

Lynne rubbed her eyes clear and straightened herself — she needed to let Jeff know what was happening. But first, she would have to collect Danny from school before any suspicions were raised. She checked the time, she still had six hours before the end of her shift, but she couldn't wait until then. Calmly, she left her office and walked to the main reception desk where a ward nurse was sitting. Lynne swallowed deeply, trying to remain calm and appear as normal as she could. "Hi Debbie," Lynne said, smiling.

The nurse looked up from the paperwork and smiled before answering. "Hello, Sister."

"I need to run a message to HR, if anyone asks tell them I'll be a few minutes," Lynne knew that the HR, or Human Resources offices, were next to the staff car park so her walking in that direction shouldn't raise any alarms with the ward staff.

"I can take it Sister if you want me to?" Debbie answered with a question Lynne hadn't expected or anticipated, and for a short while, it threw her off.

"No, it's fine, it's a message really, I just need to deliver it in person," It was the best she could do. Debbie nodded and smiled.

Lynne breathed heavily with relief once she was out of the ward, and by the time she reached her car, the quick walking had turned almost into a run.

She turned the key and pulled on her seatbelt. She felt sure as she moved the automatic gearstick to the drive position, there would be a knock on her window, and her boss would be asking where she thought she was going. But as she lifted her foot off the brake, and the SUV pulled away, she sighed with relief and exited the hospital. Lynne was now heading for Danny's school, and she knew that when she got there, she would need a plausible excuse for taking him out of lessons. A doctor's appointment was always the safest bet.

It's not often that the school would question such an appointment, especially given the way Danny looked and was behaving, so she felt sure that this wouldn't be questioned. Before she picked him up, she needed to call Jeff. Lynne touched the Bluetooth icon on the car's touchscreen display and selected voice recognition. Calmly and clearly, she said "Jeff." after a second's delay the car responded. "Calling Jeff Eastwood."

"Hello, everything okay?" Jeff answered, and he sounded anxious.

"Hi, can you get home now?" Lynne didn't stand on the normal pleasantries, there was no time.

"What's the matter?" He asked.

"Not on the phone, I need you home and as soon as you can, Jeff," Lynne said.

"I'll be there as soon as I can." He replied.

Lynne cleared the call. Normally she would have selected music to soothe the journey, but not today, she hadn't the time or mindset to do so. She pulled into the school's car park and entered the reception. As she did Jackie Wharton, one of the school secretaries approached her.

"Hello Mrs. Eastwood, we didn't expect to see you today."

"Yes, hi Jackie, I'm here to collect Danny. He has a doctor's appointment." Lynne said, calmly.

"I'll check to see what lesson he's in, and we'll bring him here."

Lynne sighed again, she expected the usual routine of appointment cards and confirmations, but after what was, in fact, a short wait, but what to Lynne felt like time had stood still, Danny was brought to reception. Lynne put her arm around him to guide him out of the school, and as she did, she smiled and nodded to Jackie. As they walked to the car Lynne moved her hand from his shoulder to the nape of his neck. A cold chill ran through her as she moved her hand up and to the base of his skull. As she reached it the cold chill turned to a sensation of warm trepidation and fear. A fear of what she believed, and yet with all of her being hoped she wouldn't find. But as her fingers searched, her worst fears were confirmed.

As with the young girl in the hospital, Danny had the distinct Occipital Bun. Lynne pulled her hand away as fast as her reflexes allowed her. Fighting the tears, she guided her son into her car, beginning the silent drive home. Once home, Lynne drove into the garage and made sure the electric door was closed behind her before she exited the car with Danny. She wanted to make sure that her car was hidden. Even though Joceline was going to seconder her through the official channels, she knew that normally took weeks, and Danny simply didn't have that long. And so, with the car hidden, she knew if someone from the hospital was to drive by, they wouldn't stop.

As she entered the house through the link door that leads to their utility room, the garage door opened. At first, she panicked, had someone seen her? But she calmed when she saw the front of Jeff's' Lexus enter the double garage. She rushed Danny inside and told him to go to his room.

She heard the clank of the garage door as Jeff entered the kitchen. She expected that she would have to convince him of her plan and that he would insist that she should stay and carry on as normal. But the look on his face matched the tone of his voice when she'd called him earlier.

"Are you okay?" He asked,

"Sort of," Lynne answered.

"How are things at work?" Jeff asked.

"Hectic, but why do I think you know that?"

"Things are about to go south, and quickly. Much quicker than we had thought they would and planned for. Police forces around the country are reporting that staff are not showing up for their shifts, that some are infected, and others are running with their families. It's the same with the armed forces. We're about to lose control. We think seventy-two hours, maybe less, and we won't be able to maintain order."

Lynne shuddered, her concerns for Danny faded just for the briefest of moments. "What does that mean?"

Jeff shrugged. "It means that this country will descend into chaos. We expect London will be the first to go, followed by Birmingham, Manchester, and then Liverpool. But the domino effect will be quick, days not weeks," Jeff paused and then continued. "Fuel is already running low, food deliveries will stop, and then the rioting will begin. Shortly after the power will fail, and the national grid will collapse. Any emergency generators will only keep the lights on for a short while. They're evacuating the Prime Minister and members of COBRA to Balmoral tomorrow. The Royal family is already there."

"But you're a member of COBRA," Lynne said,

"Yes, they want me to go with them, they're sending a car in the morning. Once we're there, they're closing the airports and borders."

Lynne felt the panic rise again, she was hoping to have one last night at home, as a family, before she left for Washington with Danny. Danny, how could she have forgotten about him?

"It's Danny," Lynne said before Jeff could say anything else. It worked; Jeff looked afraid.

"What do you mean, it's Danny?"

"That's the reason I called you. I spoke to Doctor Mercier about him. She thinks he's infected."

"But I thought the headaches, physical changes..." Jeff sounded confused.

"No, in the cases of small children there are no headaches, and she wants me to take him to Washington," Lynne said.

"Washington? Why would she say that?"

"I asked her," Lynne answered. "We don't have the facilities here. She said she would officially seconder me, but that could take weeks, and if this country is going to go to shit as quickly as you think there'll be nothing we can do to protect him."

"Then you have to go tonight," Jeff said.

Lynne nodded and began to cry. Jeff pulled her into his chest tightly and kissed her forehead. "Take him to Washington, I'll be safe at Balmoral, and after a few days, I'll get a flight over. We'll find somewhere, we'll be fine. I promise."

"What about mom?" Lynne asked.

"Call her and tell her to go to the cabin, it's off-grid, she'll be safe there. I'll get her before I fly out."

Lynne knew that what Jeff said was just reassurance. There could be no guarantee put to his words, but they did what he'd intended, they gave her the strength to do what she needed. Lynne picked up her phone. "Mom? Mom, it's Lynne, how are things?"

Jeff watched as Lynne listened to her mom, she looked concerned. Lynne interrupted her. "Mom listen, this thing that's happening, it's going to get much worse. I'm flying out with Danny to the U.S. tonight, and Jeff is leaving with the PM and COBRA tomorrow. You must pack and leave for our cabin tonight, don't hesitate, mom, time is running out."

Jeff leaned against the counter and watched Lynne's reactions as her mom tried to understand the severity of what Lynne was telling her.

"Mom, there is firewood at the cabin for the range and fire, and Jeff left the solar panels charging the batteries, so you'll have light and freshwater from the rain collectors. The key is in the usual place, go there, hide your car around back, and don't tell anyone you're going. Take the food you have at home and fill your car when you leave. You'll get there on a full tank. Just sneak out later tonight and don't stop until you're there.

It is important you do exactly as I've said. Jeff will come for you in a week or two. And mom, I love you." Lynne placed the phone down and smiled at Jeff. "You will go for her, right?" Jeff smiled and nodded, and with that final assurance, she headed up the stairs to pack.

A short time later Lynne and Jeff were at the front door with Danny and their luggage. They'd decided it was safer to call for an Uber to take them to the airport, electing to keep her car hidden in the garage, where it would stay with Jeff's until they could return home.

As the Prius pulled up, Lynne turned to Jeff and held him tight. But this wasn't a normal hug, she clung to him as if her very life depended on it, and for the briefest of moments, she felt that she had no worries in the world.
The Prius sounded its horn again, and she pulled away kissing him as she did. Jeff picked up Danny and hugged him while he carried him to the car, but Danny didn't respond with any kindness or emotion. To Jeff, it didn't matter. What did, was that his son knew his dad loved him and that he would do whatever it took to keep him safe.

With the luggage in the trunk, and Danny safely belted in the back seat, Lynne hugged Jeff one last time, and under the light of the streetlamps, Jeff could see her eyes watering. He smiled and opened the car door.

"I love you," She said.

"I love you too, and I'll see you both soon, we're doing the right thing. Remember that and you'll stay strong," Jeff answered.

Lynne pulled the door shut and the Prius pulled away. Jeff watched them leave until they had turned the corner and disappeared. Wiping the tears from his eyes he'd tried so hard to hide from them both, he entered the house, closing and locking the door behind him. He knew now he too had to get ready to leave in the morning. Jeff couldn't sleep. He listened as the rain tapped against the large bay window of their Victorian house. The shadows of the trees against the orange streetlamps danced across the walls as the wind gathered strength. He lay for as long as he could, but still unable to sleep he left his bed and made his way downstairs and into the garage to get a few items from his car. As he switched on the lights, he saw Lynne's car and fondly remembered how excited she was on the day she'd collected it from the dealer. It was her first *new* car. Before that, she'd had to settle with buying used cars, but after a promotion at work she could finally afford to buy new, and the Toyota SUV was the only car she wanted. Her dad had bought the same model when Lynne had lived with her parents, and she'd often spoken to Jeff about the family trips.

When her dad had died five years ago, his RAV4 was eight years old, but her mom had refused to sell it, it held too many sentimental memories. It wasn't just a collection of metal and plastic. It was part of the family. And though Lynne's new model had only the name in common with her father's, that was enough for her to feel as if her dad was with her every time she was in it. Jeff placed a hand on its hood and smiled.

As with the bedroom windows, he could hear the wind and rain tapping on the metal garage doors that kept the weather out, and the contents of the garage dry and safe. He took the items he would need from his car, and making sure that both cars were locked, he switched off the lights and locked the small door that joined the house and garage together and went back to bed.

As Lynne boarded the plane with Danny it seemed bizarre to her that even though the general populace heard the news, and more importantly these days, had access to the internet to give them knowledge of what was happening, they still seemed to have no real idea of how serious things had become. As the plane took off into the night sky, and the lights of London fell away beneath her, Lynne held Danny tight. She knew deep down this would be the last time she would see England.

The following morning, and after finishing his breakfast, Jeff loaded the last of the dirty dishes into the dishwasher and switched it on.

He'd already showered, packed, and dressed, and with the house clean, all there was to do now was to wait for the government car to collect him. And the wait wasn't as long as he thought it may have been. After only a few minutes of waiting, he saw the black Jaguar XJS pull up outside.

"Alexa, begin cleaning," Jeff said. Immediately, the Roomba began vacuuming. Then he picked up his suitcase and exited the house, pulling the large door closed behind him. He locked it, and then using the app on his phone, he set the security system and left. The chauffeur smiled politely as he opened the rear door, and then closing it softly once Jeff was in. As the car pulled away, Jeff took one more look at his home and smiled.

Claire Banks @claire_banks87 -12mins
Been a few weeks since Africa & meeting with @WHO. I was told to keep quiet! But now shits going down. Guess I don't need to!

Since Claire had been released by Joceline, she'd kept her end of the deal, changing the stories on her blog, and going back to posting political disparagements, and satire. She'd always believed that she could not be bought, persuaded, or threatened into making changes to what she published and tweeted about.

But after the attack in Mozambique, and the footage she captured, Claire realized just how small a fish she really was in the huge pool of what was happening. And so, on Joceline's instructions, she had fallen silent on the matter. But things had changed dramatically since they'd last met, and the human world was beginning to come apart at the seams. Claire decided that the authorities would now have enough to do without checking up on her, and her blog. And so, twelve minutes ago, she announced with a tweet, that she would no longer remain quiet. Because of her deal with Joceline, Claire no longer had the upper hand with the video evidence. Clips had begun to appear on YouTube, though initially they were dismissed by the public as hoaxes or even trailers for an upcoming movie. But as the number of clips began to increase and more people were having first-hand experience of the hybrids this was no longer the case. The term victim was the official rhetoric used by the World Health Organization and the Government. But Claire, and the general public, as in all good fiction stories and horror movies, used the term *the infected.* But this was no movie, and it was not fiction. This was real.

Some people had begun to go out, looking for those that had become a hybrid, hoping to film them, and put them online. Social-media *celebrities* were using the outbreak to increase their notoriety, while others documented the changing of loved ones and posted that online. In a world where you are more likely to be photographed or videoed while being mugged, rather than helped, it seemed that even this outbreak wasn't out of bounds for some. Claire had taken much the same approach, but she reassured herself that for her it was about telling the truth, and not to increase her online presence.

She'd set out with her assistant Emma daily to try and capture video footage of the infected. It seemed inexplicable to her that only a few weeks ago she was hiding from these things in a remote village in Mozambique, terrified at not knowing what they were. And yet, after what amounts to a short time later, here she was, in her native New York actively hunting them. And it was becoming easier with each passing day.

In the office *Verum Indicium,* located on 54 West 47th street, New York. Claire and Emma were editing and uploading the latest footage of a hybrid attack on an army Humvee. Though the army truck had been discarded, like many vehicles now were, the group of 6 hybrids seemed to single out this particular truck. As they watched the footage in the early evening, the power to the office block failed.

"Shit!" Emma said as the PC crashed.

"What happened?" Claire asked, looking around the now silent and darkening office.

"Power's out, must be the breakers," Emma replied.

Claire looked out of their window and along the street. "No, it's not, look the whole block has gone dark."

"Do you think this is local?" Emma asked.

"I don't know. I doubt the whole of Midtown is out."

"What do we do now?"

"The backup generator should be kicking in. I don't know why it isn't." Claire said. Still looking out and across to 6th Avenue.

"I'll go check," Emma said.

"Be careful."

Claire watched Emma leave the office and then turned back to her desk. The sun was low, and the office was becoming darker with each passing moment. With all the power off, Claire's only contact with the outside world was her cell phone.

Claire Banks @claire_banks87 -1min
Power failed; intrepid Emma gone to sort problem. The office is getting dark, but it's kinda peaceful.

She placed her cell down and sat back in her chair expecting the lights and systems to come back on at any moment. She never doubted that Emma would walk back in triumphant in her quest to get the office back up and running. But as the minutes passed, and the sun descended behind the high rises, doubt began to creep into her mind. And along with doubt came fear.

Claire stood and made her way to the exit, which led to the stairwell Emma would have used to check the generator room. Standing, listening, and hoping for some sound, perhaps Emma's voice shouting up the stairs, telling Claire, it was all sorted, or even just her light footsteps tapping on each step as she made her way back up. But there was only an eerie silence. Claire entered the stairwell and bent forward over the rail. Peering down, she could see through the gap in the stairs as they circulated around the five floors to the basement.

She stepped onto the first stair. "Emma?" Still only silence. Claire looked back to her office, it was still in darkness, as was the stairwell, except for the emergency battery-operated lighting. Claire moved further down to the next level. "Emma, you there?" Still no answer.

The feeling of terror began to wash over Claire as it had in the village. She was rooted to the spot. She didn't dare move farther down the stairwell, but she couldn't go back to her office without knowing that Emma was ok. Her hand gripped the guard rail tightly, and she could feel the cold sweat of panic forming on her forehead. She swallowed hard. She knew she needed to go down, to know if Emma is okay.

Perhaps she's just having difficulty with the switch.

These older buildings weren't designed for ease of use. It's probably just that. Claire reassured herself. Or maybe she wasn't sure which switch it was, and she was looking for the building manual. *Do buildings even have manuals?* Claire thought to herself as she continued her journey down the staircase. She stopped. She'd reached the basement level and the door that led to the generator room. She reached out a hand and began pushing it. The old door's return spring groaned in protest as she opened it. "Shush!" Claire demanded the spring be quiet, but it didn't comply. Now inside she let the door go and it closed softly behind her.

"Emma, are you in here?" Still no response. Claire moved toward the center of the large room, and to where the generator override switch was located. She stopped dead in her tracks — Emma was lying face down. The back of her skull was crushed, and Claire could see that it had happened quickly, and without Emma knowing the attack was coming.

She moved back slowly, and as calmly as she was able with her body pumping huge amounts of adrenaline around her. She had not heard anything on the stairwell, or move through the doors on the levels, that led off the stairwell, and she certainly hadn't seen anything. And then she realized.

That could only mean one thing. It was still in the room with her. Claire dug deep. This was a big room, with the building's plant machinery in it, but it wasn't big enough to play hide and go-seek with a hybrid. That would be a game she knew she wouldn't win. She needed to get back to her office, and she could either try and do it silently, the way she'd come in, or she could turn and run. She chose the latter.

Her legs and lungs burned as she forced herself up the stairs. Trying to take two steps at once and pulling herself up on the guard rail. It was when she was halfway up the staircase, she heard the sound she'd hoped she would never hear again. The whooping sound she'd heard back in the village. Then came the sound of the plant room door smashing open. As she ran, she dared to look down. A flash of black fur passed the bottom stair. "Shit, shit, shit!" She repeated as she willed herself to the top floor and the perceived safety of her office.

Claire knew to make it out of the building and to her car with the power out, she would have to use the other stairwell, but she knew she wouldn't beat this thing that was now pursuing her. Her only chance was to outthink it and hide in the office, hoping that it would give up the chase. Finally, she burst into her office. Spinning around she locked the door and then ran for the stationery cupboard.

It was metal, and the crude lock could be operated from the inside, it was the only hiding place her mind could think of. She opened the doors and stepped inside. Pulling them closed, she slid the lock down and tried to slow her breathing. Through the small crack in the cupboard door, she could see into the darkened office. She could see the main office door. It moved slightly, groaning under the strain. The hybrid seemed to be testing its resistance. Then it became quiet. Claire dared to think that it had given up, unable to pursue her. As she let out a sigh of relief the door smashed inward, and the hybrid entered the room. It was huge, massive, and she could clearly tell it was male. It walked slowly around, sniffing the air as it did. Claire reached into her pocket and pulled out her phone. She wrote two tweets. One she sent out immediately, and the other she wrote on *Tweetout,* timing it to be sent out later. She slid the phone into her pocket and looked out between the slits in the metal door directly into the eyes of the hybrid. She screamed and tried to bury herself in the back of the cupboard. But it was no use. The door was ripped away with ease. She felt herself being pulled from her hiding place with a force she had never experienced. She was like a ragdoll in the hands of a large primate.

Confused by the speed and ferocity of the attack she realized she was tumbling through the air. Her eyes focused in time to see the large window approach. She felt the impact, and pain in her right side as she smashed through it.
The last image Claire would see was the roof of her car as she fell toward it.

Claire Banks @claire_banks87 -1min
Trapped in the office with one of these monsters. Send help, Emma already dead! help!!!!

As it had around the city, the power had also failed at the Meadowlands Sports Complex, home to the New York Giants, and New York Jets NFL teams. On this evening, the Giants were playing the Philadelphia Eagles. As the stadium plunged into darkness the attack came from a large group of now fully transformed hybrid males. The ferocity of the attack and the impunity with which they targeted meant that families were separated, and children attacked as their helpless parents tried to defend themselves. The teams were not immune as the hybrids broke through the security barriers and charged the playing field. The players, still in their protective gear fought back, and a few of the hybrids were killed. But the sheer savagery of them meant that eventually, only one species remained alive inside the stadium. The night air was filled with the cries and whoops of victory, as the triumphant hybrids ran amuck throughout the stadium, mutilating the dead, and destroying all that they came across.

8

Following Brad's escape, and the attack on the guards before being shot dead, the atmosphere in the center had not been the same. A large proportion of the staff had now left, either because they had begun to exhibit the early onset of the transformation or members of their families had, and having the first-hand experience of what was to come proved enough for them to leave. As a result, the center was running on a skeleton crew. The living quarters and the outer labs had largely been abandoned. Only Joceline Mercier, Rob Pinkert, and two lab technicians, Emily and Terry now remained. And though the facility wasn't large, it had an eerie feel as they made their way through it. In the main laboratory, Rob was struggling to find what they believed was the best promise of a cure. A way to isolate the pathogen that was causing the mutation. But so far, whatever was causing this was eluding them. They had run every known test and procedure on the samples collected from around the world. Rob removed his glasses and rubbed his eyes, he was tired — desperately tired. Since the last meeting with the World Health Organization, and FEMA, the numbers of those affected had increased exponentially and it was clear that humanity, and our civilization, was close to that tipping point. And yet for of all their work, they were no closer to an answer.

As fewer people continued with the day-to-day business that sustains and maintains our way of life, the effects were now becoming tangible. Food supplies had become more erratic, gas too was becoming more difficult to come by, and filling stations began to run dry. Partly because the tanker drivers themselves were no longer showing up for work, but also because the filling station owners and staff were becoming absent.

The refineries were also now undermanned, and the safety systems that prevented any potential disasters from under-demand and oversupply were automatically shutting down the production processes. It was the same with the power stations. With fewer people to maintain them, system after system shut down, and power production was ceasing. Stock markets around the world began to collapse because with no production, there was no product to buy and sell, and no *one* to buy and sell it to.

As people ran out of gas and feared for their safety, and as the numbers of now fully transmuted hybrids began to increase, the highways, shopping malls, and town centers became empty and abandoned. Even the small back roads were quiet.

Cars, trucks, and buses were parked neatly where their drivers had last parked them — on driveways, in compounds, and in garages. They had become too ill to drive. This illness that was taking mankind directly toward extermination didn't come on quickly. Most people had made it home when they began to feel the most severe symptoms, and as a result, the chaos we always assume would happen when society failed had begun quietly, behind closed doors, and drawn curtains.

Rob had started to get the headaches a few days ago, but he'd ignored them, putting them down to the lack of sleep and the pressure they were under. But they were becoming more frequent and intense, and his personal fear of becoming a victim and ending his life strapped to a table in the second laboratory where they now kept the sedated victims, filled him with more fear than what he would eventually become. As he reclined back in his chair stretching his arms Joceline entered the lab. He watched her as she made her way to her desk. She smiled politely at him and sat, lifting the lid of her laptop, and placing her cell phone down next to it. Rob continued to stare at her. Joceline hadn't noticed, she was going through the usual sequence of connecting her computer to the facility's main server, while thoughts of what this day may bring, and the hopes and fears that came with them, swept across her mind.

Rob began to feel some resentment toward her which was quickly followed by anger. He could feel his outstretched hands curling into fists, which became tighter with every pulsating feeling of hatred. Then he noticed her staring back at him, he flinched and relaxed, the palm of his hands felt sore. He looked at them and was disturbed to see how deep his nails had dug into his skin. He felt sick to his stomach, it had been like a daydream, he was aware of his sudden hatred toward Joceline, but it came on him in a daze, and now he was fully mindful he felt a wave of regret wash over him.

He stood, and without saying anything left the room, and made his way to his quarters in the accommodation unit. As Rob made his way along the corridors, the automated lamps switched on as he approached them, but the end of the long passageway was still in darkness. His mind began to drift away from him again, and he began to imagine shapes looming out of the darkness. The corridor itself seemed to be stretching out before him. He didn't recall it being this long. Surely, he should be in his room by now? He thought. Rob stopped, his thoughts were his own again, and the headache returned. But this time the pain didn't stop increasing, and it became more severe with every passing moment. It felt like someone was trying to open his skull with a blunt blade, from the inside. He clasped his hands to his head and squeezed hard, trying with all of his strength to dull the excruciating pain that now pulsated and surged around his head. He closed his eyes trying to shield them from the harsh fluorescent lights that now seemed to fizz and crackle. He slid down the wall, sitting, curling up as tightly as he could into a fetal position, sobbing as the pain continued to increase. Then Rob passed out, as his brain in one last effort to protect itself caused Rob to faint, and he slumped to the floor. With no movements detected, the lamps switched off, leaving Rob's unconscious body lying motionless in the pitch dark.

Joceline hadn't paid much attention to Rob's abrupt exit from the lab. He hadn't been the same since Helen had been admitted and was now one of the victims that lay in the main lab, sedated, and wired to a machine. She also hadn't noticed the way in which he was watching her, and though Rob had mentioned a headache a few days back, she hadn't paid much attention to that either. Like Rob, Joceline put it down to stress, and the short sleeping hours they'd both kept since this had started. What she was paying attention to was the results of a simulation that had been running on the mainframe for the last two days. With the absence of any obvious external factors causing the changes, Joceline had on her own, and against the wishes of her superiors, ran simulations on spontaneous gene mutations that could be caused by environmental factors. She hadn't put much hope or credence in there being any real chance that this could be a possible answer, but as Rob had taken the lead on the external possibilities of it being a mutated virus or pathogen, Joceline had decided to follow a different route. As the results unfolded on her screen, she held her breath. What she was seeing was unprecedented. The theory she'd worked with was relatively new. Epigenetics studies cellular and physiological phenotypic traits caused by external, or environmental influences. Joceline, as with everybody in her field knew that damage to the human DNA occurs around sixty-thousand times a day and that these damages are easily repaired, but any epigenetic changes can remain, and these epigenetic changes can impact evolution. Maybe they had been looking at this from a completely wrong angle. They had assumed that the DNA itself was being re-written, and that the dormant DNA we all carry had been awakened, and that it was this which was causing the physiological and psychological changes. But this had always troubled her. She knew the actual sequence of DNA cannot be changed, or at least that was always the presumed principle, but through gene expression, the way genes work can be changed by altering the way molecules bind to DNA, or by changing the proteins that wrap around it. Joceline sat back, still somewhat overwhelmed by what this would mean if it could be proven

that this is what's causing this devolution of our species. She needed air, and she needed to tell Rob that they should put all of their combined efforts into this new theory. They had an update meeting planned the following day with the World Health Organization, and with FEMA.
If they could at least have a plausible working model that this could be the cause, then they could in theory take a huge step to finding a way to stop it, and even reverse it. Joceline stood and left the lab. Turning, she headed for the exits. Before she spoke to Rob, she would clear her mind.

Outside the sky was a deep blue and the air seemed clearer than normal, and there was also a distinct lack of human-made background noise. The everyday hustle of life that filled our populated and civilized world with a constant backdrop of sound had dimmed, and Joceline noticed how quiet it had become. It reminded her of the early days of the Covid pandemic and subsequent lockdowns imposed. Perhaps this should have given her an idea of what was to come. But her mind kept racing over the new theory, and without paying any more attention to the new quietness, she went back inside, pulling the heavy fire door shut behind her. She guessed that Rob had gone back to his quarters after leaving the lab this morning, after all, the recreation room wasn't much fun by yourself.

She followed the usual route that would take her by the large lab, which is where they now kept the sedated victims. The lights were kept on only to allow any staff that passed the room to visually check on the patients. After the attack, the internal policies had been changed to ensure that staff only entered with an escort. But even though Joceline knew the glass was ballistic resistant, and the door was heavily secured, the sight of the sleeping victims, and the recent events, gave her chills every time she passed it. She arrived at the electronically sealed doors that separated the accommodation block from the rest of the facility. She typed in the required numbers on the small security pad and entered the corridor that would lead to Rob's room. The ceiling lamps switched on as she walked the corridor. As she reached the halfway point, she noticed Rob curled up on the floor. Joceline rushed to him. Carefully, she turned him onto his back, and it became instantly obvious why he was unconscious. Joceline had seen these early symptoms before, his breathing was fast and shallow, and he was covered in sweat. His heart rate was fast, and for a brief moment, Joceline felt helpless. She was almost sure that her new line of investigation would be the answer they needed, that we all needed, but she also knew that she needed Rob's help to complete it. Neither Terry nor Emily had the knowledge required to help her.

But right at this moment, she needed to get Rob with the others, sedated and secure for his safety and for theirs. If she was successful, she may even be able to save him. She pulled the small walkie-talkie from her pocket and called for help.

"This is Doctor Mercier. Can anyone hear me?" She released the talk button and waited.

"Doctor Mercier, this is Terry."

"Terry, Doctor Pinkert has begun to show early onset, I need a stretcher in the living accommodation main corridor."

"On my way doc."

Joceline lay Rob back down and sat herself against the wall. There wasn't much she could do now until Terry arrived with the stretcher. As she sat motionlessly, the lamp switched off. She smiled to herself. *Great! now I'm sitting in the dark.* She thought. Movement would be the only way to switch the lights on again, but for now, she would enjoy the quiet and the dark. As she sat for a few moments, enjoying the solitude, a lamp flickered at the end of the corridor. Initially, she thought it was Terry with the stretcher, but then she realized it was the wrong end of the corridor. Terry would come in where she'd entered. Joceline stared, but the pitch-black between her and the solitary lamp made it impossible for her to make out any detail. The lamp went out, and she heard a thud she recognized as a footstep.

Another came, and another lamp flickered to life shining down a single beam of fluorescent light. She heard another thud and another but it followed much quicker than the last, and she realized whoever it was, was picking up their pace and moving quickly toward her. She stood and moved back a little, the lamps above her came on, as did the lamps above the now running shape. As each sequence of lamps illuminated the corridor, Joceline could make out more detail, and she realized with horror that it was Rob. She could now see a trail of dark-red mucus leading away from where she'd found him lying, and she realized that Rob had crawled to the end of the corridor after the lamps had gone out, his slow movement hadn't been enough to trigger them. But now he was almost on her. She walked backward as quickly as she could, unable to turn around, she was fixed on him. Partly through fear and partly because she didn't want him attacking her from behind. She fumbled in her pockets for anything she could defend herself with, she felt something sharp and pulled out her steel nail file. Rob was close, only a few feet away, he'd covered the length of the long corridor much quicker than she thought possible. She screamed at him, hoping to distract him.

"Rob, no!" She yelled as loud as she could. It had no effect.

Rob's outstretched hands grabbed her by the throat, and he began to squeeze.

She fell backward, landing heavily, and he fell on top of her. She was gasping for air as his thumbs pressed down on her windpipe, and she knew if she did nothing, she would die here and now. Clutching the nail file, she swung her arm around with as much strength as she could muster with no aim or target. Just at the point of unconsciousness, Rob released his grip and slumped to her side. Panting, and gasping for air she turned her head. Rob lay next to her, his lifeless eyes staring at her, and buried deep into his temple was her nail file. The doors behind her banged open and she sat startled, scurrying around to see what or who it was. To her relief, it was Terry with the stretcher. Rob's body was now lying on the same table they had used only a few days ago to examine Brad. Joceline looked down at it with a sense of great sadness.

She and Rob had started to form that rarest of relationships. One based on mutual trust and respect for each other, not only as professionals in their respective fields but also for the people they were. But Joceline knew there was still work to do, and answers to find. She needed to understand why it had affected Rob as quickly as it did, whilst she was showing no signs of infection, not even the tell-tale headaches. She pulled the large lamp down over his face. There were no physical changes, nothing that she could have seen sitting across from his desk. And even as she reached around the base of his skull there was no occipital bun, at least not prevalent enough for her to feel. Joceline decided against a full autopsy, partly because there just wasn't the staff available to perform it, but also because he deserved much more than being sliced up. But she had to know why his psychological changes had happened so quickly, and why he'd become so violent toward her. All of the reports they'd read, and witnesses they'd spoken to, all confirmed that even when the mind started to lose reasoning and communication skills it was gradual, quick but gradual. But Rob's had been like a light switch. She decided to perform an MRI scan, it would be less intrusive and quicker than removing and dissecting his brain. She turned to Terry who had found them after the attack, and who'd stayed with her since.

"Terry, please run an MRI scan on Doctor Pinkert's brain, and then move his body to the morgue."

"Will do Doctor Mercier," Terry replied softly.

"Please, just Joceline, I think we're passed titles at this stage." She said as she removed her gown and gloves.

Terry didn't answer. He smiled and nodded his acknowledgment. The next few hours were a blur to Joceline as she ran model after model based on her new theory that it was environmental influencers and factors that were causing the changes in humans only.

No other species were being affected by this condition that was taking mankind to the very precipice of collapse. Slumped at her desk she was awoken by the sound of the computer, it was chiming repeatedly, letting anyone who was close by know that it had finished its given task. She opened her eyes slowly, blinking as she did and lifting her head from her folded arms.

Sitting back in the chair and placing her glasses on she started to read the results, slowly at first but as she became fully awake, she began to skim-read it, her eyes moving quickly left to right, and then back again to the next line. She stopped and took a deep breath. Was she seeing this right? Did she fully understand what it was saying? And if she was, did she fully understand what it meant for our species? She paused, trying to collect her thoughts. She needed someone to read it, to give her a second opinion on the information that was on the screen, but there was no one. No one other than Rob would have understood what this was. She needed to read it again, but not here, not on a screen, she needed to see it spread out in front of her. Joceline sent the data to the printer in her private office, then backed up the file to a flash drive she kept on a chain around her neck. Once the print was confirmed, and the backup complete, she logged out of the computer and left the lab. Her private office was directly attached to her quarters.

As the lead scientist appointed by the World Health Organization, Joceline had the largest and grandest accommodation, though, in the outside world, it wouldn't be considered either large or grand. But here, amongst the bland magnolia corridors and white square ceiling tiles of the facility, it was an oasis of calm.

Joceline showered and wrapped her large dressing gown around her, picking the fifty-five pages of data up from the laser printer she walked to a large wingback chair and sat. Elsewhere in the facility, the automated procedures were shutting down non-essential systems for the night ahead. Terry and Emily were now in their own quarters with their doors firmly locked. Lamps in the unused labs were switched off, as computer workstations went into hibernation mode, waiting for the next user, which for most would never come. In the recreation room too, only the blinking lights of the assorted video games and slot machines were visible in the pitch-black windowless room. Only two rooms outside of the accommodation block had any kind of lighting on — the small security office which had been empty since most of the staff had left and the laboratory which held the victims. And the small canteen attached to the Labs.

Under the facility, the staff parking lot was now largely abandoned, with only a few vehicles parked in it. Two belonged to Joceline and Rob, the rest were staff pool cars.

Both exits were sealed by large electric shutters which were locked, and like the rest of the facility, the ceiling lamps were switched off. Only the green glow of the exit signs offered any kind of relief from the dark. Joceline wasn't sure what time she'd finally fallen asleep or how long for, but the soft alarm of her bedside clock woke her at precisely 6:45 a.m. as it had since she'd been here. It was today she would have to go before members of FEMA, and the World Health Organization, and not only tell them of Rob's death but also that all of the research they had done since this started had been wrong.

All of their assumptions, ideas, and quests for a cure, or even a vaccine, had been based on incorrect supposition and conjecture. And Joceline knew that news like that wouldn't be received well and would be met with skepticism. But the proof she needed to persuade them that this new theory was correct was in front of her, and if they doubted her still, she could send the data to the labs in Munich, Geneva, and Mozambique to confirm it. There was a soft knock on her door. Puzzled, Joceline answered to find Emily standing patiently.

"What is it?" Joceline asked.

"There is a woman and child at the main gate asking for you," Emily answered.

"Who is it?"

Emily looked down at the piece of paper she was holding.

"She said her name is Lynne Eastwood, and she's with her son Danny."

Joceline had forgotten about the conversation she'd had with Lynne the previous day. So much seems to have happened since then her mind scrambled to accept that it's only been twenty-four hours. She also realized that she hadn't formally requested Lynne as she said she would. But it was too late now, she couldn't send them away, she'd have to bring them in.

"Tell the gate to allow them in. You meet them at the main entrance and bring them to me. Remember to secure the main doors behind you."

"Will do," Emily said, as she turned to leave.

Joceline was in the main lab preparing for her conference when Emily brought in Lynne and Danny, and though Joceline had not previously met Danny, she recognized Lynne.

"Ah Lynne, how are you? How was your flight?" Joceline asked smiling.

"Doctor Mercier, thank you for taking us in," Lynne answered.

"Please, we have dispensed with the formalities, just call me Joceline."

Lynne smiled and pulled Danny forward, "This is my son, Danny, we spoke about him."

"Yes, I remember," Joceline kneeled and turned her attention to him. "Hello Danny, how are you?" Danny didn't answer, he looked at Joceline sullenly, and she recognized it as the same look Rob had given her before she'd found him in the corridor. A chill ran down her back. "Emily, why don't you show Danny our wonderful recreation room?"

"Sure, come on Danny, come with me." Emily took Danny's hand and led him out of the lab.

Joceline stood and smiled as they left, then she turned to Lynne and her smile left her. Lynne knew this wasn't a good sign. She gestured to Lynne to sit which she did, and Joceline sat next to her at one of the long desks that skirted the lab walls.

"I am sure, there is no doubt in my mind that Danny is infected, I saw the same look yesterday in Rob's eyes, Doctor Pinkert. You may remember him," Joceline said calmly.

"Yes, the American you were with at my hospital, is he infected? Is he okay?" Lynne answered.

"Yes, he was infected, he's dead now," Joceline's soft tone was replaced by sadness.

Lynne looked down, gathering her thoughts. "How?" She asked.

"He attacked me, I stabbed him. I killed him," Joceline answered.

Lynne nodded, she didn't say anything more about it, there was nothing more to say. Death and destruction had become common news now. All over the globe were reports of it, and it was becoming more widespread.

"How are things in London?" Joceline asked,

"Not good. My husband Jeff works for the government, for COBRA. Well, you know that you know him," Joceline nodded confirmation, while Lynne continued. "He said the government is closing the airports today, that's why I'm here now, he's with the Prime Minister. They've taken him and the cabinet to a safe location, along with the Royal Family to Balmoral Castle."

"What about the police and the army?" Joceline asked.

"No better, most have become infected. Those that haven't are showing up less and less for work, staying with their families. Who can blame them? I don't think the UK will hold out much longer,". Lynne's tone became more distraught as she continued.

"We have a cabin in the Lake District, it's off-grid. I told my mom to go there, to wait for Jeff. I hope she has. But even so, how will he get her here with the airports closed?"

Joceline sighed heavily. "It's no better anywhere in Europe Lynne, yesterday the Eastern European countries went dark, Romania was the first to go, and then it spread east into Moldova, Ukraine, and then western Russia. Moscow was communicating yesterday, but I have no idea if they still are."

"Are you close to a cure?" Lynne asked.

"No. It seems we were looking in the wrong place. Our ideas and theories were way out."

"What does that mean?" Lynne asked.

"It means I'm starting again. We all have to start again. I have to convince those in charge to drop all the research we've been doing and start on a new premise."

"Do you think they will?" Lynne asked, cautiously.

"Honestly, I don't know if there is time," Joceline said as she shrugged.

The room became quiet. Lynne was less unsure now than when she'd been at home. With Rob dead and the facility all but empty, she wasn't sure if coming here had been the best thing. As far as she knew the hospitals back home were still operational, if chronically overcrowded. But what Joceline had said about Eastern Europe was now reverberating around her mind. She had seen first-hand how easy it was for economic migrants to move across the European continent, and eventually make it across the English Channel, or under it by the Euro-Tunnel. And if Europe was starting to fall from the east, it would be fair to assume that people would move west to escape the coming nightmare, and Britain was the most westerly country. As a thousand if's and what's rampaged through Lynne's mind, she was interrupted by Terry entering the lab.

"Joceline," Terry said.

"Yes," Joceline answered with a polite but very fragile smile.

"They're ready for you in the conference room."

"Thank you, Terry."

Joceline turned to Lynne. "You should come in and be a part of this Lynne. With your medical training and experience of treating these victims, you will be invaluable to me."

Lynne shrugged. "I'm not sure how much help I can be, genetics and DNA? It's all beyond me, I just run a ward in London," She hesitated for a second. "Did run a ward in London."

Joceline stood. "Non-the-less come with me. You may as well hear what I've discovered, and what I now know."

Lynne followed Joceline out of the lab and along a short corridor to the conference room. Near the lectern where Rob had stood the last time they'd met, now hung a large white screen from the ceiling. On it were three live video feeds.

One of them had the World Health Organization's logo in the bottom right corner. The other two screens had FEMA in the top left. Lynne sat toward the front of the room while Joceline stood at the head of the table directly in front of the screen.

"Hello, nice to see you all again," Joceline said.

The three-people responded in kind. Sean Macleod from the Federal Protective Service, who sat in at the last meeting was the first to speak. "Where is Doctor Pinkert?"

Joceline looked back at Lynne and then back to the screens. "I'm sorry to report that Doctor Pinkert became infected and can no longer take part in our efforts."

"That is a shame," Sean said.

Doug MacAskill, an Emergency Management Specialist who had also been at the previous meeting was the next to speak. "Tell me, Joceline, what progress have you made on finding a cure or vaccine?"

Joceline looked between the three faces that she knew were hoping and praying she would tell them that she'd found a way to mask or change the DNA-altering virus, or better yet, a way to stop it. But their prayers had been false ones, based on the wrong theories they had been working with. There was no masking or changing it, or ways to stop it. She cleared her throat. She was as ready as she ever would be to deliver her findings.

"What we thought, what we spoke about at our last meeting, everything we thought we knew is wrong." She said.

There was a silence before Doug spoke again. "What do you mean everything is wrong?"

Joceline looked back at Lynne and then back to the screen, her eyes began to fill, and her voice became dry as she fought back the wave of dread that washed over her. She gathered herself and cleared her throat. "This is not a virus or a pathogen, it's something ancient, something we have not seen before, and never will again."

There was stunned silence in the room. Joceline stared at the three faces on the screen, and all of them without exception showed the same expressions — Confusion and utter disbelief. Sean was the first to speak.

"What do you mean, there is no cure?" Sean demanded.

"What I mean is that there is no cure! There never was. This is Mankind's extinction event. There will be no coming back from this."

9

Elizabeth Shaw asked the next question. She too had been at the previous meetings. "But at our last meeting, you said you could mask it, making our bodies fight the pathogen. What has changed since then?"

Joceline sighed before answering, this was the part she was dreading, she would now have to tell them that since their last meeting, she had been working on her own initiative. Her theory of what could be happening, even though they had explicitly told her not to follow this line of inquiry as it was one that was not sanctioned by any of the world's health or emergency response departments. But she'd had a hunch that this was not a virus or pathogen when they had first seen Brad. The theory she followed had first been put forward in the nineteen-sixties by the British Scientist, Doctor James Lovelock while working for NASA on the possibility of human colonization of other planets. But this theory, the Gaia Hypothesis, had largely been ignored by mainstream science, and so to investigate it, Joceline had to work in secret. But following the results of the final model tests she'd run yesterday; she now had no doubt in her mind.

"Since our last meeting, I have been running models based on the Gaia Hypothesis. This states that the planet earth is a single living organism, rather than a rock in space that supports individual life forms. It suggests that all living and non-living components of earth's biosphere are regulated to a very high degree, so much so that it can be viewed as a single living organism in its own right." She paused and waited for the inevitable reprimand. She didn't have to wait long.

"And who was it that gave you the go-ahead for this particular line of exploration?" Sean asked sternly.

"No one, as I said I did it on my own, which is why the results that convinced me enough to tell you what I have, have taken this long to collect and interpret," Joceline answered with the same uncompromising tone.

"You know if you'd proposed this theory, we would have taken you off this project," Sean said.

"That's why I didn't tell anyone, including Rob. But now we have the results, and I have no doubt in my mind that what they've shown me confirms my initial thoughts and fears. If you don't believe me, then I'll send the data to Munich, or Mozambique. They can and will confirm my findings."

"Mozambique went dark twenty-four hours ago, most of Africa is now quiet, and we're receiving no radio traffic or any broadcasts of any kind from most of the continent," Elizabeth said.

"Okay, Munich or Geneva" Joceline argued.

"We don't have time. If what you're proposing is actually what is happening, we have no choice but to work to your findings, but you'll need to convince us beyond any doubt. Because ultimately, you'll be asking us to put in a contingency for our eventual demise," Elizabeth paused and then continued. "So Joceline, if you're one-hundred percent sure that what you're about to tell us is fact, it's really what is happening. Then go ahead."

Joceline paused and looked at Lynne, she was expressionless. She stared back at Joceline and nodded. Joceline took a deep breath and turned back to the screen.

"As I said, think of the earth much like a human body which is composed of trillions of cells, and yet we consider ourselves to be one single organism. The Gaia Hypothesis puts forward that this is the case with any planet which has life on it. The most famous experiment to prove this theory is the Daisyworld simulation. A world covered in either white daisy's which reflected heat, or black daisy's which absorbed heat. Therefore, the black daisy would heat the atmosphere, whilst the white daisy would remain cool, and not add to the heating of the atmosphere. This is one basic way of showing how one individual thing can alter a state not physically connected to it, in much the same way a small change in our bodies can lead to the symptoms that seem to have nothing to do with the initial problem. We thought this thing was a virus or a pathogen, especially given the way the initial outbreaks were patterned, they mirrored the earth's wind patterns, but this hypothesis proves this is not the case."

"Okay, so you've told us the principle behind the theory, and that it's not a virus. So, what is it?" Asked Sean.

"It's nature," Joceline said. "If you accept that the earth is a living organism, and everything, like our bodies, is connected, then the earth, the body on which we live, has a cancer. This is planet earth fighting back."

"Then what is the cancer, and why are only humans being affected?" Sean asked.

"We're not being affected. We're being infected," Joceline paused and looked around before she continued. "We are the cancer. Mankind, Homo-Sapiens, whatever label we have put on ourselves, nature has labeled us as a pest, a disease, and we're being eradicated in the same way our bodies send anti-bodies, white blood cells, to kill unwanted organisms." Joceline paused again, waiting for another question.

"But why this way, why not turn the animals against us if nature can really do this?" Sean asked.

Joceline smiled. "How could it, we're the apex species, we can defend ourselves from almost any animal attack, and anyway why would nature risk another species? Think of this, what gives us dominance over all other animals? As a predator, we can't run very fast, we're not good swimmers, we can't climb very well, or fly, and compared to other species of similar size we're physically weak. We don't even have natural weapons, such as sharp claws or teeth. What we have is intelligence, and that is what nature is targeting. That is what nature is taking away from us."

"You've said this can't be cured. Why are you so sure it can't be?" Elizabeth asked.

"Because we're already infected, all of us, the whole human race is infected at the fetal stage. Nature built a safeguard into us. If you like we were designed, evolved with a reset button, much like your home computer, so that if we started to go, well wrong, we could be reset. It just needed the right environmental factors for the switch to be flicked," Joceline answered.

"But how and why has this switch not been seen before?" Sean asked.

"Simply speaking we never looked for it, why would we?" Joceline shrugged as she answered.

"But why so suddenly?" Doug asked.

"Truly it isn't. Cultures around the world have reported a drop in intelligence in parts of their societies. How many of you here have thought, why does it appear that some people are stupid? The way they react to situations —— speak or are even unable to hold a conversation. We know our intellectual and emotional skills are reliant on a web of genes that are intricately linked. According to a paper published by Stanford, these genes are susceptible to dumbing down mutations, and it follows that within societies the less intelligent have more children per family than their more intelligent peers. We thought this was just about socioeconomic factors but it's not. The natural urge to breed was stronger in the people whose genes had been affected by the dumbing down process. Nature has been moving its chess pieces, waiting for the right time."

"Essentially, what you're saying Doctor Mercier, is that as a species we're de-evolving, our DNA is being re-written?" Sean protested.

"Actually, the term de-evolving in modern biology is now redundant, though it's as good a phrase as any to describe what's happening, I guess. But the idea of devolution assumes that evolution needs a determined path toward more complexity. This ties in with anthropocentrism, the idea that our presence is the point of all universal existence. We now know that evolution is a continuous process.

Had this not happened, it's fair to assume that eventually no human would be born with wisdom teeth. Another example is the tale of the cetacean, whales, and dolphins. In fact, all sea-based mammals. We know that the tale of these species is essentially the evolved spinal column of land-based mammals, which they are related to after they returned to the sea from living on land. This could have been classed as devolution, a backward step, from land to the sea, but still needing to breathe oxygen without the use of gills. But from an evolutionary point, it is absolutely evolution. According to Dollo's law, evolution is not reversible, and so from a perception of the earth being an organism, it is evolving us backward, and into a non-evasive and benign species."

"But that is almost opposed to everything we thought we knew," Sean said.

"Darwin believed that evolution was progressive, that it was directed toward one goal — Human perfection. He was wrong." Joceline answered.

"That's a big statement to make," Elizabeth said.

"It's the truth. Nature has allowed us to get this far, and now it's taking back what it has given us. If evolution was indeed the single directional path to human perfection, then this, what is happening to us, could not be," Joceline answered.

"I still don't understand why you think us becoming some kind of human-Neanderthal hybrid would be classed as evolution," Doug said, with a frustrated tone.

Joceline sighed. "Okay, let me put it this way. Devolution relates to an ancient idea that life either came into being by a creator or that humans are the ultimate goal of evolution, as Darwin suggested. That, as I have said is essentially anthropocentrism. In the late nineteenth century, some scientists discussed degenerative evolution, but those theories are no longer used today. Evolution isn't like time, it's not linear, it doesn't have to travel in one direction. Our jaws are much less complicated than the sea dwellers all life on land evolved from, and yet we believe we are more evolved than them. If you still believe less is devolution, then surely we have devolved?"

"If we accept that the earth is doing this and that it is one organism, then why and how?" Elizabeth asked.

"As I've stated, because it sees us as cancer, a risk to all other life on it, to its own survival." Joceline sounded frustrated.

"How is it? You said we were born, made with a reset switch in our genetic code. So how is it resetting us, and how did it trigger it?" Asked Doug.

Joceline sat in the large chair that was at the head of the table and rubbed her hands over her head.

"We know that DNA itself cannot be altered, but environmental conditions can affect it indirectly by modifying epigenetic factors. These are the compounds that are attached to the DNA. They interact with the genetic material but don't change the underlying DNA sequence, rather they are genetic tags indicating what, where, and which genes should be turned on or off. Some of these epigenetic factors are actually encoded in the DNA and form part of the gene regulation, that's how these factors control which genes are active in particular cells, and are implicated in social and behavioral traits, hence the aggression we've seen," She paused and took a drink of water. After hydrating her throat, she continued. "The epigenome is vital as it is this which is the primary location of gene-environment interactions, and it can be altered by certain environmental stimuli. For instance, an environmental agent such as a chemical toxin could enter the cells of a tissue, and interface directly with the genetic material."

"And you believe this is how nature has started the re-set sequence in humans?" Elizabeth asked.

"Essentially, yes. We know that Methylation is how a cell knows it needs to grow into a leg, or fingernail, rather than an eye or toenail. And I believe that it is the process of methylation that nature is using against us."

"If you know how it's doing this, then surely you can stop it?" Sean asked.

"No, because the agent that started the interaction was released slowly over the last five years. It was hidden amongst our own pollution, that's why we didn't see it, and because it was a slow release and the effects are only now being seen, it is, I'm afraid, too late. This is irreversible," Joceline answered.

"But if it's been over that time scale, why is it affecting all generations, surely newborn babies, and children under five should not be affected?" Elizabeth asked.

"Darwin's central premise was always that evolutionary changes happened over millions of years through natural selection. But our new model of epigenetic characteristics means that changes are memorized and transmitted through to new generations." Joceline answered.

"Is there proof of this theory? Or is this just conjecture?" Sean asked.
Joceline smiled and nodded. "Yes, there is. There are many studies of fearful memories that are passed to the next generation. Toward the end of World War Two, the allies attempted to push across the Rhine, to end the war early. This was called Operation Market Garden, and it failed. Because of this, the Germans blockaded Dutch towns across the western Netherlands. This became known as the Dutch Hongerwinter.

On average, every person had only five hundred and eighty calories a day, and many starved to death. Thousands of babies were born underweight. What surprised researchers after the war was that the children's children of the underweight babies, who were well fed were significantly underweight. It seemed the famine had scarred the victims' DNA. In other words, through epigenetic characteristics, the grandchildren of the Dutch Hongerwinter suffered the same fate as if they had been there at the time. That's why children conceived even after the release of the chemical toxin will be affected in the same way."

"Can you tell us how the planet has attacked us? How has it instigated this change in our genome?" Asked Sean.

"I believe it's through the levels of carbonic acid in our blood. As you know carbonic acid is used to transport carbon dioxide in our blood, and it is also the by-product of carbon dioxide being absorbed by our oceans. As the levels of carbon dioxide have risen dramatically due to man-made climate change, I believe those levels reached a saturation point which triggered our genetic re-set," Joceline paused. "In other words, we have flicked the switch on our re-set."

"But we can reverse climate change, we can reverse the changes. We are reversing the changes." Sean protested.

"But we haven't done it quickly enough, and nature, the organism that is the earth, is resetting it for us, taking matters into its own hands. As a species, we've poisoned the oceans, hunted animals to the brink of extinction and beyond, carried out tests on them, and experimented on them. It is estimated that eighty-eight percent of the world's species are yet to be discovered, and there are at least ten animals at least the size of the Great White shark, or bigger, yet to be discovered in the oceans. Imagine what we would do if we had found everything. We pollute the very air we breathe, kill ourselves in the name of Gods that no one could ever prove exist, and we have put more resources into ways of killing each other than in ways to live in harmony and peace. We are suffocating the planet we call home, killing it for our greed and short-term goals. Tell me that is not the behavior of cancer or of a parasite that any of us would want to have removed from our own bodies?" Joceline answered angrily.

Elizabeth calmed her. "Tell us, Doctor Mercier, how do you see the Earth ten years from now?"

"On that day, the seas will be full, the forests lush and green and the air will be clear. The animals of Earth will live without the memory and fear of man and in harmony with each other. On that same day, mankind will have long been dead." Joceline Replied.

All of them looked bewildered and frightened.

"It's not just this that should concern us," Joceline added. "I believe there's something else at play, something more we should consider."

"What is it?" Elizabeth asked.

"I believe this has happened before, and I believe there is evidence around the world to prove this theory," Joceline answered.

"You mean with another species?" Doug asked.

Joceline looked between the small screens and cleared her throat. "No, I mean Homo-Sapiens. And more specifically, a duplicate civilization."

"Can you please clarify what you mean by that statement?" Doug asked.
"The Earth is not only re-setting us. It is re-setting evolution. Again." Joceline whispered.

"Please, explain further Joceline," Elizabeth said.

"Creationists believe in the Pre-Adamic man theory or Pre-Adamites. They believe that a human-like species, at least as advanced as we are now, once lived on earth before God put Adam and Eve here."

"You're a scientist doctor, surely you don't believe in God. Do you?" Doug interrupted her.

"No, but there is fossil evidence to suggest that it could be true. Not that a God created the planet, and put the first two humans, Adam, and

Eve on it. But that a human-like species was once here. However, much of the evidence found is just fragments - teeth, jawbones, and limbs though they are considerably larger than modern man, leading to the belief by some that the earth was once inhabited by giants." Joceline said.

"Giants?" Elizabeth asked.

"Mainstream science has always debunked or even just plainly ignored things which don't fit into the fossil record as we think they should. And the evidence is often locked away or even destroyed. But what if Pre-Adamites did exist? And what if nature pressed the re-set button of them too?" She paused. "What if, as a species, this isn't our first time here? What if we've been on this ride before?" Joceline said.

"Apart from hear-say and religious ramblings, what evidence is there to support that theory?" Sean asked.

"During my research into the Gaia Hypothesis, I stumbled upon the possibility of the Pre-Adamites theory. And so, I began to look at this in detail, and the evidence exists of human civilization and technology millions of years before humanity is thought to have evolved. Two hundred-million-year-old modern shoe prints have been found, and documented, as well as the metallic spheres found in South Africa." Joceline replied.

"And you believe this is enough to state that we are on, some kind of universal merry-go-round?" Elizabeth asked.

"No, not on their own, but one of the most condemning pieces of evidence is the *Cenozoic Era Proof,"* Joceline answered.

"Please, explain." Sean encouraged her to continue.

"It follows the time of the Mesozoic era which is then divided into the following time periods. They are the Tertiary Period and the Quaternary Period. The features of the Tertiary period are considered under the time periods called the Epochs, which are made up from the earliest to the latest. In order, these are the Paleocene, Eocene, Oligocene, Miocene, and finally the Pliocene. Do you follow so far?" She asked.

"Carry on," Elizabeth asked.

"The accepted view of evolution is that human beings, Homo sapiens, began appearing in the Cenozoic Era around one and a half million years ago, and human civilization only around ten thousand years ago. Yet scientific finds present a very different story. For instance, a *modern* human skeleton was found in Tanzania, and carbon dating showed it to be over eight hundred thousand years old, but what was most interesting was that the skull was embedded in rock that dated back over one million years.

Our distant ancestors of this era were very different in certain features to us, but this skull was modern," Joceline paused, taking another drink of water. "Another modern human skull was found in Italy in the late nineteenth century, which was dated over three-million years old, and a small figurine was found of a modern human female skillfully made from clay in a well boring hole, which has been dated and confirmed to be over two million years old."

"They could be hoaxes," Doug said.

"Or time-travel?" Sean added.

"Really?" Elizabeth interrupted them.

Joceline looked between the small screens. "I know this is a lot to take in, and had we had more time we could have investigated it further. Every other scientific investigation that has tried to gain ground on this theory has been shut down by the establishment, every time, and I believe it's because it is a plausible answer to what is happening to the human race now.
No other species is being affected, only Homo sapiens, so it's not out of the realm of possibility that this is what is happening."

"But you can understand our skepticism?" Elizabeth asked.

"You mentioned a footprint," Sean said.

"It is a shoe print found in Utah shale, which was aged at around five hundred and nine million years old," Joceline said.

"To sum up Joceline, this is not a virus, or a pathogen, whether it is man-made or naturally occurring. What you're proposing is that nature, the earth to be exact, is a single living organism that is fighting a cancer that you claim is mankind and that you also believe this has happened before in the earth's history?" Doug asked.

"This is not a proposal. This is a statement of fact. The earth is wiping out an infectious bacterium that unstopped will kill every living thing on this planet, and yes, I believe it has happened in the past. This is not mankind's first existence." Joceline answered.

As Joceline continued to watch their reactions as they each started to comprehend what they had just been told, the three small video links crackled and hissed with static. Before any of them had a chance to say anything further, the large screen became blank, and the message *Transmission Lost-No signal* scrolled across it. Joceline turned to Lynne who had the same dazed look on her face.

"Is that true?" Lynne asked quietly. "Is the earth a single organism, is it clearing us away like some disease?"

Joceline nodded slowly. "I'm afraid it is, yes."

"So that's it, there's nothing we can do?" Lynne asked.

"I'm sorry Lynne. There isn't."

Lynne stood and took a deep breath. "I need to be with my son, and I need to call Jeff, if this is it, we should be together."

"Of course," Joceline said.

Lynne left the conference room, leaving Joceline to look at the static that had now covered the entire screen. Joceline expected this to happen.

As the population fell, the technology we had become so proud of, the thing that had allowed us to achieve so much would also be our greatest downfall and the first casualty of our modern civilization. She picked up the small remote and pointed it at the ceiling-mounted projector and pressed the small red button. With a small whir of its fan, the bulb was extinguished, and the screen became blank. Joceline took one last look around the large conference room before she switched off the lights and closed the door behind her. Knowing now there was nothing else to be done, she would let Terry and Emily go, along with the guards on the main gate.

With the barriers in place and the windows protected by steel shutters, the facility was almost impossible to gain entry to, and as the population continued to regress to a hybrid-Neanderthal state, she knew that Lynne, Danny, and herself would be safe, at least until one of them started to show early on-set and became violent. Before she could send Terry and Emily away, there was one last task to perform.

"You wanted to see us," Emily said as they entered.

"Yes. There is little point in you both staying here now, society will soon break down, we have reached the tipping point of chaos, and I think you should both be with your family and friends. But before you leave, I have one last task I need you both to perform."

Terry and Emily looked between each other, somewhat puzzled. "What is it?" Terry asked.

"I need you to give each victim a mixture of the following drugs, Thiopental, Pancuronium Bromide, and Potassium Chloride. Is that understood?"

Terry looked concerned "That will kill them." He said.

"There is nothing that can be done, this is the kindest way." She replied.

Neither Joceline nor Terry nor Emily spoke as they entered the lab that held the sleeping victims. With the three syringes ready, Terry injected the chemicals into the intravenous drip of the first patient. As the last syringe emptied, Joceline looked at the patient's details. She was a woman in her twenties, her name tag showed L. Lou, and she was admitted to the hospital with severe headaches only four weeks previous. Joceline watched as her heart rate stalled and flatlined. One by one they followed the same procedure until they reached the last two victims.

As Emily began to administer the first of the drugs the victim opened his eyes. Startled, Emily jumped back, dropping the cocktail of drugs. Its body convulsed, a reaction to the first injection, but she hadn't given it the full dose and its body was fighting the paralyzing effects of the drug. Abruptly, the convulsing stopped, and its eyes closed again. Joceline, Terry, and Emily stood staring at the large hybrid-Neanderthal male that seemed to be unconscious once again. Joceline moved toward it.

"Careful," Terry whispered.

Joceline didn't verbally answer, she nodded slowly. She reached out and took the large right hand in hers. Carefully she reached around and checked the wrist for a pulse, she couldn't feel one. But she didn't know if that was because there wasn't one, or that the skin was too thick to feel it. She squeezed the wrist harder, tightening her grip, but still, she couldn't feel it. Out of the corner of her eye, just in her peripheral vision, she thought she saw something move. Unsure she turned her head slowly, relaxing her grip as she did. It moved again; it was the index finger of the hand she was holding.

She swallowed hard as she felt the same fear rising in her that she had when Rob had attacked her. She kept watching as she slowly and gently released her grip and lowered the heavy arm down.

The index finger curled again, this time it was followed by the rest of the fingers. The hand now made a fist.

"Back away slowly," Joceline whispered to Terry and Emily as she let go of the now tensed arm. Joceline looked along the body. When she reached its head, she was met by its stare. Its eyes were dark brown, almost black, and they looked full of fear and hate. Joceline moved her gaze down its face and she could see clearly that it was snarling at her, in the way a rabid dog would do just before it attacked. Joceline's adrenaline was now coursing around her body, her legs shook as she backed away, she wanted to run for the door, to lock it inside, hoping that the door and glass would hold it, but she didn't get the chance to turn and run. Before another thought, and another scenario where she managed to get to safety had crossed her mind, the large hybrid screamed at her. The noise split the air and vibrated in her ears. She'd heard cries like this before in the animal kingdom, and she knew instantly what it was. It was a battle cry. As the cry continued the other victim they had not yet euthanized awoke, instantly it joined in, instinct seemed to have told this one it was in danger too.

The large male broke the straps that held it down and it leaped from the table with a speed that Joceline had not seen in large bipedal animals before, especially humans.

It struck out at Joceline knocking her backward into a large metal cabinet. Hitting her head, she fell to the floor unconscious. Terry and Emily now stood motionless, afraid, and unable to think of what to do. The hybrid took a step toward them and then stopped. It studied the room, and Terry could see that it was trying to understand why there were so many others like him, but only one other had responded to his cry.

Then its gaze fell upon the monitors which now showed the flat lines of those they had euthanized. *Surely it couldn't understand what it was looking at.* Terry thought to himself, but it seemed to recognize the collation between the still bodies and the continuous flat line on the monitors. Slowly, it turned and walked toward the female that was still strapped tightly to the table. It looked at the moving wriggling creature before it, and then at the monitor which showed the spiking lines of its heart rate. Emily reached out slowly and picked up another syringe as quietly as she could, Terry grabbed her arm to stop her, but she pulled away and stepped silently toward it. It had its back to her as it tore apart the straps holding down the female.

She got within striking range and began to lift her arm, taking aim at the middle of its back, knowing that if she needed to let go it wouldn't be able to pull the syringe out.

As she brought her arm down it spun around and caught it. Spinning her around it towered over her. Grabbing her head, it twisted it with the ease you would twist open a bottle top. Terry heard the snap of her neck. That was all he heard, it happened so quickly, Emily hadn't had the time needed to scream. Her body collapsed to the floor lifeless. Turning back to the table, it pulled the last strap off, and the female stood next to it.

Terry lowered his head, hoping and praying that averting his eyes would be enough for it not to see him as a challenge. It seemed to work. He watched as best he could from his viewpoint, as both hybrids walked from the lab and turned toward the conference room and to the now redundant and abandoned part of the building. He waited until they had turned the corner and were out of sight before he made for the main terminal in the lab. Entering his passwords, he clicked on the building security icon and selected lockdown.

This protocol would separate each part of the facility with reinforced magnetically sealed doors. The section the two hybrids had entered was made up of the administration, and communications block. They would now be separated from the lab and living quarters. Though how long for he wasn't sure.

He turned his attention from the terminal and to

Emily's body. He couldn't leave it where she'd fallen, and the morgue was in the section which was now sealed off.

The lab was airtight once the door was sealed and locked so the decomposing bodies would not pose a threat to the rest of the facility. And besides, by the time that happened, they may not care, or be alive themselves. Carefully, and as respectfully as he could, he lifted her from the floor and placed her on the table the large male had escaped from. He straightened her body and head, and pulled the thin white cotton sheet over her, covering her completely. Terry then turned his attention to Joceline who was starting to come around, moaning softly and holding her head. She stood and looked at the empty table.

"Did he get out?" She asked Terry.

"Yes, they did." He replied.

She looked confused. "They?" She pointed at the one empty table and Terry realized she didn't yet know about Emily. He pulled the sheet back revealing her head, which still lay at an unnatural angle to her body. The bruising had already begun, and the skin around her neck resembled a badly wrapped package. Joceline then looked to the table that had held the female and then looked up at the monitor that had been attached to it. On it was the name, Helen Pinkert. She brought her hand to her mouth and gasped. "Where are they?" She whispered.

"They went into the admin block; I've secured the building. For now, they're locked in there." Terry reassured her.

Joceline nodded and Terry re-covered Emily. "We should leave the lab and seal it." She said.

Terry sealed the only door to the lab. He knew that whilst the facility had power the magnetically sealed doors would hold. But if the power was lost, all of the doors and electric shutters would open in case the power outage was caused by a fire. And he knew this would mean that their two prisoners would not only have free reign of the facility, but they would also be able to leave it, and more would be able to enter.

They walked silently to the accommodation block. They entered it through the only access, a heavily reinforced steel door that needed a five-digit pin to open it. As they entered, and the door began to close, Joceline could see the corridor on the other side of the glass façade, and she imagined the two large hybrids running toward the slowly closing door. A shiver ran down her, but she was interrupted by Terry.

"I forgot to tell you, the MRI scan showed that Rob, Doctor Pinkert, had a brain tumor pressing on his frontal lobe. It was small, he probably didn't even know it was there, but it could explain why he acted violently so early on in the process."

Joceline felt sick to her stomach. The frontal lobe controls amongst other things, our behavior. With a tumor pressing on it, and the physiological changes this transformation brings, it was no wonder he acted the way he did.

"Thank you, Terry. You can leave if you wish, go home perhaps."

Terry smiled. "Thanks, doc, but I'll stay, there's only an empty house waiting for me."

Joceline placed her hand gently on his arm and smiled at him. "Sleep tight and lock your quarters tonight."

"Will do doc," Terry answered.

Joceline stood in the empty corridor, and her thoughts turned to Lynne and Danny. She knew Danny was already starting the transformation, and that she couldn't offer Lynne what she'd come for — Salvation for her son. All she could offer her was comfort and security. She found Lynne and Danny in the recreation room. Danny was asleep. It had been a long day for all of them, and the little boy that was curled up on the large sofa was still on British time. To him, it was past midnight. For Joceline, she had no idea what time it was. It didn't seem relevant now, what was the point of watching the clock, every minute that passed was just another minute closer to what was coming. She smiled at Lynne as she sat opposite her on one of the large armchairs.

She decided that tonight she would not speak of Emily's death, or of the two hybrid-Neanderthals which now roamed freely around the administration block.

"Did you manage to speak to Jeff?" She asked.

"I couldn't get through, he didn't answer. I'll try again later." Lynne answered wearily.

"Do you wish you had stayed home?" Joceline asked.

Lynne sighed. "No, I don't think so anyway. If Jeff was right, we wouldn't be safe."

"It won't be safe anywhere soon," Joceline said.

"No, but at least here it'll be quieter I guess," Lynne said softly.

"You want me to show you where the accommodation is?" Joceline asked.

Lynne shook her head. "No, Danny's comfy there, let him sleep. I'll curl up next to him. Maybe show me tomorrow, we'll get settled in then."

Joceline stood and walked to the door. "Goodnight." She said as she left the room.

Lynne didn't answer, she was too tired, exhausted from the journey, and from what she'd learned from Joceline. She lay next to Danny, and in no time, she fell into a deep and dream-filled sleep.

Joceline had reached her quarters. She checked her computer station, and it confirmed that the building had been locked down.

The building resources would now be controlled by the building itself. All non-essential areas would be in darkness, and the secured doors leading to them would be locked. But to Joceline that didn't matter. The laboratories were of no more use. Checking that her own door was secure, she climbed into bed and yawned heavily. Her mind was now blank, exhausted from the last twenty-four hours.

After months of research and weeks of running models secretly, the truth that she'd learned, and shared today, and its consequences for all of us, had left her empty. She lay down and rested her head on the soft pillow, and like Lynne, she was soon asleep.

Two days had passed since Joceline had delivered her revelations, and the two hybrids had woken and killed Emily. Though she could hear the faint banging of their attempts to break free, she knew that if they managed to break out of the administration block, they would still have to get into the accommodation block.

The routine had become much the same. Hunkered down in the facility, waiting for contact from FEMA or any part of the federal government or even her employers at the World Health Organization, but no such communication had come. News had become sketchy, and when reports had been coming in, they were generally confusing and nothing more than hearsay and conjecture. Some governments still denied the fact of what was happening, regardless of the cause, while others were trying to play it down in a misguided attempt to keep society going.

With the UK, and especially England being the country most surveyed by security cameras, and CCTV, the majority of the footage came from there. And what it showed only confirmed to Joceline that she'd been correct, that this was not a virus or pathogen. Even the mnemonic plague which had hit England as late as the nineteenth century had not spread this quickly, and neither had the Coronavirus pandemic of 2020 which lasted until late the following year until enough people had taken the vaccines. However, as with the Covid-19 pandemic which brought countries close to economic and social ruin and had forced major rethinks on open borders — especially with the EU trading block, as well as how closely countries should be linked economically, there had been deniers of it. People foolishly believed it to be some sort of unilateral government conspiracy to de-populate the world and gain more control of the remaining populace. Joceline, as well as every other professional working to stave off this new threat and the previous threat from Covid-19, had been dismayed and yet not completely surprised by just how dumb some of the supposed most intelligent species on the planet can be in times such as these. However, there could be no doubt now, this was nature, and it was taking back what we had begun to destroy.

On the third day, Joceline awoke at her usual time. She showered, dressed, and made her way to the recreation room where she would, as always on a morning, find her guests. Danny was at one of the video game consoles shooting hordes of mutant zombies, whilst Lynne was watching the large screen TV that was mounted above a small orange sofa. Joceline sat next to Lynne holding her coffee cup closely. The CNN reporter looked haunted as he relayed his report using a video phone. The majority of the communication satellites used to relay high-definition pictures were now inoperative, and most if not all of the ground staff that kept our 21st-century communications and entertainment systems running were no longer at their posts. But the older technology, perhaps because it's more robust, seemed to be faring better, and so that was the only way to continue reporting the events as they happened.

They both watched as over the next few hours different reporters from around the world told of cities going dark, communities crashing, and the complete collapse of law and order as police forces and armed forces stretched beyond capacity could no longer control those who had devolved, and those who would as always, use such a time for their personal self-indulgence.

As the hours ticked by and more feeds began to show the violence that had begun only a few months before with some isolated incidences scattered around the globe, but which had now spread to every corner of it, every town, street, and home, it was clear to them both that we had now passed the point of no return.

Hybrid-Neanderthals, regardless of the stage of devolution they were at, now outnumbered the rational and more intelligent, but physically weaker humans. Those that had been lucky enough to have had the symptoms start later or progress more slowly, were now being actively hunted and slaughtered by those that had lost their humanity. Families and friends turned on one another.

Parents who had sworn to protect their children now attacked and killed them with the brutality and disdain a predator would attack its prey in the wild. It was clear now that the battle was lost. It was now purely about survival and hanging on as long as your own humanity stayed with you. Silently, Lynne and Joceline watched as one by one the reports began to fade. This civilization that humankind had calved out from our earliest days, and that had taken a millennium to build, was about to be lost in the blink of an eye. Our Eldorado, our golden city that is our entire civilization with everything that was virtuous, and corrupt in equal measure, was about to be lost to the passage of time.

Africa was the first continent to lose all communication. The Middle East, Asia, Russia, and Australia soon followed, and then mainland Europe.

As time passed, Canada became quiet, followed by the South American countries, falling one-by-one like dominos. Argentina went first, and Mexico was the last. Ireland and Scotland too fell quiet, quickly followed by Wales. As the clock passed 2:00 p.m. local time, the only countries that continued their broadcasts were England, parts of the U.S., and Iceland.

By the time the next hour had passed, the news Joceline had been expecting and dreading was announced. The president and most of the federal government were dead, and martial law was now in effect across the entire United States. Shortly after, the remaining countries lost their voice. For the first time since Christmas Eve 1906, when the first radio program was broadcast, and those signals traveled out into the cosmos, the earth had become silent.

"You had better try to call Jeff," Joceline whispered calmly to Lynne. "I think it's about to happen."

"What is?" Lynne asked.

"The U.S. will go down soon. Infrastructure will collapse, and there will be chaos in the streets. All power and communications will fail very soon. We may only have a few minutes, or hours if we're lucky."

Lynne scrambled to get her cell phone from her pocket. She dialed Jeff's number, but there was no connection. She tried again desperately, but the phone was useless.

Joceline handed her the facilities Satcom phone. "Try this, it can connect to multiple satellites, it has the best chance of getting through."

Lynne took the phone from her and dialed. It rang and Jeff answered. "Jeff? Jeff? It's Lynne are you okay? Where are you?" Lynne shouted down the phone.

Jeff whispered "I'm at Balmoral Castle. I'm just about to leave. I have transport to the States. Where are you? Are you both okay?"

"We're at the facility. Danny's getting worse, there's no cure, Joceline said it's the planet wiping us out, it's not a virus, there's nothing we can do." Lynne was frantic.

"She said what? It's the planet? What does she mean by that?" Jeff couldn't understand what Lynne was telling him.

"Danny will change, we all will." She continued. But as she began to explain, she heard him scream, and then the line became dead.

10

Jeff had joined up with COBRA at Balmoral Castle in Scotland. After being collected from his home, he'd been driven to RAF Northolt, a base close to Heathrow airport. From there he took a flight with two other consultants, in a short-range transport aircraft to Aberdeen airport. A military escort had then taken him to Balmoral Castle, where what was left of the British Army, and Royal Air Force had established a main operating base to protect the remaining members of the government and the Royal family. After what seemed the longest night of his life, tossing and turning in his bed, unable to sleep with the last image he saw of Lynne and Danny, as they had left home still burning in the back of his closed eyes, he finally gave up trying and got out of bed. Perhaps a warm shower and wet shave would relax him, but it didn't. Rather, he found himself looking out from the large window across the manicured lawns and gardens of the estate as the sun rose. He pushed open the door and stepped out onto the balcony. The air smelt clear and clean. Maybe it was the location. Or more likely it was because industries had shut down, and motor vehicles of all kinds were being left on their drives and in their garages. The smog that he, and all of us, had become so accustomed to had already begun to clear.

In the distance, he could hear the soldiers being put through their morning drill. He smiled to himself. *Even with all that's happened, and that's still yet to happen, the British Army still maintains its discipline down to the last man. Perhaps that's why it's the best army.* He thought to himself — rather patriotically. Smiling at his own statement, he turned and went back inside his room. He dressed in what Lynne used to jokingly call his serious blue suit and then left his room tucking his cell phone into his pocket. Protocol meant it shouldn't be seen or heard while he was attending the meetings. But set to vibrate, and pushed deep into his shirt pocket, it was well hidden. Overhead he could hear the pulsating drum of the helicopters that were now patrolling the grounds. Two soldiers on foot patrol had run into a group of hybrids the day before he'd arrived. One had been killed and the other escaped with serious injuries. And Jeff had been told by the over-eager driver who'd picked him up from the airport the story of the private that had emptied a full clip of his assault rifle into one of them before it had dropped dead at his feet. Since then, foot patrols had been limited to within the grounds, whilst exterior patrols had now become the job of the gunships.

Inside one of the large halls of the castle that had once seen kings and queens entertaining their peers from across the world, there was now a makeshift operations room.

Jeff sat next to the cabinet ministers and other consultants that made up Britain's emergency response council; COBRA.

As reports came in it was clear that across the United Kingdom society was beginning to fall. All of the UK's police forces had now either collapsed completely, or simply disbanded, as officers no longer showed up for their shifts, and with Britain still heavily reliant on the Trans-Siberian gas pipeline to feed many of its power stations, they had started shutting down when Russia had gone dark. The gas reserves held in the UK were simply not able to cope with the demand during one of the coldest winters the country had seen in almost a decade. Though the occupants of most of the households were no longer capable of using the technology we use without a second thought, modern heating systems continued to function automatically and would do so until either the gas or electricity ran out.

They had been here for two days, and the absence of the Prime Minister, along with the ever-increasing empty chairs around the table was obvious to everyone. But it wasn't just the table that they sat on. Jeff had noticed that most of the army Land Rovers hadn't moved, and he wasn't sure if it was because they didn't need them now that the helicopter gunships were carrying the patrol load, or it was because there weren't as many army personnel to drive them as there had been.

And that's what he feared the most. The army had set up makeshift barracks in the grounds of the castle, which were close enough to respond to a threat to the government or Royal family, but also far enough away that they kept a respectful distance. If it was the case that more soldiers were becoming to this condition, that in itself would pose a much larger threat to all of their safety than the odd few breaking in from outside of the castle walls. As these thoughts ran through his mind, the deputy Prime Minister, Johnathan Davies entered the room. And as is the custom, all those at the table who were waiting on him stood to show their respects. As he sat at the head of the table, they too sat.

"Let's begin," He said.

Jeff looked at the five seats which were now empty. It had been explained when he'd arrived that whenever a member of the government or Royal family began to show symptoms, they would be confined to their rooms and two armed guards would be posted outside. Jeff had no access to the wing of the castle that housed what was left of the Royal family, but if five empty seats meant ten soldiers guarding rooms, and the army itself was losing men and women, this place that now held the last threads of a once-great nation, that once had the largest empire the world had seen, and which had given so much to the world, was no longer safe.

His thoughts were brought back by the minister for the interior.

"It's not good news sir." The young minister said nervously. This was a new post created to deal with the infrastructure and social problems this pandemic was causing.

"Can you qualify exactly what that means?" Johnathan asked him.

"All of the police forces have collapsed; the Navy is reporting that all-but-two surface ships and one Sub are no longer operational and effective. The air force is grounded. What few pilots we have left have aircraft that cannot be maintained," He sighed.

"And what about sanitation, power, the NHS?" Johnathan asked.

"Much the same — the NHS staff that were here on visas fled back to their own countries when it became clear that this was more than the Covid pandemic and the remaining staff couldn't cope, and now they too have largely abandoned their posts, so to speak. As for power and sanitation, we have reports that all of these services are shutting down systematically. Almost seventy percent of the country is now without power, fresh water and sewage treatment are now out of action, as is the rail network, and all public services and infrastructure."

The young minister sat back down, he looked scared, and Jeff thought he should be.

Johnathan turned to the army captain who now represented the highest-ranking officer left of the country's armed forces.

"How are we here?" He asked.

"We're down forty percent, sir. The men and women that are left are either guarding those that are showing onset symptoms or are in the early stages themselves sir, another forty-eight hours and we'll lose Balmoral, sir. The remaining personnel won't be able to mount a successful defense if we are attacked from the outside, or from within. Sir," The captain looked as frightened as the young minister, and Jeff knew him.

A veteran of the Falklands, and the first Gulf War, he was as tough a man as Jeff had known, and if he looked scared then everyone else should be terrified. As the Captain had been talking one of the red *incident* phones had rung, and a young female private that had answered it now handed Johnathan a small, folded piece of paper. Jeff watched as he opened and read it, firstly to himself, and then with a look of foreboding to the room.

"This is from the royal quarters. The Prime Minister, the King, and Queen are dead. The PM escaped his room and attacked and killed them before being shot dead himself. Prince Charles has declared that with our infrastructure collapsing and no working police or armed forces, that we are to abandon

Balmoral and try to get to our families, those who have any family left," He paused and looked around the room, everyone without exception now looked at him.

All of the activity that had previously been going on around them had now stopped. He continued. "I declare the United Kingdom lost, and her government dissolved. Good luck to you all."

Jeff looked to Johnathan who had crumpled the piece of paper in his hands and held it tightly in his fists. He looked lost, without his boss, and now without a country to serve he was without direction.

Jeff turned to the Captain. "I need to get across to the U.S. is there any way?" Jeff asked him.

The Captain looked at Jeff blankly. "The U.S? Do you think it's better there because I can assure you it's not?"

Jeff shook his head. "No, my wife and son are over there. I should be with them."

"I'll check and let you know."

Johnathan stood, placing the piece of paper down carefully. "Attention everyone," Every person in the room became quiet again and gave him their undivided attention. "The Prince of Wales, Prince Charles, has dissolved the government and declared the UK lost. Please stop what you're doing immediately and leave to be with your families or friends. And may

God be with you all." With that, he left the room.

Jeff turned back to the Captain "I need to get across, can you find out? I'll be in my room packing."

He stood and said a solemn goodbye to a few others before returning to his room. It was only when he was back in his room that what had just happened, and what it meant hit him, and Jeff broke down. Shaking, he sat on the bed and wept at the thought of how quickly this had spread across the globe and taken down the most intelligent species that had ever lived. Perhaps if only they'd done something differently, stopped international air traffic and managed the ports and borders better, reacted quicker, then perhaps it could have been stopped, even beaten. But now it was lost, and this it seemed was the end of humankind.

Jeff had always known our reign at the top would end one day, every reign does. But he hadn't imagined that it would have been in his lifetime, let alone his sons. His son, Danny, he must try and get to him and Lynne. He stood, wiping the drying tears from his eyes, and packed his small bag. Just the essentials, there was no use now for suits and ties and dress shoes. Once packed, he would get changed, by then the Captain should have news.

It was another thirty minutes before Jeff was ready.

Out of habit, he hung his suit up, and neatly tidied his room. He hadn't made a conscious decision to do so. At this point, he was running on instinct alone. He'd tried his best to switch off any cognizant thoughts because they always lead back to Lynne and Danny, and that was too distracting for now.

Now changed into a pair of jeans, jumper, winter jacket, and his *mountain boots,* as Lynne called them, he sat waiting for the Captain.

There was a knock at his door, Jeff sprung from the chair and opened it. It was the captain. "There's a transport leaving Newcastle airport on Wednesday, at 11:15 a.m. I've told them to expect you, but Jeff. They won't delay it for you."

"What's the destination?" Jeff asked.

"JFK New York. Where are your wife and son?"

"In a CDC facility in Washington."

"JFK is as close as we can get you, from there you're on your own. The transport is taking the last of the U.S. service personnel that were based in England back to the U.S. You're lucky, if they'd already gone, you'd be swimming over there." The Captain smiled and placed a hand on Jeff's shoulder. "Good luck!"

"You too Paul," Jeff said, smiling.
Paul smiled back at him, his rank was obsolete now, there was no army, there was nothing left of the country he loved and devoted much of his life to.

Jeff picked up his bag and opened the door. Walking out into the main hallway he placed his room key on a small table just inside the door and closed it behind him. He wouldn't need the key anymore. As he walked along the corridor, he heard the sound of gunfire crackling. At first, it seemed to be outside, but as it continued and became more intense, he realized it was inside. He stood rooted to the spot as the gunfire continued. And with it, the cries of people, along with the cries of something else, and they were becoming louder and getting closer. Jeff didn't know which way to turn, or where to run. He was confused. Where were the sounds coming from? The gunfire was reducing, not only in frequency but also in intensity.

That could be good he thought, they've killed them all, but then another thought pushed its way into his mind. What if the soldiers are all dead, what if they've been overrun? Footsteps approached from around the corner that led to the elevators. He backed away slowly not knowing what he should do. A shadow now appeared. Jeff froze.

It was Paul. He was injured but alive. "Come on!" He shouted to Jeff as he ran past him "They're coming this way."

Jeff dropped his bag and turned, following Paul back along the corridor and to the stairs.

Paul burst through them and stopped, he checked upward, and then he looked down the stairwell. He signaled for Jeff to follow him. Both of them made their way down the metal staircase. At the bottom, Paul stopped. "On the other side of this door are four Land Rovers. The keys will be under the sun visor. Get to the nearest one and get to Newcastle airport, and don't stop for anyone, or anything. I'll get to the gatehouse and open the main gate for you."

"Come with me," Jeff said.

"No, what's left of us need to protect the Royal family, if anyone does find a cure for this, we'll need them."

Jeff nodded and slowly opened the door. The first Land Rover, painted in the usual colors of the British army, was parked close — only a few feet away. He turned back to Paul and smiled and then slowly stepped outside and crept toward it. He made his way around to the driver's door and with a metallic click, he was sure all the hybrids close by would hear, he climbed in, closed the door, and locked it. He sighed, allowing himself to relax just enough to concentrate on pulling the keys down from the visor. He slipped them into the ignition and started to turn them. As the ignition lights came on, he noticed a movement in his passenger door mirror. It was three large hybrids. He let go of the keys. If he started the engine now, he would be surely pulled from the car and killed before he could engage a gear and drive away. But he was also visible sitting in the driver's seat. He slumped down, and as quietly as he could he crawled between the seats and laid in the back. The large figures passed by the front of the Land Rover and Jeff could see for the first time just how large they were. As he hid, he felt his phone vibrate. He checked the screen, but he didn't recognize the number. Nervously, he checked around. He couldn't see them from where he was lying. It seemed clear and he answered it. It was Lynne and she sounded hysterical.

"Jeff? Jeff? It's Lynne are you okay? Where are you?" Lynne shouted down the phone.

Jeff whispered "I'm at Balmoral Castle, I'm just about to leave. I have transport to the States. Where are you? Are you both okay?"

"We're at the facility, Danny's getting worse, there's no cure, Joceline said it's the planet wiping us out, it's not a virus, there's nothing we can do." Lynne was frantic.

"She said what? It's the planet? What does she mean by that?" Jeff couldn't understand what Lynne was telling him.

"Danny will change, we all will."

He took a breath. He needed Lynne to quieten down, to tell him calmly what she meant. But as he started to ask her the Land Rover was hit hard.

The steel panel that Jeff was resting against bowed inward, and he was knocked to the floor. He screamed in pain, as his phone was knocked from his hands. It landed and skidded to the back of the truck. Another hit and this time the steel seam split, and Jeff could see the large fists pounding the Land Rover. He couldn't get to the phone, he needed to escape. He scrambled to the driver's seat and turned the key, stealth was now no longer an option, it was time to run. As the engine started another hit came and the Land Rover shook violently. Jeff engaged first gear and let out the clutch, pushing his right foot to the floor. The Land Rover spun its rear wheels before digging in and setting off. Second gear, but the three hybrids were keeping up with him. The leader shoulder-charged the Land Rover, and Jeff struggled to keep it from spinning off the road. Third gear and they started to drop back. Jeff thrust the truck into fourth and at forty miles per hour the hybrid-Neanderthals gave up their pursuit. Jeff sighed and hoped that the security gates would be open.

Paul had made it to the security gatehouse that was located inside the compound, but he was badly injured. The attack had come from behind, a female, a former soldier had bitten him hard on his right shoulder, severing his nerves and muscles, and as a result, his arm was useless.

It now hung from him, nothing more than dead weight. But it was his shooting hand, and his aim with his left hand just wasn't as good. As blood dripped from his dead arm he staggered to the door and pulled it open. Inside he could see the monitors which were still being fed by the cameras at the gate. He placed his gun down and made his way over to the control panel and pushed the green button which had the word *gate* written next to it on a piece of tape. He smiled as he watched the gates open. From the bottom of the picture, he saw the Land Rover approaching them. "Go get your family," He said softly. He watched as the truck sped through the gates and out of range of the cameras. He pressed the button again, and the gates began to close. Then turning, he picked up his gun and left the gatehouse, and started back toward the Royal quarters.

It was Monday afternoon, and Jeff knew that normally the journey to Newcastle airport would take around five hours, but these were not normal times. His overriding instinct was to head straight for the airport, but he'd made a promise to Lynne that he would bring Susan, her mom, with him. He knew he couldn't face Lynne without at least trying. He reached the junction and stopped. It was deserted. There were no abandoned cars or trucks, just quiet, just silence. It was now or never.

He could continue south toward Edinburgh, and eventually the border with England. From there it was a straight shot to Newcastle-upon-Tyne and the airport. Or he could turn west and toward Stirling and Glasgow, and eventually to where their cabin was. He sat — the only sound was the continual churning of the Land Rover's diesel engine. He sighed. In the end, the decision was easy. He turned the wheel and headed in the direction of Sterling.

He pushed the Land Rover hard along the small and narrow country lanes. Its diesel engine, more used to pulling heavy loads than high-revving fast driving, eventually consumed the fuel in its tank, and with a cough, it died. It couldn't have happened at a worse time for him. The daylight was starting to fade, and the last place Jeff wanted to be in the dark was in an unprotected metal box. He pulled the stricken Land Rover off the road and freewheeled onto the moorland as far as the momentum of the dead truck was able to carry him.

Thirty or so feet from the road it came to a lumbering halt. "Fuck it!" Jeff cursed as he slammed his hands on the steering wheel. There was no choice now, he'd had no time to prepare for this journey, it all seemed to go wrong so quickly back at the castle. Staring at the countryside around him he knew that soon it would be pitch black and he wouldn't be able to see his hand in front of his face, never mind an approaching hybrid, and he couldn't risk walking. If he became lost, he would spend days wandering around in circles. He had no choice but to stay with the car tonight and walk on to Sterling tomorrow. Resigned to his fate he flicked the headlamp switch and the warm glow they had put out in front of him was extinguished. His best strategy now was to hide, and become invisible to any wondering hybrids that may be out there. Pulling off the road meant that he wouldn't be silhouetted against the skyline, and with the headlamps out, the olive green and brown camouflaged Land Rover became almost invisible in the low fading light. Jeff reached over and locked the doors. He knew that wouldn't stop them, but it made him feel a little easier for some reason he couldn't and didn't want to think about it at this time. Moving into the rear of the truck, he unpacked a Bergen, which had been left by the previous occupant. Inside he found a sleeping bag and a gas stove with a choice of field rations.

After eating what was labeled *Hunters Chicken with New Potatoes'* he climbed into the sleeping bag and wondered what the following days would bring. As he stretched, he touched something under the bench seat, and he remembered the phone that had been knocked out of his hands earlier

"Lynne." He whispered to himself. He pressed the small button at the bottom of the screen, and it lit up. But there were no missed calls, no emails, no text messages, and no service. It was nothing now but a useless collection of intricate electronics. He tossed it aside and closed his eyes.

Jeff was woken the following morning by a shaft of bright sunlight which found its way into the back of the Land Rover where the weld had split when the large hybrid had attacked it. He sat bolt upright. It was Tuesday. He picked up his phone and checked the time, 10:48 a.m.

"Shit!" His instinct was to rush from the Land Rover and run to Stirling, but he couldn't, he needed to be careful. Jeff climbed through to the cab and checked the horizon. To his relief, it seemed clear. He unlocked the driver's door and climbed out, closing it softly, but not before he took the map from the door pocket. The easiest way to find Stirling, and he thought another car, would be to simply follow the road, but that would leave him vulnerable and easy to spot. No, there must be another way, he had to be clever, quick, but clever. He laid the map over the hood and figured out the route he would take.

Walking as the crow flies, and just hoping in this sparsely populated area that he would be lucky. Pulling his coat tightly around him he set off. He wasn't sure how long he'd been walking when he realized he'd left his phone back at the

Land Rover. "Shit, ya Fuckin idiot!" He called himself out loud, as it dawned on him. He hadn't meant to. He'd put it on the hood when he'd planned his route and just forgot to pick it up. Besides, according to his rudimentary map reading skills, he figured Stirling couldn't be much farther. He was right, *it can't have been more than an hour he* thought to himself when he saw the small town ahead of him. He stopped to observe his destination. The streets looked clear. He couldn't see any people and more importantly, he couldn't see any hybrids.

He walked quickly — he was hungry and cold. As he approached from the east, he could see a large supermarket. He skirted the parking lot, not walking directly across it, making sure nothing was watching him. Walking through the main entrance it was as he imagined it would be. This wasn't a place hit by a sudden panic. Nothing abrupt had happened here. Shopping carts were neatly stacked, though the shelves for the most part were almost empty. There had been no panic buying and no mad rush to grab and loot food, water, and luxury items that for some reason people grab when disaster hits. His first stop would be the toilet. He entered the windowless room. Thankfully, the power hadn't run out just yet, though whether that was the national grid supplying it, or the store's emergency backup generators he didn't know, and right now he didn't care.

As he sat in the small cubicle his imagination ran wild. Images of large hair-covered hands grabbing at him from under the door ran shivers up and down his spine.

Outside he heard banging and grunting, and he realized with dread that this was no longer his imagination, the sounds were real. As quietly as he was able, he exited the cubicle. Was it muscle-memory, or just habit that made him want to wash his hands before he left? He didn't know, but if his mother would ever have allowed him a one-time pass on doing so, he guessed this would be it.

As carefully as he was able to, he walked around the aisle that faced the large front doors. Any sound now would bring whatever was outside bursting into the building, and he knew he would stand no chance against their strength and ferocity. Jeff ducked down behind a magazine stand, waiting to see if they would simply pass by. He hoped that they would because if they had the main entrance covered, he would be trapped in here, and he wouldn't dare to use the emergency exits. He knew if he did an alarm would sound and that would surely attract more of them. He breathed deeply, trying to slow his racing heart.

He felt adrenaline coursing around his body as his muscles tingled and ached ready to be called upon, to give him as much speed and power as they could muster.

But he remembered the previous day, it was only when he'd reached forty miles per hour that they had given up the chase, and for all of his readiness, he couldn't compete. The only way this ends with him alive was to use his intelligence and outthink his opponent. As he watched, the large glass entrance doors slid open as the sensor above them detected movement. He could now see shadows. The sun was behind them casting the long shadows ahead of them. He counted three, no, make it four shadows. He closed his eyes and sighed before opening them again. Then he heard voices, a strong Scottish accent with an east coast inflection, and he dared to peek from his hiding place. It was people. Thank God it was people — four of them. An older and younger couple wearing light clothing. That meant they were either local or they had transport or both. Jeff stood from his hiding place and smiled at them.

"Hi, boy I am glad to see you." He said, smiling as he walked toward them.

The older of the two men smiled back and held out a hand, taking Jeff's and shaking it firmly. "Likewise, we thought we're alone ya ken?" He said, the strong accent throwing Jeff a little.

"Ya ken?" Jeff asked.

"It means ya know. Ah, he's an English da, he does'na know what ya mean." The younger of the two men said.

The older man smiled. "I'm George, my son Greg and my wife Mary, and this is Greg's wife, Angela," He pointed amongst them and continued. "You're a long way from home?"

"I am. My name is Jeff, I was at Balmoral with the government, but it fell apart. I'm trying to get south, to pick up my wife's mom, and then over to Newcastle." Jeff stopped short at telling them there was a flight to the U.S.

"The government?" Mary asked,

"What's left of it? But with the prime minister dead along with the King and Queen and most of the cabinet, the government has been disbanded. There's nothing left."

"Aye, that's a shame, the King and Queen that is, I'm no bothered about that ponce the PM. Shame it didn't happen when that bastard Blair was in power if you ask me." George snarled.

"This isn't the time for politics George," Mary said. "We're here for Angela, remember?"

Jeff looked across at her. She was ashen white and cradling her head. He could see beads of sweat collecting under her hairline and running down her neck. "Does she have a headache or migraine?" He asked.

"Aye. Why do you ask?" Greg asked.

"It means she's infected with whatever this is," Jeff answered.

Greg stepped in front of her as if to protect her from Jeff. "She's just a headache is all, she'll be fine when we get some painkillers in her." Greg insisted.

Jeff backed down, he was happy to see other people, but this was no longer his job, he didn't need to protect them anymore. All he had to do was grab supplies and get to their cabin.

"Do you know where I can take a car from? I must get south, mine ran out of fuel back up the road."

George looked out at the car park and pointed to a Range Rover parked in the closest bay. "See that?" He asked.

"What about it?" Jeff replied.

"That belongs to the manager of this store, the keys will be in his office. I never did like him. I won't tell him who took it." George laughed.

"And his office?" Jeff asked.

"I'll get them," Mary said. "I work here, or I did before this mess." She turned to George. "You take Greg and Angela, get what we need, and I'll meet you back here. That applies to you too." She said turning back to Jeff.

"Thank you," Jeff replied.

Jeff pushed high-sugar drinks and food into a bag and made his way back to the entrance. As good as her word,

Mary was waiting and dangling the keys to the Range Rover in her right hand. She smiled as she handed them to him.

"Thank you," Jeff said.

Mary smiled. "Best be on your way now," And with that, she turned and headed toward the back of the store.

Jeff paused, should he stay and help them? Every fiber of his being wanted to, but he knew what was coming. He'd seen Angela's symptoms too many times before, and it wouldn't be long before she attacked whoever she came across, and that included her parents and husband. But if he tried to stop her now, George and Gregg would stop him. The biggest cruelty of this was just that. People hesitated too long, unable to take action against the people they loved and whilst they hesitated, the victims, the infected, these hybrids didn't. He tightened his grip on the bag and walked out of the store. Pressing the key fob, the lights on the Range Rover flashed and Jeff climbed in.

This time he would check it for fuel. He turned the key and the V8 petrol engine purred to life, "Full tank!" He said smiling to himself. He looked back at the store one more time before he put it into gear and left.

11

Lynne put the Satcom phone down. She was shaking and sobbing heavily. She wiped her eyes and turned to check on Danny who had taken no notice of her cries when Jeff had screamed, and the line had gone dead. In some ways, Lynne was relieved Danny had not paid any mind to her, but in another, it only reinforced what Lynne knew was happening to him. His lack of interest and empathy wasn't because he was too young to understand or too engrossed in the video game. It was simply that he didn't care. To Danny, Lynne was no longer his mother, his protector, and shield against the world, she was a no-one. Danny had no more feelings for her than for the game console he was using, and he had no more love for her either.

"What is it?" Joceline asked.

"I don't know, he was whispering, as if he was hiding. He said he was leaving Balmoral Castle, but I don't know why he didn't say. I don't understand, he should have been safe there." Lynne replied — her voice cracking as she tried to swallow more tears.

"Can you call him back? Did you try?" Joceline asked.

"The line's dead, even this phone has no signal now," Lynne replied, with defeat in her voice.

Joceline picked up the phone and looked at the screen, she was right. The words *No Signal* confirmed it. She placed it on the side and sat next to Lynne to comfort her, though how she would manage this she had no idea. They all knew their fate. What is it she can say?

Lynne broke the silence. "The worst thing is, he doesn't know."

"What do you mean?" Joceline asked softly.

"He doesn't know what we do, that there is no cure, that this never was a virus. If he's still okay, he'll be heading here expecting Danny to be better. I tried to tell him, but I..." Lynne stopped abruptly and shrugged.

The door to the recreation room opened and Terry entered. "Any news?" He asked as he poured himself a coffee.

Joceline turned, moving away slightly from Lynne. "The news isn't good. They've reported the President and most of his staff are lost, and the country is under martial law, for now, at least as long as we have an army, but that won't be for too much longer."

A distant banging could be heard coming from the administration block, and it was clear to Terry that Joceline was concerned. "Don't worry the doors are strong, it will take them a while to break through them, and they still have to get into the accommodation block."

"What do you mean?" Lynne asked. "Who's trying to break in?"

Joceline looked at Terry and then turned back to Lynne. "When we tried to euthanize the subjects we had in the lab, two broke free. But they are confined in the Administration block, and as Terry has said the doors are incredibly strong. We're safe in here."

Lynne stood, alarmed at the news that two hybrid-Neanderthals were loose in the building, the one place she thought she and Danny would be safe until Jeff and her mom could join them.

"Can they get out, get to us?" She asked.

"No, well possibly, but it's unlikely," Terry answered, unsure of what to say.

"Oh, that's great!" Lynne shouted.

"No, if they managed to get out, and it is if. They still have to break into here." Joceline tried to calm her.

"But what about the power? If that goes out will the doors open?" Lynne asked.

"Technically, yes," Terry answered. "Technically! What the hell does that mean?" Lynne snapped.

"If the power fails." Terry started, but Lynne interrupted him.

"You mean *when* it fails," She said.

"Yes, *when* it fails the building UPS will kick in, and the doors will be secured again," Terry replied.

"UPS?" Lynne asked.

"Uninterruptable power supply," Terry answered. "It means that all the systems, data, and everything else will continue to function if the main grid goes down for any reason. But there is a gap in supply. It's only a second, but technically, if they happen to be pushing on the door at the time the grid goes offline then they could, in theory, push through the door before it's resealed by the UPS."

Lynne sighed heavily and sat again, holding her head in her hands. She looked back to Terry and Joceline. "Then let's hope their timing is crap!"

Terry noticed the Satcom phone and picked it up. "Is this working?"

Joceline shook her head. "No, Lynne was using it and it died, it seems all communications are down now."

"Who were you speaking to, Lynne? Is it any better anywhere else?" Terry asked as he put the phone back into its charging cradle.

"It was my husband, Jeff. He was in Scotland. He said he had transport to the U.S. so maybe things are getting better." Lynne said a fresh tone of optimism in her voice.

"Maybe," Joceline said, knowing that the truth was that things wouldn't be better and that they would become much worse. But she couldn't take that straw from Lynne, right now she needed to grasp onto something.

"I'm going to do my rounds, and make sure the external doors are secure," Terry said.

"Okay, that's fine, I have some work to finish in my room," Joceline answered. "Will you be okay here Lynne?" She asked.

Lynne smiled and lay down on the large sofa, pulling a blanket over her. "We'll be just fine. He's on the video game. I'm going to have a sleep. You never know, I might wake, and this will all have been a dream." She answered, yawning.

Joceline and Terry left the room. As she did Joceline pulled the door closed. It couldn't be locked, but if the hybrid-Neanderthals did break out, they may walk past a closed door. It wasn't logical, she knew, but as she walked back to her quarters it made her feel a little better.

Jeff had crossed the border into England, and now he didn't have far to go before he would be in the Lake District national park, where their cabin was located. He had no idea if Susan had made it there, but it didn't matter, even if she hadn't the cabin was as good a place as any to rest up before heading east to Newcastle. With an early enough start in the morning, he'd be there before 11:00 a.m. Even with the roads clear, it would be cutting it a little close, but he didn't dare risk driving across the Pennines at night. Not now. The Pennines are referred to as the backbone of England for a good reason.

They're a mountain range which separates the North West of England, from the East, and they're a bleak and unforgiving place at any time of the year. The weather can change in a heartbeat, and especially in early March. The thought of running into wandering hybrids at night, up there, where there is only the odd scattered farm building for shelter, didn't bear thinking about. No, his safest bet was to make it to the cabin, it's secure, bed down for the night, and then cross the mountain range in the morning. He turned off the last of the main roads.

From this point on, it was single-lane country roads to the cabin, with twisting tight corners and high hedgerows. Even with the elevated view the Range Rover gave him, he couldn't see around each bend as it loomed, and the light was dimming. Tuesday seemed to him to have vanished in the blink of an eye. From leaving the stricken Land Rover to finding the supermarket to now, this moment in time, it all seemed a blur. As he pulled around the last bend and turned off onto the track which would lead him to the cabin, he sighed with relief that this day at least was over.

By the time he reached the cabin, the sun had set behind the mountains, and the high beams of the Range Rover were the only light source. As he approached the cabin. he could see that Susan's car was not parked outside.

He stopped and turned the Range Rover around, reversing up to the door.

If he needed to make a quick getaway, he didn't want to be performing a three-point turn in a blind panic and under attack. He waited for a moment with the engine ticking over. The high beams still sent their shafts of brilliant white light out into the surrounding woodland, but even so, the areas they didn't penetrate were pitch-black, and his imagination told him monsters were watching him. He pulled his keys for the cabin from his pocket and switched off the engine, but not the headlights. He knew these were on a timer, and in a minute or so they would switch off, allowing the dark to reclaim the night.

He checked one last time, it was now or never. He opened the driver's door and ran for the cabin. Slipping the key into the lock he tried to turn it, but it wouldn't move. He tried again. Nothing. "Come on you bastard!" He said as he turned the key forward and back as he imagined at any moment a hand would grab him from behind and pull him into the darkness. Then he realized the door was unlocked. He turned the knob and pushed the door open. Once safely inside he spun around and slammed it shut. The feeling of the imaginary hand that had tingled his shoulder left him as he locked the door. Jeff stood with his back pushed against the door, breathing heavily while his heart rate returned to normal.

He hadn't seen or heard anything, but the things we fear the most are the things we can't see and can't hear, and right now he was terrified of them. He looked around the cabin. The lights were on and the shutters were closed. The TV was on, playing a Clint Eastwood movie on the DVD player. He was Susan's favorite actor, and the reason she'd taken to Jeff so well when Lynne had brought him home to meet her, or at least that's what Jeff always suspected. He moved through into the kitchen. The oven was cold, as was the kettle, but that didn't surprise him too much, and beside the cabin was warm. She had been here recently. But why had she left? There were no signs the cabin had been attacked, and with the shutters closed very little light escaped. Any passing hybrids would have been lucky to notice any shards of light as they walked through the woods. He walked up the short staircase and to the master bedroom. The bed was made, and her clothes and toiletries were still here. Whatever had happened had not been too long ago. The movie was about to finish, but that would only mean she was here two hours ago to start it. He was unsure of what to do. Should he go back outside and look for her? But what chance would he have in the dark? He could pass within a few feet of her and not see her, and if she had taken her car, and Jeff didn't have a reason to believe otherwise, she may well be miles away by now, and the car would at least provide some protection. He sat on the bed, confused and alone. He wasn't a hero, he wasn't particularly fit or strong or fast, or even good at running. He was a middle-aged man, a normal married man, and a father. What the hell was he doing even thinking about going out there in the dark? Her best bet, and his best bet to find her, was to wait until morning when he'd have daylight on his side. He just hoped she would survive until then.

Jeff checked the cabin once again making sure in his mind it was secure. There was only one door in and out, and he'd checked it on five separate occasions that it was locked and bolted. With the TV off and the single light in the corner softly illuminating the cabin, he felt safe for the first time since he'd left home. The wood-burning stove in the corner was keeping the cabin warm. He climbed the stairs and got into the king-sized bed. Through the skylights, he could see the stars in between the wisps of light cloud that floated across his view. He was tired, exhausted and it hit him like a train wreck. Within seconds of pulling the heavy blankets over him, he was asleep.

For the first few seconds after waking, Jeff had completely forgotten what was happening around the world. For the briefest of moments, as the sun shone through the skylight and he lay in the large soft bed, warm and relaxed, the terrors of the last few weeks were gone from his mind.

But it didn't last, and sooner than he would have liked it all came flooding back. It was the opposite of waking from a bad dream to feel the relief when you realize it was just that, a bad dream. This time it was the nightmare that was real. He pulled himself from the bed and dressed and put on a watch he kept at the cabin as a spare. Making his way downstairs, the bright light of the early spring morning found its way through the small cracks in the shutters, flooding the room with splinters and streaks of light.

The fire had long since burned out and that was the first thing Jeff attended to. Throwing on the last of the logs that they kept neatly stacked next to it, he lit a firelighter, and the cabin warmed again. After breakfast he checked his watch, it was 08:32 a.m. He would have thirty minutes to look for Susan, but if he was to make the airport in time, he would have to leave whether or not he had found her.

He unlocked the thick wooden door that had kept him safe while he'd had the much-needed rest, and carefully stepped outside, locking it again behind him. It looked very different in the daylight. There were no hiding places amongst the shadows as there was last night. The air was damp, but clear and fresh, and the sky was a deep blue. He breathed in heavily and smiled, *maybe today might be a good one*, he thought to himself as he climbed into the Range Rover and started the engine.

As he reached the end of the private track that led from their cabin, he was faced with a choice. To either turn right, which was the way he came in, or left. It would take longer to get back to the main road, but he hadn't seen Susan's car last night. He didn't have a choice; he turned the wheel to the left and started along the single-track road.

On the right of him was a steep incline, where the side of the cliff met the road. She wouldn't have gone that way, no car would be able to drive up it, and Susan certainly couldn't climb it. To the left of the road was a steep bank which was mostly grass, and rocks. But after a few hundred feet from the road, the woodland began again. Halfway between the cabin, and the exit to the main road which would take him to Newcastle upon Tyne, he spotted something just inside the tree line. He stopped and got out of the car.

Walking around to the front of it he squinted trying to make out the shape. It was Susan's SUV. Its hazard lights were flashing, and he could see that it was up against a tree. His heart sank. Maybe she'd made a run for it and lost control? If she had, was she dead inside the car? Or had she been dragged out by whatever she was running from? Or worse, had she abandoned the car and ran? If so, he would have no chance of finding her. He hesitated and looked around, checking to see if he was being watched.

He wouldn't know if he was, but there was little choice, he ought to go down and check it out. Leaving the engine running, and the driver's door off its latch, in case he needed a quick escape, he stumbled down the steep bank and reached the car. It was obvious to him now, that it had hit the tree head-on, and with some force. The front was crumpled up to the firewall of the passenger's side, and the engine had lost all of its fluids – oil, coolant, and brake fluid pooled under the front of it. Inside, all the airbags had deployed, and the windshield was smashed. But there was no blood, no signs of a struggle, it seemed she had survived the crash and left the car.

He couldn't understand why she hadn't made her way back to the cabin. He moved around the back and opened the tailgate where she always kept winter clothes, and emergency food in a plastic container, if she'd had time to walk away rather than running for her life, she would have taken the contents. But it was full, nothing had been moved. He slammed it shut in frustration. "Susan," He shouted. "Susan!" Again, there was no reply. He checked his watch — 08:51 a.m. he was running out of time.

One last look, then he could tell Lynne he did the best he could. He moved back to the front of the car and made his way a little farther down the slope. "Susan!" He shouted.

He knew he shouldn't, shouting was a bad idea, but when you're desperate, any idea is generally a good one. Even the bad ones. Still nothing. "Okay that's it, I've done all I can." He said to himself. He turned and started his way back to his car. As he did, he heard a rustling of the trees behind him. He stopped cold, a shiver ran down his spine, and he could feel his adrenaline once again starting to pump around his body. He spun around and there she stood. It was Susan. Disheveled, and with dry blood matted into her hair, but it was her. His heart lifted.

"Thank God I found you." He said, relief pouring through his words.

"Me too, I thought I was done for." She said.

He moved down to her and held out his hand. She grabbed it and they started to claw their way back up the bank toward the waiting Range Rover.

"What happened?" Jeff asked.

"Last night I was about to make myself supper when I remembered I'd left something in my car. I went out to it, and when I turned around there was one of those things on the porch, between me and the cabin, it growled and snarled. I was frightened, so I got into my car and left, but I lost control and, well ended up there." She pointed back to the car wreck.

"What the hell was it you'd left in the car that was so important it meant you went outside in the dark?" Jeff asked.

"It's silly really, I wanted my slippers." She said.

Jeff sighed and almost laughed. "Well, at least you're safe now."

They reached the top of the bank and stood at the front of the Range Rover.

Susan looked back down at her wrecked car. "Such a shame, I'll miss that car." She said.

Jeff shook his head. "Miss the car? Christ!" He said under his breath.

He turned and made his way to the driver's side and got in. Susan was still looking back at her car shaking her head. As Jeff looked down to fasten his seat belt, through his peripheral vision, he saw a dark shape flash across the front of the car, then he heard the scream. He scrambled out of his seat, but he was too late.

All he could do was watch as two large hybrids carried her back down the bank. He stepped forward, he wanted to chase after them, kill the things, and rescue her but he was scared. Every ounce of his fiber told him to get back into the car and drive away, but he couldn't just leave her. Could he? His fists clenched from anger and frustration, and then the screaming stopped. She had been calling his name, it was a shrieking cry for help that echoed around the forest. But now everywhere was silent. He stepped forward again and found himself at the edge of the road. His eyes darted from side to side, but he could see nothing.

Then he heard a growl. A low-pitched primeval guttural growl. It was clearly a warning to back off. He did, he took a step backward, but the growl came again, and he still couldn't see where it was coming from. Suddenly, something was coming at him, flying toward him, high, with the sun behind it.
He tried to focus but it was silhouetted. *What the fuck was it?* Had they thrown a rock at him to chase him away? He'd heard of Gorilla's throwing things to chase people, and those *Myth Seeker* TV shows Danny loved to watch, they always claimed that's what *Sasquatch's* do if you believe in that sort of thing. The object spun through the air, coming closer and closer, Jeff ducked, holding up his arm to shield him. It hit the hood of the Range Rover with a dull wet thud. He turned and realized what it was.

Susan's gaunt eyes stared back at him; terror still registered across her face. Jeff turned and his stomach emptied. The growl came again, and this time Jeff didn't need another warning. He scrambled into the Range Rover and put it into reverse. He planted his foot on the gas and watched as Susan's severed head rolled forward and off the hood. All that remained were the bloody streaks and dent the impact had made. He stamped on the brakes and selected drive on the auto-box. Then stepping on the gas again he sped away to a chorus of hybrid-

Neanderthals chanted, whooping, and cheering in celebration. Once he was sure that he was clear, Jeff brought the car to a halt. He was in shock. He sat motionless shaking. He didn't cry for her, he couldn't, what had happened was so horrific his brain simply couldn't process it. He switched on the wipers and washer jets, frantically trying to clear the blood that had sprayed up onto the windshield. His sorrow and frustration turned to anger, but there was nothing he could do now, he must get to the airport and catch the last flight out. Now more than ever he needed his wife and son.

The route across the Pennines was, for the most part clear. The deep blue sky of the lowlands was now replaced by thick white clouds as he climbed the road to the top of the mountain range. In some places, the clouds rolled down from the top of the peaks and flowed across the road like a stream, but there was no time to slow down, he had to push on. He wasn't too far now, he could make it in time, and he knew the runway they were using well, he'd used it himself. Away from the commercial runways, you can drive almost up to the aircraft, he would not need to park and make his way through the terminal. The cloud that lay across the road started to thin out and Jeff picked up speed. Ahead he could see something. The thinning cloud obscured it from clarity just enough to make him unsure.

He took his foot off the gas and the Range Rover began to slow. As the low cloud thinned, and he got closer he was able to make the object out. It was a hybrid-Neanderthal standing in the middle of the road. Jeff smiled, this time he had the advantage. He gritted his teeth and planted his foot hard down. The Range Rover picked up speed. The supercharged V8 pushed the two-ton SUV forward like a missile. Jeff put the high beams on and blew the horn. The hybrid spun around and tried to avoid the oncoming missile, but it was too late. The Range Rover's front left fender hit it hard, tossing it up into the air like a rag doll. It screamed in pain as it flew past his passenger window. Jeff hit the brakes hard. The Range Rover came to a stop thirty yards from where the hybrid lay. It was alive, crippled, and badly injured, but alive. He slowly climbed out and walked to the back of the car, lifting the tailgate he opened the plastic lid that held the emergency tools and removed the tire iron.

Gripping it tightly he walked toward the injured animal and stood over it. Even in its badly wounded state, it was aggressive, growling and spitting at him as he looked down on it. Jeff lifted the tire iron over his head and screamed "You fucking cunt!" as he brought it down with as much force as he could on its forehead. He hit it over and over, as the rage of what had happened to Susan, Danny, and how things had fallen apart came out of him, right there, at that moment. Exhausted, Jeff dropped to his knees beside the dead hybrid and let go of the tire iron. It slipped from his limp hand, blood-soaked, from the dead creature, and Jeff's own injuries when his hands had hit the shards of sharp bone that now protruded from the smashed skull. He looked at the lifeless hulk. He could see where the Range Rover had struck it, its leg was smashed, and its arm broken. Then he looked to where he'd vented his rage upon it. There was nothing left. The face that snarled and growled was gone. Instead, there was now just a pulp of bone, tissue, and brain matted together by the thick black hair. "Fuck you!" He whispered as he stood. He spat on it and walked back to the car. Pulling the door closed, he looked down at his blood-soaked shirt and smiled to himself as he set off for the airport.

Terry was almost finished checking the facility. The entrance to the underground garage was secured as were the exterior doors. The last area to check was the door that sealed the administration block from the rest of the facility. As he approached, he could hear movement through it. The small glass viewing porthole allowed only the smallest of glimpses of the large beasts on the other side. He walked up to the door. He could see dents bulging out toward him where they had struck the door repeatedly, trying to break out, to get to them.

But so far it was holding. He placed his face on the porthole. A few feet away the female stood with its back to the door, and it looked to him like it was cradling something though he couldn't make out what it was. Smiling he tapped the glass. "Hey, you, yeah you, ugly bitch," He said taunting it, but as he expected it took no notice. "Yeah, you're too fucking dumb."

As he said it the female turned slowly and faced him, it seemed to be smiling, Terry looked harder, it wasn't cradling anything, it wasn't holding anything. As he tried to understand what it was, the glass smashed, and the male's hand grabbed at him. Terry pulled back quickly. Stumbling, he fell backward, landing heavily on the concrete floor. The hand which only just squeezed through the porthole frame grabbed at the air, searching for the face that had been pushed up against it. Then it dawned on him, they had set a trap for him, or for anyone that would be so close to the window. He swallowed hard, this was new behavior, and realized that they're learning, and adapting.

He had watched as the male seemed to understand the flat lines back in the lab, but he hadn't believed it. He'd put it down to coincidence or just luck, but this wasn't. This was a trap, and only the higher-intelligence animals used such things for hunting. As he hauled himself back to his feet the large hand pulled back through the porthole and was replaced by the male's face. It was too big to see all of it, but Terry could see the eyes clearly, and he could see that it was smiling at him.

But this was no friendly smile, it was a, *I'll get you another time* smile. Terry knew this had to be reported, Joceline must know what he'd just witnessed.

Joceline was at her desk when Terry knocked on the door and entered, gasping from running the distance between the administration block and her quarters. He was doubled over trying to catch his breath.

"What is it?" She asked.

Terry pointed back from where he'd come. "It's the hybrids, they're becoming organized," He gasped.

"What do you mean, organized?"

By now Terry had regained his breath and composure. "When I checked on the door, to make sure it was holding, I noticed that it was buckled, dented from the inside where they had been hitting it, trying to get through. They must have known I was there. When I moved closer, the female stood with her back to the door a few feet away."

"What was she doing?" Joceline asked.

"It looked like she was cradling something in her arms, so I moved closer, put my face against the glass porthole to try and see," Terry paused.

"And then?" Joceline pushed him to continue.

"The male must have been against the door. I didn't see him. The next thing, his hand came through the glass and nearly got a hold of me, it was only because it couldn't fit past the wrist that I managed to duck out of the way." Terry answered, visibly upset.

"Are they still behind the door?" Joceline asked, with a concerned tone.

"Yes, they are." He said.

"I need to see."

"Okay, I'll come with you."

They approached the door slowly, and quietly. Joceline could see the smashed glass on the floor, and the indentations Terry had mentioned from their attempts to break through it. She moved closer.

"Careful doc," Terry whispered.

Joceline put her hand up. to indicate she would be. She approached the porthole and stopped. She pulled out her phone and switched on the video camera, holding it at arm's length she moved the phone through the porthole and scanned up and down the door. She couldn't see anything, nothing seemed to be moving. She turned back to Terry and shrugged, pulling the phone away she placed it back in her pocket.

"Are you sure they can't get through now that the glass is smashed?" She asked.

"No, they can't reach the handle, besides with the doors locked the handle is no use even if they could." He answered, reassuring her.

Joceline nodded in agreement. "Okay Terry, keep an eye on this door as often as you can, I'll be back in my office." She smiled and walked away.

Terry stood staring at the door, moving closer to it he examined the hinges one last time. They looked solid. For all of the force these hybrid-Neanderthals had exerted, the hinges were holding. Satisfied, he turned and made his way back to the accommodation block, and his quarters. He needed sleep. The headache they all knew was a precursor to this transformation, this de-evolving had started, and Terry knew deep down he didn't have long. But like everyone else, he was also trying to convince himself it was because of the stress of the situation they found themselves in. But even in his own head, he didn't sound too convincing.

Lynne had woken from her late sleep, the screams of Jeff had haunted her dreams, and she imagined the worst of things that would explain it. She checked the large clock on the wall, it read 05:42 a.m. She'd slept through most of the previous day and the night, but it didn't surprise her. She knew with the time difference it would be 10:42 a.m. in the UK, and wherever Jeff was, she could only hope that he was okay.

She looked to the other couch where Danny was still asleep. He must have put himself to bed after Lynne had dozed off. She smiled at him and stood. She left the room and made her way to the toilets. When she returned, Danny was sitting up staring at the flat-screen TV. Lynne watched him, it was as if he found it familiar, but he didn't know why. She knew this was the start of the end game for him, she should really tell Joceline, she should make sure Danny wasn't a danger to himself or to any of them. She should do this, but she couldn't. Not yet, just another day. *Give me one more day with my son,* she thought to herself.

"Do you want it on son?" She asked moving back into the room.

Danny didn't answer, he gave her the same look as he did the TV. Lynne smiled at him, she didn't react, she didn't know how to. She sat next to him on the floor and switched on the game console, and the TV came to life. Danny slowly picked up the handset, he looked at it, turning it and pressing the buttons as he did.

"That's right son, just like that." She said. The game menu loaded, and though Danny was no longer playing the game, the changing graphics on the screen and sounds seemed to keep his attention. Lynne stood and made her way to the coffee machine and began to cry. She knew this would be the last day she would have with her son.

She looked back up to the clock 05:53 a.m. "Where are you, Jeff?" She whispered to herself.

12

The time on the dashboard clock showed 10:53 a.m. as Jeff pulled the battered SUV onto the runway. He'd made it, but only just. The collisions with the hybrid had damaged the car's cooling system, and it finally gave up in a cloud of hissing steam as he entered the airport. As he limped the struggling and overheating SUV into the hangar where he'd been told to meet the crew, the Range Rover's engine knocked one last time before it died. He climbed out shutting the driver's door behind him. As he did a tall athletic-looking man wearing a U.S. air force flight suit came into the hangar and walked toward him.

"Are you our guest passenger?" He asked.

"I am, yes. Thank you." Jeff replied.

"No problem, you're on time but only just by the looks of things." He pointed to the damaged Range Rover.

"Yeah, shame it's a nice car," Jeff said smiling.

"Okay, come on then, we're the last flight out. Oh, I'm Aircraft Commander Glades." He said holding out his hand.

"Jeff, Jeff Eastwood," Jeff replied shaking his hand.

"Any relation?" Glades said, smiling.

"No, none at all," He replied. Not that he'd been asked that before!

Jeff was shown to the Lockheed C-5 Galaxy transport plane. He entered with Glades and the rest of the flight crew. There were eight of them in total, including Jeff.

Glades introduced them. "This is Rodriguez, he's the pilot, these two are Sully and Stuart the flight engineers, and these three sad sacks are the loadmasters, but you don't need to know their names," He laughed, and then continued "Okay, okay their names are Connors, Brady, and Givens, God help me they'll sulk if I leave em out." He turned and pointed to Jeff. "And this is Mr. Eastwood, and no, he's not a relation, but he is our guest and a *VIP* from the British government. Or what's left of it."

Jeff was strapped into one of the folding seats that lined the large cargo bay. As the rear door closed, he got a last look at the airport, and he knew he wouldn't step foot in England again. But as the plane took off and climbed, all he felt was relief. For now, at least, no hybrids could get to him, and he could rest easy. He was woken by a jolt of turbulence. Yawning and rubbing his eyes he looked around at his surroundings. In the cargo hold with him was an Army Humvee which seemed devoid of the usual gun that sits on the top, and next to him sat Loadmaster Brady. Jeff smiled at him, nodding in polite acknowledgment.

"Y'all catching a ride with us sir?" Brady asked, shouting over the noise of the aircraft.

"Yes, yes I am. And please it's Jeff, not sir." He answered, trying to match Brady's volume.

"Do you have family in the States?" Brady asked.

"My wife and son are in Washington."

"You know we're landing in New York, right?" Brady said smiling.

"Yes, thank you I know, I'm hoping to find a rental I can commandeer," Jeff answered.

"No need for that sir, take the Humvee, the army has no use for it. Hell, there is no army."

Jeff looked at the armored Humvee that bounced in its straps with every bump of turbulence. Remembering the damage caused to the Range Rover, he agreed it would be the best thing to use, better than a rental car anyway.

"Don't mind if I do, you sure they won't mind?" Jeff asked.

"Who's to mind? As I said, there's no one to mind." Brady confirmed.

The conversation stopped, and what was the background din of the aircraft while he'd been talking filled Jeff's ears, while his mind filled with thoughts of what he may find in Washington D.C. He needed a distraction, anything, even if it meant pestering poor Brady for the remainder of the flight.

"This is a big aircraft," Jeff shouted while pointing around it.

"It is, but she's an old bird, sir, most have been retired. This one was due for a re-fit, but not now I guess, this will be her last flight sir. Like the army and navy, there is no air force anymore. We're the last out of the UK, and probably Europe." Brady shouted back.

"Once you land, then what?" Jeff asked, desperate to keep the conversation going.

"Once we're down and secured, we go our separate way, that's it." Brady's answer was cold.

Jeff pointed back to the Humvee "Won't any of you need it to get home?"

"No sir, we flew out of JFK when this started, we left our own transport there." He answered.

Brady hesitated; Jeff could tell he wanted to ask something. "What is it?" Jeff asked.

"Do they know what this is sir? I mean how it even started." Brady asked.

"The last update I had, we had at COBRA." Brady interrupted him. "COBRA sir?" Brady asked.

"I was part of the UK government's emergency council. The last update we had from The World Health Organization was that they still believed it was a pandemic of some kind, viral or a pathogen."

"When was that?" Brady asked.

"Seems a lifetime ago now they were meeting with the two scientists that led the search, Joceline Mercier and Rob Pinkert, but we didn't hear back from them, so God knows what it is," Jeff shrugged, then continued. "But it's beaten our best efforts."

"Funny isn't it, all the might we have, and this is how it ends," Brady said.

"Every dominant species on Earth has a due date, even the dinosaurs, arguably the most successful species ever to live had their sell-by date. I just hoped I wouldn't be alive when ours came. That we'd have more time — we'd find resolution in our differences, religion, culture, and history." Jeff said.

Brady laughed. "When you've seen what I have sir, you don't hold out much hope."

"What do you mean?" Jeff asked.

"Well, I'm not a scientist, but it seems to me you don't see animals killing each other over a God we all know doesn't exist," Brady said.

"How do you know?" Jeff asked.

"Take a look around sir, the world's gone to shit, and the only animal that's been affected is also the only animal that believes in a God. I don't see sharks being infected, or apes or dogs sir, and they don't pray to anything. Do they sir?" Brady replied.

Jeff sat in silence. This was only affecting mankind, and there had been no reports of any other species being infected. Even when they tried to experiment on monkeys when it first started, their bodies didn't react. "Maybe that does prove there is one," Jeff replied.

"How so sir?" Brady asked.

"As you say, we are the only species to pray, and the only species to be infected, so maybe there is a God, just one God that appeared differently to different cultures to best represent that culture's own beliefs, and maybe that God is fed up with us killing ourselves in his name, and he's doing it for us," Jeff said.

"Yeah, and it may be aliens too sir," Brady said sarcastically.

Jeff laughed with him, and Brady elaborated. "Maybe humans are their experiment sir, or a game and they're bored with us so they're resetting it."

Jeff nodded and sniggered. "Thing is Brady, with the world going dark now, the power is failing around the world, and the humans that haven't been infected by whatever this is, are dropping in numbers. I guess we will never know what brought about our downfall."

"Well, whatever it is sir, I'm one of the lucky ones. Once we land, I'm off to my bug-out cabin, and I'll do just fine, living off the land." Brady said.

Jeff sighed, he wasn't infected either, at least that's what he believed, and why wouldn't he? The true reason why this was happening had never got any farther than Joceline Mercier, and the members of FEMA she'd had the meeting with. After their screen had gone dark, all their communications had failed. They simply hadn't been able to convey Joceline's theory of the Gaia Hypothesis.

As Jeff settled back down to try and sleep some more, Brady's words about being one of the lucky ones resonated with him. His ignorance of the facts gave him comfort and optimism for his family's future, at least for now. He woke and drifted back to sleep as the flight continued, and in his waking moments, he watched the Loadmasters attending to their various duties. The aircraft wasn't comfortable, and it was cold, but he was out of danger and on his way to be with his family the fastest way possible. Though this aircraft wasn't a commercial jet, and it wasn't built for speed or comfort. Jeff had been told the flight time would be around nine hours, not the seven or eight hours it would normally take. But it didn't matter to him. All that mattered was that he'd made it. Against all the odds he was on his way, and soon he'd be able to see his wife and son again. And that above all else was all that mattered.

Joceline entered the recreation room and found Lynne sitting quietly watching Danny pushing the buttons on the game console controller and staring at the images on the TV.

"Is he playing that game?" Joceline asked.

"No," Lynne whispered, not taking her eyes off Danny.

Joceline moved around to the side of him and looked back at Lynne. "His physical changes are starting, Lynne; he may become dangerous," She said.

"I know," Lynne whispered her answer again.

"His eyes are set deeper, and his skull is reshaping, and like all of the others his skin is darkening," Joceline said as she looked closer at the little boy who sat motionless on the floor. Only his arms moved as he wielded the game controller through the air. She continued. "His hair is becoming much thicker, matted almost. Do you see this?" She directed the question to Lynne.

"Yes, I do, I noticed this morning," Lynne spoke normally now.

"His cognitive reasoning is reduced also, that is why he's not recognizing that he's not actually playing the game. The machine is only screening the demo, it's infantile almost." Joceline said.

"I just wanted one more day with him. Jeff is on his way, I know that now, I can feel it." Lynne said, her tone sharpening.

"It's too dangerous, for you and for Danny, you know this, and we don't know if Jeff is on his way, we don't know if he even made it out of Balmoral Castle," Joceline said.

Lynne sighed and slumped into the sofa; she knew Joceline was correct. Of course, she was right, and if Lynne was back at the hospital in London, she would be giving any parent the very same advice. London! That seemed such a long time ago now, where did that normal boring life go?

She would give anything to be bored and stuck in rush hour traffic right at this moment. London had its faults. She'd seen the old city change a lot in the years she'd been living there. Area's she remembers as a child on holiday now seemed unrecognizable, but she would take it all back, the good and the bad. She knew it was lost, she knew when she'd left that night for Washington that she would never see her home again, and she'd come to terms with it, and that she would never see her mom again. She'd told her to go to the cabin, and Jeff promised he would bring her, but she didn't expect either of those things to happen. The world was full of badness now, tragedy, and heartache. Why would this be any different?

"Okay!" Joceline brought Lynne back from her thoughts. "One more day, but we keep a close eye on him."

Lynne smiled. "Thank you."

Joceline poured herself a coffee and turned to leave, as she did Terry entered the room and both of them could tell he looked worried.

"What is it?" Joceline asked.

"You'd better come see this." He said to her. Joceline placed her coffee down next to Lynne and left with him.

Terry led Joceline to an office that was situated close to the door where the hybrids had set a trap for him the previous day. In the office, a monitor displayed the images from a security camera inside the lab, which held the dead hybrids they'd euthanized. Terry had remotely moved the camera's viewing angle, and standing outside the lab, looking into it, were the two hybrids. And it was clear to both of them that they were mourning their dead. The female was pacing up and down, the behavior often seen in animals suffering from stress and loss, and the male was standing with both arms resting on the glass. In the silence of the empty facility and this close to the block, they could hear them howling. But this wasn't the aggressive howling that they had witnessed previously, this vocalization was mournful.

"You seein' this?" Terry asked.

"Yes. I am." Joceline answered, still staring at the screen.

"What does it mean?" Terry asked, concern growing in his voice.

"It means that the transformation takes longer than we originally thought." She answered, not breaking her concentration from the images from the camera.

"I don't follow," Terry replied.

"We always thought the transformation finished with the physical, but obviously, it doesn't. After that comes the social development, it's as if they're almost new-born."

"In what way?" Terry asked.

"Once the physical changes are manifested, we know the brain also goes through a physical change of its own, and it would now seem that includes the re-connecting and re-arranging of the neural pathways. Once this stage is complete, only then are they fully formed and functioning hybrids, though they are much more Neanderthal than human." She explained.

"But didn't you say that they would all die out, that they didn't have the capacity to carry out the basic functions to preserve life, hunting, keeping warm, building, or even finding shelter?" Terry asked.

"That's what we thought, but it would appear that we were wrong, as we have been about this all along," Joceline said.

As they watched them in silence, the facility was plunged into darkness as the power from the main grid finally went down. Around the facility lights went out, computers shut down, and in the recreation room, the TV that had kept Danny occupied switched off, and without any external windows, Lynne was in darkness. Within seconds the emergency generators came to life, and the lights came back on, but the emergency fire protocol had already unlocked the magnetically sealed doors including the door that had been securing the administration block. The computer Terry and Joceline had been watching re-booted. When it did, the security feed came back on, and the two hybrids were no longer in view.

The Lockheed C-5 Galaxy transport touched down at JFK airport eight hours and forty-two minutes after it had left Newcastle.

Jeff watched from the small window as it lumbered to a halt outside a VIP terminal once used for when world leaders, dignitaries, and Royal families from around the world visited. He unfastened his belt and stood, stretching his legs from the cramped position he'd been in. The rear door began to open, and as it did the crew joined Jeff in the cargo hold armed with assault rifles. As the New York morning air flooded in, Jeff smiled. He was here, he'd made it, now he just had to get to the facility in Washington, and in an armored Humvee, he was more than confident about his chances. Commander Glades approached him and offered him his sidearm. Jeff looked down at it and took it from him. He'd had some small arms training, it was a prerequisite of being a member of COBRA, but he hadn't been much good at target practice, and hadn't fired a gun since. But still, *better to have it and not need it*, he thought to himself as he pushed it into his belt.

"Okay gentlemen let's get this Humvee off for our friend, and then we're out of here," Glades ordered.

Jeff watched as they pulled it out of the aircraft. He followed it down the huge ramp and onto the tarmac.

With everyone now off the Galaxy, the ramp began to lift, sealing the aircraft shut.

"Welcome to America and thank you for flying with the U.S. Air Force, we hope you had a pleasant flight," Glades said smiling.

"No, thank you for bringing me" Jeff replied, though more sincerely. He really was thankful to them.

"Don't sweat it, but you're on your own from here. Good luck, I hope you find your family," Glades said.

Jeff smiled and shook his hand. "You too."

The other crew members had already left, and as Glades turned and began to walk away, a U.S. Air Force armed transport vehicle appeared. As Glades climbed in Jeff waved once more, and then watched as the large vehicle disappeared from view. He stood, alone on the tarmac in what was once one of the world's busiest airports, and yet other than the sound of the Humvee's engine ticking over there was silence. Huge airliners, as well as smaller private planes and helicopters now sat abandoned. Nothing moved, the radars that would rotate, tracking the thousands of flights that came in and out were motionless. He could see shuttle buses, aircraft tugs, and luggage cars parked neatly — Another sign of how the effects of this had taken their toll gradually rather than in an instant. In the distance, he could begin to hear the howls and cries of hybrids that had been attracted to the airport by the Galaxy touching down. It was time to leave. He climbed into the Humvee and pulled the solid door shut, he smiled sitting in it. "There was no way any of those bastards would be able to get in here." He said to himself as he set off. He checked his watch which was still on Greenwich Mean Time. It read 7:35 p.m. which he knew meant it was 2:35 p.m. local time. He was tired, but there was somewhere he had to be. He pulled away, and headed for Washington, and what he believed to be the safety of the facility.

Joceline looked at Terry, the security feed had come back on, and the hybrids that had been mourning their dead in the lab were no longer in view. Terry moved the camera to the right, and still, there was no sign of them, then he moved it to the left, and he could see the female. He sighed, *at least one of them was in view,* he thought to himself.

"You stay here and keep an eye on the female, I'll go check that the door has re-scaled." He said to Joceline.

Joceline nodded. "Okay, but be careful, if they have now fully developed, they're smarter remember."

"Yeah, I know." He said as he left the small office pulling the door closed as he did.

Joceline watched as the female walked back and forth along the glass wall of the lab.

Every so often she would stop and lean on the

glass with her forearms, though it was clear she wasn't pushing against it, and she didn't seem to be testing its strength. Contented that the female was going to continue this pattern, Joceline moved the camera. She wanted to try and find the male, but as before, he was nowhere near the lab. She selected another camera, the one in the large conference room, and again there was no sign of it. She checked the camera that covered the administration offices, and while there were signs that this is where they had nested, the male was not there either. Joceline had one camera left to check, the camera that looked along the corridor where the door was. She switched over to it and she could see Terry making his way along the corridor toward the door. Pulling the small joystick to the left, the camera began to move until it was facing the door. Joceline jolted back from the screen in shock. The door was wide open. Terry stopped by the open door and turned to the camera shrugging, he pushed it closed, but it was clear he was having trouble. He turned back to the camera.

"Can you see where they are?" He asked.
Joceline checked each feed, but she couldn't see them. She moved the camera left and right to signal no.

"The hinges are bent, it won't close. I'll have to try and adjust them." Terry said.
Joceline moved the camera up and down and then watched Terry.

He took a long screwdriver from his belt and moved toward the hinges. She could only see the back of him, and because she had the camera trained on him, Joceline couldn't see the corridor on the other side of the door. "Come on Terry!" She said to herself. He backed away from the door and pushed it closed. This time it worked, and the door closed with ease. The magnetic lock reengaged and Joceline sighed. "Thank God." She said.

She watched as Terry turned away from the door and then stopped. Joceline placed her hand on the joystick and moved it right. As she did the camera turned, and into view came the female hybrid. They had tricked them, set a trap. Terry had repaired the door, but he hadn't locked them back in the administration department, he'd locked them out of it. Joceline watched as Terry took a step back toward the door, stretching his left hand out behind him, he was fumbling for the keypad, but as he did the female moved forward, mirroring him step for step. Terry stopped and lowered his arm. In his right hand, he still had the screwdriver, and he was gripping it tightly.

When the lights had gone out in the recreation room, Lynne hadn't moved, she'd remained perfectly still, she knew the generators would kick in, Joceline had told her it would only be seconds before they did. But as the fluorescent lights flickered back to life and the room was bathed in the harsh light once again, Danny was not sitting in front of the TV.

"Danny?" Lynne said his name quietly. She turned to check the door, it was still shut, and she hadn't heard it open in the dark. She stood, turning around on the spot. Her instinct told her that this was her son, and she should have nothing to fear, but her conscious told her he was no longer the little boy who loved Coco Pops in the morning and playing soccer with his friends on a weekend, and she should have everything to fear. She moved forward slowly toward the kitchen units that held the microwave oven and coffee machines, her head turning, spinning from left to right, looking, and listening for the smallest of movements. There were plenty of places to hide in the room for a small child, behind one of the arcade games, or the large sofas. She continued gingerly forward until she reached the kitchen area. She turned. She could now see the full length of the room. Only some of the lights had come back on. The building systems did this to preserve power, and to stop the generators from burning through the diesel reserves too quickly. But now the room was littered with shadows and dark corners. The arcade games and all but the main TV had also been denied power, they weren't essential. "Danny?" Lynne spoke softly. "Are you there sweetheart?" Still no reply. "Mommy has Coco Pops."

A noise, a rustle from behind the Pacman machine, Lynne craned her neck, routed to the spot she couldn't move. "Danny?" She was now whimpering. "Are you there, is that you?" She reached out and grabbed a packet of cereal from the worktop — she didn't know what it was — it didn't matter. It just had to sound like Coco Pops. She shook it. The noise came again, and she took a step forward shaking the box. "Danny?" A shadow appeared from behind the game's machine. It was Danny.

His head was down, and he looked at Lynne through his furrowed brow, with a menacing threatening stare. He snarled and growled, and then Lynne saw his hand. He was holding a large bread knife with an eight-inch blade and serrated edge. Lynne stopped and held out her right hand. "It's okay baby, put the knife down, I'll get the games working again." She said, as softly and calmly as she could manage. But her voice trembled. Danny looked at the knife in his hand, and then back at Lynne. And then he smiled.

Jeff had left the airport behind and was making good time toward Washington and his family. As with Scotland and England, the roads were for the most part clear. Did he dare to believe he could be with his wife and son tonight, safe and in a military-grade facility that in theory at least, could support them for over a year. The Humvee trundled along; any small obstacles were easily knocked out of the way. Inside most of the military equipment had been stripped out, the gun that is usually seen atop was gone and the hole the soldier would stand through was covered over. The radio and communications equipment too was gone, but he didn't care, he would have no need for them, this was only to get him where he needed, and where he wanted to be. He looked across at the passenger seat and wondered if he could have done anything differently to save Susan. How would he explain it to Lynne who had counted on him to bring her to safety? He couldn't tell her the truth, he couldn't tell her what actually happened, what they did to her, she wouldn't be able to process that, and he was convinced that in the facility, locked away from what was happening outside, they would have no real idea of the violence and brutality that these hybrids were capable of. No, it was settled, he would simply tell her that he found her car smashed against a tree and that when he looked for her, he couldn't find her. After all, that was the truth. Kind of. As he continued along the I-95 South, he could see ahead that the road was blocked by the small amount of traffic that had been abandoned. As he got closer, he could see that a gasoline tanker had jack-knifed across the width of the highway. He stopped as close to it as he dare. It could be a trap, set by other people looking for any unsuspecting travelers fleeing the cities. He looked around for any would-be bandits, but he could see nothing from inside the Humvee.

Jeff switched off the engine and climbed out. He approached the tanker slowly holding the gun down by his side, his right hand gripping it tightly and his thumb ready to flick the safety off. Standing next to the cab of the truck, he stepped up and looked inside it, the keys were in the dash. He opened the door and climbed in, checking the bunk in the back of the sleeper cab as he did. It was clear.

He turned the key, and nothing happened, its batteries were dead. "Shit." He said. "I fucking knew this was too easy." sitting in the cab he looked for a way across, but there wasn't one, if he was to continue in the safety of the Humvee he would have to turn around and double back, find another way, and he didn't know if there was enough fuel for that, and if there wasn't the last thing he wanted was to be vulnerable at a filling station. He looked passed the truck, maybe there was a car on the other side of it?

He climbed out of the cab on the passenger side, through the gap between the cab and the trailer he could see the Humvee, but it was no use to him anymore. He turned and began walking along the highway toward the closest car. He opened the driver's door, no keys. He slammed it out of frustration. Seconds later he heard a cry, and it wasn't human. He spun around, not knowing which direction it had come from, but it came again, followed by another cry, and another but from the opposite side of the highway. Should he turn and run back to the Humvee? He knew he'd be safe, but he didn't know if he'd make the distance.

The next car was five hundred yards ahead of him, he'd probably make it, but if it had no keys or its battery was flat, he'd be out in the open, and the small BMW soft top would offer him no protection. The cries came again, this time they were closer, but he still couldn't see anything, he needed to move, he had to do something. As the next cry came Jeff turned and ran back to the semi and scrambled into the cab locking both doors. He climbed into the sleeper compartment and closed the curtain that separated it from the rest of the cab. Jeff lay on the bed, trying to slow his breathing, he was panting, and his heart was beating fast. He gripped the gun tightly pointing it at the center of the curtain. If anything came through, he would fire, point-blank range, he didn't care how big they were. A 9 mm would make a big hole this close. The cries now turned to howls and vocalizations, and they were close, very close. Outside of the cab, he could hear sniffing, and he could hear them testing the metal of the truck.

Through a gap in the curtain, he was able to see the side mirror, it reflected a nightmarish sight. Two large hybrids were working their way along the truck. Eventually, they reached the driver's door. The leader climbed up onto the step, hanging onto the mirror as he did. Jeff could see the shadow of its large head cast into the cab as it moved, looking for its quarry. He pulled back into the bunk. There was nothing he could do now but pray and hope that the truck would keep him safe.

Joceline was trapped in the room between the administration and accommodation blocks. Terry had closed the door when he'd left but it didn't lock, it was an open office for anybody to use. Splitting the screen display, she could see along the corridor that led to the room that she was in. So far at least, that corridor was clear. But Terry was still face to face with the female hybrid. As Joceline watched the video feed, the terror and fear for Terry rose inside of her. She couldn't look away, she needed to know he would be safe, but if it attacked him, that was something Joceline wouldn't want to witness. As she stood, fixated on the screen, she heard something. It was footsteps, and they were becoming louder. She checked her screen again, the corridor still looked clear, but there was no mistaking the sound. She looked around the office for something, anything she could defend herself with, but it was empty, just a desk, four chairs, and the PC. She darted behind the door, squatting down under the glass that filled the top half of it, pinning herself as hard as she was able against the door. She waited and held her breath. She could see the monitor from her hiding position and now she could see the male hybrid on the screen, and it was on the other side of the door. Its breathing was heavy and coarse, and as it breathed out, she could hear a low grumble resonating in the back of its throat. The glass partition fogged up as it exhaled on it. It sniffed the air and from the point of view of the camera, she watched it as it turned and looked through the glass in the door. It cast a huge shadow across the room and Joceline knew if it realized she was behind the door, there would be nothing she could do to defend herself. The shadow moved again.

From her hiding place, she watched as it continued along the corridor on the monitor. Somehow, it had evaded the camera as it had approached. She wasn't going to be caught out that easily again.

Terry didn't know what to do. His mind scrambled at any and all options. If he turned his back to unlock the door, he knew she would pounce, and he'd have no way of defending himself, but he also knew he couldn't remain in this stand-off. Was she keeping him here until the male arrived? Where was it? Why wasn't it here? Why wasn't he already dead? A thousand thoughts raced across his mind. He'd already begun to have the headaches, and he knew what followed, and that, he'd promised himself he wasn't going to allow. If he was to die, then it would be saving Joceline who he knew was trapped in the small room. He gripped the screwdriver tightly and screamed at the female. "Come on then you fucking ugly bitch!" It worked, the female shrieked back at him and charged. She hit him hard knocking him backward and against the wall, he was winded, but she had her back to him now. Before she was able to turn, Terry jumped onto her back and brought the screwdriver down as hard as he could. The flat-headed screwdriver embedded itself into its left shoulder. He pushed hard and forced the shaft down until he felt the mattered hair of her body against his hand. The female screamed in pain as Terry twisted the handle. She ran backward squashing him between her and the solid concrete wall, he let go, the wind knocked from him, and he fell to the floor. Spinning around she pulled the screwdriver out and flung it to the floor, and then she turned her attention to Terry.

Danny smiled at Lynne, but it wasn't the sweet smile of a child looking at the mother he adored. This was a menacing, cold, and unsettling smile. Lynne was shaking, she'd heard what Brad, the original victim had done, and just how strong he had become, but none of that mattered. This was her son, regardless of how this thing had changed him, he was still her little boy, and from the second she'd held him in her arms, Lynne had promised him that no one would ever hurt him. He stepped closer to her, a guttural growl formed in the back of his throat and beneath his now darkened skin and thick black matted hair, he was bearing his teeth.

"Danny, stay there son." She whispered, smiling through her fear.

He took another step toward her. Lynne was pinned against the kitchen counter. She could not move farther back. Then the attack came. Danny rushed her, slicing through the air with the large knife as he did. Lynne tried to move out of the way and passed him to the door. She almost made it. But as she sidestepped him, Danny spun around and wielded the knife. It sliced deep into the back of her calf muscle and she went down smashing into the glass coffee table as she fell. The pain was intense, a white-hot burning pain that seared through her muscle. She lifted her leg and turned to look; the blade had cut deep, down to the bone. Facing down she crawled for the door, if she could just get out and lock him in, she might be able to talk him down, bring back the boy she knew was still in there. He attacked again, driving the knife through the back of her left shoulder, Lynne cried out in pain, gasping for breath as Danny pulled the blade back out and ran behind the arcade machine. She turned over and lay on her back, her left leg now useless, and she knew she couldn't make the door. Lynne lifted herself against the couch she'd been sleeping on just a few hours ago. Sitting on the floor with her back against it she looked to the door, it was only a few feet away, but it may have well been a few hundred. She heard the growl again, and Danny emerged from the dark corner, the knife he'd struck with now dripped with her blood. He smiled and raised the knife again.

Jeff's hands were shaking, the weight of the gun was now becoming too much, but he didn't dare to lower it, he knew if he did, at that very moment he would be charged and he wouldn't be able to draw it, aim and fire quickly enough. He looked at his watch, 5:48 p.m. He'd been trapped in here for nearly fifty minutes, it was vital he got out, to get to the facility. He began to panic, and he felt sweat running down his face and the back of his neck. The early spring sun was beating down on the truck's windshield heating up the cab, making his throat dry and tickly. He tried his hardest not to cough but he couldn't hold it in. Immediately, the lead hybrid wrenched the driver's door open and climbed up and into the cab. Its large primal head burst through the curtain and Jeff instantly squeezed the trigger. As the bullet hit it and went through its skull the back of its head exploded across the dash and windscreen before the remains of the bullet smashed it. Inside the cab the sound of the gun discharging disorientated Jeff. His ears rang and his eyes watered. He dropped the gun as he pressed his hands against the side of his head, trying to stop the ringing. Outside he heard the howls of the other hybrids as they cried for their fallen leader. Without an alpha they were disorganized, each of them tried to scramble into the truck, but the dead body of the large male blocked their entrance. Now, with his head clear and the disorientation gone, Jeff knew he had to escape. He picked up the gun and pushed it deep into his pocket. Kicking and pushing against the large heavy carcass, he managed to get past it. As he pushed out from behind the curtain the thrashing arms of the other hybrids grabbed at him, one managed to grip his trouser leg, and he hit it with the butt of the gun, he didn't want to fire it in the cab again, any delay now and he would surely be ripped to pieces. It let go and he managed to open the passenger door and climb down and out of the cab. Two other hybrids had now made it into the cab, but they were still blocked by their fallen leader. His instinct was to turn and run, try for that BMW that he'd spotted earlier, but he knew if he did and they got past the truck he wouldn't make it. He couldn't outrun them or outfight them, and the gun would run out of bullets much sooner than he would need it to. He turned around looking for anything to give him the edge. It was then he noticed the trailer of the rig for the first time, it was a gasoline tanker. Looking back at the cab he could see that they were still trapped, so enraged that he'd killed one of their own any thoughts of coming under or around the truck hadn't yet come to them. He ran for the tanker and turned the outlet taps. Gasoline immediately gushed from them and Jeff turned and ran, he must be far enough away. *If they just stay in the cab for a few seconds more*, he thought to himself. He heard a cry and he turned back around. The first hybrid was almost out, and he wasn't as far away as he wanted but it was now or never. He pulled the gun from his pocket and aimed. He squeezed the trigger, it missed. The lead hybrid was now past the body and in the doorway, he fired again, he missed again. He looked back to the cab, it was out, and the second hybrid was starting to climb out behind it. "Fuck it!" He shouted. Jeff emptied the clip at the tanker.

The female hybrid growled at Terry as it held its hand over the wound in its shoulder. The screwdriver was on the floor next to its foot. He looked to it, he needed it because without it he was defenseless. He mustered his remaining strength and pushed himself off the wall ducking down and below the swinging arms of the female. He grabbed it and spun around to face her. She charged him and grabbed him, slamming him down on the floor, roaring in his face. Terry could smell the warm putrid breath. It raised a fist and brought it crashing down on his chest, the pain was intense, it was like nothing he'd felt before. As it brought its fist up again Terry swung his right arm around and thrust the screwdriver through her chest wall penetrating her left lung. The female lunged to its left in agony. Terry pulled the screwdriver back out and swung again. This time with her doubled over he could reach her head. With his two hands gripping it, he mustered his remaining strength and lunged the screwdriver at her. The female cried out. It was a high-pitched cry of pain. The screwdriver had pierced her left eye. Terry pushed on it again, and this time she fell silent as the blade penetrated her brain. He watched as all the expression slid from her face, and her right eye became glazed and lifeless. She fell forward landing across him. Exhausted, his arms flopped to his side.

Joceline had heard the last cries of the female and had watched on the monitor as Terry had struck the fatal blow. But the male had also heard her and had given up its search for Joceline. It had run past her as she cowered behind the door. As the pounding footsteps had become almost inaudible, she made a decision. She would run for the safety of the accommodation block. Standing, she pulled the door open and ran. She could hear the male screaming for the female as it ran toward where she had been, and the sound drove through her with utter terror, but she couldn't stop, she needed to get back behind the reinforced door. As she rounded the last corner, Joceline could see the keypad and her fingers were already pressing the sequence of numbers in her mind. Five-three-one-six-eight, five-three-one-six-eight. She'd used these numbers for as long as she'd been at this facility, but right now, right at this moment, she was terrified she would forget them just when she needed them the most. She reached for the pad and keyed them in. The small green light came on, and the door hissed as the magnetic seal released. She pushed through it, spun around, and slammed it shut. Gasping heavily, she collapsed against the door, she was safe. But what about Terry? The thought bolted through her mind, and the panic came back.

The last image she'd seen of Terry, he was lying under the dead female. Surely, he must have pushed her off and made it into the administration block, hadn't he? She tried to reassure herself. She had to know, but she couldn't go back out there, what if the male was around the corner, what if after finding the dead female it came back for her, unable to find Terry? She stood and made her way to the closest room that had a PC that was linked to the security system.

Danny moved closer to Lynne and stepped into her pooling blood which now ran freely from her leg. Raising the knife, he straddled her and leaned forward. Lynne was weak from the blood loss. As well as her leg, the wound in her shoulder was hemorrhaging blood. He grabbed her by the throat and moved her sideways.

She was now lying flat on her back. He moved his body up hers and sat across her stomach. He squeezed her throat hard, but even in this advanced state, he didn't have the strength to choke her. Lynne's lips curled at the edges as she pleaded with her son. "Danny, please don't." She said, as the tears now ran freely down her blood-stained face. He raised the knife again and brought it down. Using her right hand, and all her strength, she caught his hand and pushed against him. He moved his body forward and leaned on the knife. It inched closer to her chest. "Please, please, please." She repeated in a whisper, but he didn't respond. The little boy that once relied on his mom for everything was now gone, and the monster that sat on top of her had only one thing on its mind. Lynne moved her left arm, her fingers searched for something, anything that she could use to stop him.

The blade was now against her skin and she could feel the pressure of the sharp point as it pushed through her jumper and bra. Her fingers grasped onto something, a piece of broken glass from the coffee table she'd smashed when she'd fallen to the floor. Gripping it she brought it up slowly. The serrated edges cut into her hand. And more blood ran along her wrist and to the puddle she was lying in. "Please, Danny." She pleaded again, but his eyes remained fixed. She put the glass shard to his throat. One push and it would sever his jugular, and it would be over, she would survive. But as she summoned the strength, she couldn't do it. She wouldn't kill her own son. Not her Danny. The fear and terror that had been with her since the attack had started washed away, and it was replaced by a calm and a clarity that she'd only ever felt once before — When he was born. She dropped the glass and looked at him in the eyes "I love you, son." She said peacefully. And then she relaxed her right arm. The knife penetrated her skin and entered her heart, stopping it instantly.

As her vision became black, the monster that was sat astride her faded, and was replaced by Danny, lovingly smiling at her. The dull white ceiling was replaced by the deepest blue sky, and the dark recreation room by the lush green fields near their home, where they would often play and picnic. Lynne felt no more pain and no fear. Then everything became black, and Lynne's body became limp.

The last bullet left Jeff's gun as the two hybrids moved away from the truck and toward him. As they did the tanker exploded, engulfing the cab and two of the advancing hybrids in a ball of fire. Jeff was lifted off his feet and flung against the BMW convertible. The force of his landing on it crushed the flimsy roof and his head hit the dashboard knocking him unconscious. When he woke, the sun was setting. He looked down at his watch. It read, 6:25 p.m. In front of him, the

fire still burned, and he could see the charred bodies of the hybrids that had taken the full blast. Lifting himself, he climbed off the wrecked roof, and pulled it back and off the car, leaving it discarded on the highway.
"Thank Christ!" He said as he noticed the keys in the ignition. "Let's hope it works," He pushed the start button, and the engine fired. This car was not ideal, it was a two-seater sports car and now it had no roof. Compared to the Range Rover it was fragile, and that had been destroyed by just one of them. If he was to come across another pack it would offer him no protection. But right now, he didn't care. What it did have was speed. Jeff stepped on the accelerator, and the BMW sped away, and toward Washington.

After a short rest, Terry regained some strength from his fight with the female and he tried to heave the heavy carcass off him.
But it was heavy, and his left hand was doubled under him. He hadn't had the time needed to react before it had fallen lifeless on top of him. He twisted his legs and pushed as hard as he could with his free hand. Slowly, the body began to move. Inch by inch. Out of breath he stopped and relaxed. "Good God, you were one big bitch." He said to it. He strained again, and again it moved slowly. As it did Terry heard a noise, he stopped and listened, trying to quiet his breathing. There it was again, and he

recognized what it was. It was footsteps, and that meant only one thing. The male was coming back. It had taken everything out of him to defend himself against the female, and she was much smaller. He knew if he didn't get from under her and through the door into the administration block, he would stand no chance against the male. He pushed again, straining, his face turned red, but he couldn't get the angle he needed to move it enough to wriggle free. He gasped and tried again, thrusting, and twisting as the footsteps became louder and louder, and then they stopped. And Terry realized why. He looked from behind the shoulder of the dead female and there stood the male. It was looking at the body that Terry lay under. He could see the anger building in its eyes, and across its face. A surge of pure dread shot through Terry's body. He needed to get out now. Terry pushed again but it was no good, the body was just too heavy. The male walked along the length of its fallen mate and stopped opposite Terry's head. It looked down on him with contempt, and Terry knew this is where he would die, and there was nothing more he could do.

His head relaxed back to the cold concrete floor and he sighed closing his eyes. The male lifted its heavy leg and hovered its foot over Terry's head. With all of its might, it slammed it down. As it picked up the female's body and carried it back from where it had come from,

Terry's feet twitched as his nerves fired their last signals to his muscles.

Joceline had watched with horror, as Terry's head was flattened, and she'd seen the spray of red that had covered the door. Terry had tried so desperately to get free. But there was nothing she could have done to save him. If she hadn't got back into the accommodation block, if she'd gone to help him, they would both be dead. Shaking, she switched off the monitor. Her thoughts turned to Lynne and Danny. She needed to see if they were okay. The image of Terry played over in her mind as she walked along the corridor to the recreation room. Joceline had seen some of the worst things nature can do to the human body, and what humans can do to each other, but it had always been the aftermath, it had always been after the event, never unfolding in front of her.

Even when Brad had escaped and rampaged through the facility, she'd arrived long after it had happened. She reached the door she'd closed earlier. Opening it, she stepped inside. Lynne's body was lying where Danny had killed her, and the knife still stuck out from her chest. She knew who had done this. It had been a mistake to leave Danny for this long, but Lynne had pleaded with her for just one more day to be with her son. Perhaps if the power hadn't gone out, it wouldn't have happened, and she would have walked in to see Lynne drinking a coffee, and Danny sat in front of the game's console. Perhaps if she'd stuck to her rules and insisted that Danny had been sedated, Lynne would be alive. But it didn't matter, all that mattered was that she didn't, and the power had cut out, and as a result, Lynne lay in front of her, dead. Joceline crouched down next to her and softly closed her eyes, perhaps death is the best way out. Like Terry, Lynne won't have to go through the transformation. Perhaps it is better this way around, that Lynne hadn't killed Danny in a primeval rage.

Danny? Joceline stood, how could she have ignored that fact? The door was closed. It meant Danny had to be in the room with her. Carefully, she stepped over Lynne and made her way to the back of the room. As she did, she heard a sound behind her, she spun around, it was Danny. He was standing over Lynne's body and he'd pulled the knife out of her chest. And now it was pointing at her. Joceline reached around and found the coffee jug. She grasped the plastic handle and moved it slowly from the hot plate. Danny screamed and charged, but this time he wasn't as fast. Joceline brought the hot jug around and smashed it on the side of his head. The glass smashed, and cut into the soft skin of his scalp, and hot coffee covered his face. Cut and scolded, Danny was knocked against the wall, dropping the knife as he cradled his burns.

Joceline let go of the smashed pot and bent down picking up the knife. As she did Danny turned to face her. He reached for her throat and Joceline brought the knife up hard and fast. Danny's expression changed from anger to surprise, and his arms dropped by his side. Joceline let go of the knife and his lifeless body fell, landing next to Lynne. Joceline collapsed down to the floor. She couldn't handle anymore, she was exhausted, and within seconds she passed out.

She woke sometime later and stood in an almost dream-like state. Calmly and slowly Joceline left the room, closing the door behind her and making her way to her own quarters, where she showered and changed. She felt immune to what she'd witnessed that day. The deaths of three people in the worst ways imaginable, and one by her own hands. It was clear what she had to do now. And once she was dressed, she would waste no more time trying to hide, to protect herself, only to wait for the symptoms to begin. After all, what was the point? Her mind is what she is. Her brilliance in her field had made her who she was. It defined her friends, social standing, and her very life. If that were to go what would she be? And in a world, which had no use for such a mind what was she now?

Joceline put on her smartest business suit, the one she kept for White House meetings and other grand occasions when only the best would do, and then she sat at her terminal and logged in. She clicked on the icon that would take her into the building's security systems. Without hesitation, she stood down the emergency protocol Terry had initiated when the two hybrids had broken out of the lab. Around the building, doors began to open, and the large steel shutters that had kept the underground garage sealed tightly shut lifted.

She left her quarters and walked along the corridor listening to her favorite music. She felt no fear of what was to come, and no thoughts of regret as she turned the corner and came face to face with the male hybrid.

As Jeff approached the building, he could tell something was not right. This was supposed to be a highly secure facility. The barriers that protected the entrance should not be raised, and the garage shutters should have been down. He pulled the BMW into the garage and switched it off. The garage was empty apart from a few cars. It should have been almost full. *What the hell has gone on here?* he thought to himself as he slowly walked across to the steel-reinforced door that would take him from the garage and into the facility. On the keypad, the green entry light was flashing. It should be red. It should have been locked. Carefully, he pulled the door, and it opened.

He climbed the stairs to the first level and entered the facility. It was deserted, but undamaged. There had been no explosions or fire, and he could see no signs of panic. The rooms looked as if they'd been left calmly. It was as if everyone had gone home at the end of their working day, and not returned. On the wall were two signs. One read *Administration Block,* in green on a white background, and the other read *Accommodation Block and Laboratories* in white on a red arrow-shaped sign that pointed to the left.

He moved forward and came across a large glass wall. Inside he could see medical trolleys. On them, he could see bodies covered by blankets, and all the monitors that were attached to them were without power. He turned and followed the corridor until he reached what should have been a secured door, but like the garage it was open. But more than that, the glass had been smashed outward. He reached forward and pushed. The door opened, and Jeff stopped in his tracks.

On the floor, he saw a body. It was a human male, and his head had been squashed. There was no face to recognize, there was nothing remaining from the shoulders up. Whatever force had been brought to bear had been immense. Along the floor and up the walls and door were the spread pattern of brain matter, bone fragments, and tissue that would normally be seen after a point-blank shooting from a high-powered gun. He moved slowly and quietly past the body, following the arrow which pointed to the accommodation block, where he was convinced Lynne and Danny would be. He passed a small office, and he noticed on the screen it displayed two live camera feeds. One showed the dead man, and the other was the back of himself. He pushed the door open, but it was empty. He continued and rounded another corner. There was another door and again the keypad was lit green. Above it was a sign which read *Accommodation Block*. Jeff's blood ran cold. This was not a good sign. He pushed the door open and found another body. It was female, and this time he recognized her. It was Joceline Mercier, and Jeff now knew that this facility had been compromised. He looked at her body. The brutality that had happened to the man had not been brought on her. Her body was where it had dropped after her neck had been snapped. Her lifeless eyes stared up at the ceiling. He moved onward and came across a room with a closed door. Above it, the sign read *"Recreation Room"*.

Jeff turned the handle slowly and entered. He stood motionless, his mind scrambling. He had risked all believing that this facility was to be a safe haven for his family – Somewhere to ride out the coming storm, and perhaps one day return home. But as he looked down on his slain family, he felt an emptiness and darkness he would not have believed possible.

The world had ended around him and now the two people that drove him, and that gave him the energy to continue when he was void of all feeling were dead. He lowered himself down and sat between them, cradling them in his arms while he sobbed uncontrollably. He didn't care who or what may be in the facility now. He didn't care that he could be killed at any moment, he would welcome it, he wouldn't fight it – More than that he was praying for it. But the facility was silent except for his weeping. He could see how Danny had transformed. How this disease, this virus, that he still thought it was, had made his beautiful son into a monster – A thing of every child's nightmares. When Danny had been afraid of the dark, Jeff had told him there were no monsters. Nothing was hiding in the shadows or under the bed. But he'd been wrong. There are monsters, and his son had become one. But as much as Danny had changed, he was still his son. With nothing now but a vacuum inside of him where once hope and love had been, a thought came across his mind. A moment of clarity in the fog that had swirled around his thoughts. He had to know how his wife and child had died, and whether it was quick. He would check the security recordings, and only then would he be able to lay it to rest. He couldn't spend what was left of his life wondering how it happened, and if they had felt any pain. He took off his jacket, and resting Lynne and Danny together, as they'd slept so many times before, he laid it over them and left the room. Farther along the corridor he came to a small office. He entered and sat at the terminal and tapped the space bar. The screen came to life and Jeff pointed the cursor at the *backup* icon and clicked on it. The first video he came across was a recording by Joceline Mercier titled: *Devolution of a Species.* He clicked on it and sat back in the chair. Joceline's image appeared, and after a few seconds of buffering the video began to play.

"Hello, I am Doctor Joceline Mercier, and for the last ten months, we've been tracking what can only be described as the devolution of the Homo Sapiens species. At first, we thought this may be viral, or even a pathogen, carried on the gulf streams, and air currents. We believed this because the outbreaks didn't seem to correspond with human movement, and migration, as would be typical for this type of outbreak. Rather, it was random, it had no genetic type or racial definition, and nor was it age-related or dependent on the individual's health. Whilst the brightest scientists around the world struggled with the idea of a virus, or parasite, I alone explored other theories, and I found what it is. But while presenting my findings, our civilization ended. In other words, we were too late. If you're watching this, then please understand that we did all we could.

But sometimes we are just not supposed to win or continue. The truth is this. This was not a pathogen, virus, or parasite from outer space or something that had lain dormant for an eon. This was nature taking back from us what Mother Nature herself had given us. I discovered that we had a reset button built into our genetic code and using our own pollution against us, nature switched it on. This devolution of our species is our fault, we brought it on ourselves. But more than that, I now believe this is not the first time this has happened. I believe mankind, as we are today, has been around before. And like this time, we were sent back to begin again. I now believe that the mysterious sightings of objects on distant planets, and those in our solar system are relics from mankind's previous state of being. And that the bone fragments that have been locked away by mainstream science are proof that Homo Sapiens have walked the earth before. But it is too late to keep researching this theory. The facility has been breached, and everyone other than myself is dead, and soon I too will de-evolve. But I can't allow that to happen. Once this recording is complete and up-loaded onto whatever is still transmitting, I will face what I would become, and I will die as a human."

The video froze on Joceline as she leaned in to press the stop button at the end of the recording. For Jeff now it all became clear, he understood, and it made sense. Everyone was infected, that's what Lynne had been shouting at him just before he'd fled Balmoral Castle. Now it was clear to him that he wouldn't survive either. There was only one choice — to turn or to die. Before he made his choice, he needed closure on the events that led to the death of his family. He found the security footage for the recreation room and pressed play. As the events unfolded, he watched as Lynne gave her life so that their son would live. Even though he would no longer be human. The emptiness returned. As he watched her arms fall to her side, he paused the video and looked at the wall clock. The time of her death. It read 5:48 p.m. It was at the exact moment he was trapped in the cab of the truck. If the truck hadn't been there, if he'd not had to stop then maybe, just maybe, he could have been here to stop Danny from attacking Lynne. He closed the video window and stood. A clear calm had now come over him again, and with the information, he now had from Joceline, what he needed to do couldn't be any clearer.

He walked slowly along the corridor and entered what used to be the main reception area. In front of him were the large glass doors that once welcomed visitors to the facility. "Bye darling, bye son." He whispered before pushing through the doors and stepping outside.

The sun was low in the sky and he could feel its warmth on his face. He looked around him. The city was quiet. Even the howls and cries of the marauding hybrids had ceased as they began to bed down for the coming night. It was more than quiet, it was silent.

Jeff was alone in a world without his family, and in a world no longer ruled by man.

Epilogue

"And God blessed them, and God said unto them, be fruitful, and multiply, and replenish the earth, and subdue it: and have dominion over the fish of the sea, and over the fowl of the air, and over every living thing that moveth upon the earth."

Around the world, civilization was falling. Communications had gone down and as the last of the power stations fell silent. The Earth from space became as dark as it had once been. Nature had indeed begun to take back its planet from the parasite that had threatened its very survival — Humankind. In the depths of space, on comets, and on distant planets, our greatest technological achievements went about their business in blissful ignorance. The information they were sending back home was now irrelevant. Robots roamed the surface of Mars. Carrying out pre-determined experiments — set by a species, and for a species. that no longer existed. In the great scheme of the universe mankind's reign had been but a blink of the eye, and yet we had created language, art, and music. We had conquered space and climbed the highest mountains of earth and searched the deepest oceans.

Voyager one and Two had passed out of our solar system and would forever carry mankind's image and humanity into the deepest reaches of space. We had learned how we worked. We could repair ourselves, and we could replace our broken and failing body parts. More than any other species, we loved and formed bonds that lasted a lifetime and surrounded ourselves with family and friends. We learned to fly higher than any bird, and we crossed oceans. We've built tunnels that connected continents, and bridges that span the deepest valleys. We lived amongst the clouds in buildings, and we've burrowed deep into the ground. We survived nature's cruelest illnesses and learned the secret of the atom. Above any other species that had come before us, we had conquered our world, and we were on the precipice of conquering others. But for all we had achieved, for all of our great accomplishments, we could not leave behind our true nature. What it really means to be human.

The things we had above all the other species on this planet, was our capacity for violence and cruelty and hatred. Not just for the animals we shared it with, but for each other. And for what? A piece of land, or a God we could never know for certain in our lifetimes existed. Oil or gas, which was never ours, to begin with, and were the remains of the ancient forests that had helped give this planet the rich oxygen we needed. We raped the oceans and took what we wanted. Not what we needed.

Driven by greed, we exterminated countless species of animals and plants. Some we eradicated before we had even known they had shared our world. We polluted, and we hunted for fun, and in the name of sport. Like a petulant child, we thought, we believed, this wonderfully rich world was ours to do with as we wanted. It is the ignorance and arrogance of man that calls all other creatures animals.

Perhaps it was all of these things or more that nature, the planet Earth, took back the gift it had given us. It wasn't a God that gave man dominion over the animals, it was nature that gave us the intelligence to ensure nature's own survival. But we misused it, and we didn't respect what we had. And because of that, it took back from us the greatest gift any species could ever have been given. Everything that signified modern life had ground to a halt. And over the decades that would follow, our entire existence would be wiped from the planet. Museums and cathedrals would crumble as the forests moved back in to reclaim the land that once was their own. Skyscrapers would fall. The banks that held our gold and money, that defined our wealth and self-worth, would become nothing more than crumbling relics of a time of gluttony and injustice toward those less fortunate.

With the ease you might wipe a fly from your arm, nature had wiped its most violent and destructive species from itself. For all of the intelligence we had been given, we only sought to advance our own personal agendas. No other species became as good as killing itself for such insignificant reasons as mankind. Animals fight and die for food or resources, or to sustain their lineage. We killed each other for a cell phone, some loose change, and because of the way we looked, the color of our skin, or how we spoke. Perhaps Joceline had been correct? There is overwhelming evidence of the existence of the Nephilim and their Bible. Archaeologists now believe that they may have found the lost city of giants in Ecuador's Amazonian Jungle. There they have found large boulders that formed a massive pyramid with a sacrificial stone atop it, too large for any human. They have found tools that would have been too big for humans to fashion and use. And of course, there are the skeletons, which are simply too big, and too numerous to just be oversized humans. Could it be that Biblical Nephilim taught humans our technology?

In the twentieth century, a cassette audio tape that had been fossilized was found with Aluminum spheres and other technological items. Such things are out of time, and beyond the abilities of our early ancestors. Many believe that it could be proof of time travel.

Others would argue that if time travel were possible in the future, we would come back and visit ourselves in this present.

Whatever the reason for these finds we will now never know. Nature had called time on our reign as the planet's top species. And if this is just a loop, that plays endlessly, have you existed previously? Lived the exact same life you live now? Could it explain why people believe they have lived more than one life? Are they remembering their own, or an earlier time of existence? Could it be that you are destined to meet the same people each time? To fall in love with the same person each time and suffer the same heartache each time? Perhaps that would explain soul mates, and why we feel we have lived this already. If this is to be the case, how can you or anyone break the cycle? And if you can't, is it possible to remember, or know how and when you will die? It could just be that nature only gives us enough to reach this stage and go no further. We may never know if we are the pinnacle of evolution as Darwin envisaged or the creation of some God that has abandoned us. Perhaps God didn't create man, but rather man created God. We may, as many believe, be the experiment of a vast alien race. Whatever the reason we are here, and what or who put us here. One thing is clear.

Not in the history of this planet has any species other than mankind been bestowed by nature the gifts to create an Eden for all. And none have failed so badly, and none have fallen so far.

Claire Banks @claire_banks87 -sent automatically from *tweetout* -1min
If this automated tweet goes out, I'm dead & humanity has fallen. Perhaps, after everything we've done, that isn't such a bad thing?

The End…

www.martynellington.com
Twitter: @MartynEllington

Thank you for reading this story. I wrote this as a comment on how we treat this wonderful planet we call ours. Even though it isn't, and never was. It belongs and belonged to all the life which thrives upon it now, in the past — and if there is one, the future. However, if we don't change what we do — and what we are — we are putting that future in grave danger for all species.

Regards,

Martyn.

Other titles:
The End of Everything
Thirstonfield Halt
Thirstonfield Halt Book Two. The Bradbury Farm
Tomorrow's Flight (2021)
The Harvesting (Coming 2024)

2020 Vision.

by

M.E. Ellington.

"What are the things you've seen last year?" She asked me, a week or so ago. I contemplated this question for a moment. I remember in February watching the news channels as the world began to change. This was different, I remember thinking to myself. It's different from the epidemics and pandemics which have come before. I recall that around the same time my youngest daughter called me from the university she was attending — for the record, it's around an hour away. "What should I do, people are getting worried?" A call no parent wants to take. "Don't worry," I replied, trying to reassure her. "We've been through all of this before; SARS, Swine-flu, Bird-Flu," I reeled them off, convincing myself as much as her. "Okay," she said. "I'll stay."

A week later, Italy and France began to shut down. Then the first cases in England began. She called me again. "Dad, there are cases here, close to the University." This time I didn't hesitate, "Come home! Grab what you can carry and catch a train, we'll go back for the rest when we can." She hesitated. "Okay, I'll let you know which train I can get."

I remember picking her up from the station on a rainy March night, relieved she'd made it out. A week later the university closed. Her halls of residence locked down along with her remaining personal possessions — it would be four months before we could go through to collect them. The foreign students and those who couldn't go home were locked down in their individual rooms. Campus security ensured no one left or entered, while their food was delivered by the local supermarkets.

My son, and the oldest child, lives on his own across town. He called me, "We're being told to work from home, there's been an outbreak in our office." From that moment we spent what time we could on the phone and Skype. I was determined he wouldn't become lonely and isolated. Yet still, I didn't see my son for three months.

It was now mid-March. I was sharing an office with my middle child who's also my oldest daughter. She has her own company. I'd agreed to share office space with her to help her get up and running, and because I wanted to work away from home. The symptoms first hit me mid-morning. They came on suddenly, it was like being hit with every flu and cold I'd ever had at once. I told her we should leave and let the building manager know. We piled what she would need to work from home in her car, locked the office, and left everything else.

I remember thinking, *at least I have my laptop.* My daughter had to drive; it had come on me so quickly that I simply was unable to. She headed for the hospital while I called the COVID-19 hotline number. They asked me a few questions, which I answered. Their advice was short. "Stay at home, don't come to the hospital, isolate, stay in bed, and rest. Drink fluids and if you begin to struggle to breathe at rest call us back." That was it, that was all they could offer. I did as I was told. Yet, I was frightened. I was used to being able to turn to our wonderful NHS at any time and always being able to see a doctor. Now I was being told, don't come, there's nothing we can do.

We got home and I made my way to bed. By the time I washed, changed, and climbed in I was gasping for breath. I could only breathe normally whilst remaining still in bed. I couldn't talk because I would become breathless before I finished a sentence. Making it to my bathroom was like running a quarter-mile flat out and I would cough so hard my vision would begin to fade. I was incapacitated in bed for nearly two weeks. It took another five to recover.

In late October, the symptoms came back. This time I was hospitalized. They ran tests, took x-rays and scans, confirmed it was COVID, and sent me home. As I write this it's early December and the fatigue and breathlessness are still with me.

They've told me, it may never fully go away.

So, what have I seen in 2020? I saw our government, and all governments struggle to contain a new pandemic in the age of easy in-and-out international flights, cross-border agreements, and open access. I saw Italy being left to manage the crisis on its own with little help or cooperation from other EU member states. I watched with horror as doctors from Spain took to social media breaking their hearts at the decisions they were being forced to make. I saw certain EU member states hoarding their stores of PPE as hospitals became overrun. *So much for collaboration*, I thought as I watched the images on the news channels.

In the early days, I saw the people of Britain come together and stand on their doorsteps every Thursday at 8 pm to clap for the NHS and other key workers. I saw people queuing patiently outside of supermarkets as the new normal became daily life. I saw empty shelves where once toilet paper, flour, soap, and pasta had once been plentiful as the new reality began to take shape. In the skies above my home, I saw no aircraft for four months and I saw the roads become quiet save for the multiple daily wails of the ambulances.

As the weeks passed, what I saw began to change. No longer did people clap at 8 pm on a Thursday, no longer were we together. I saw society begin to fracture and polarize. I saw people blaming 5G towers for spreading the virus and some were burned down, ironically destroying the masts people would need to call for help. I saw people spreading conspiracy theories, claiming the world governments had collaborated with this hoax virus to take more control and depopulate the planet. I saw people being too selfish to obey and comply with the guidance, refusing to wear masks, socially distance, and stay home. I saw the roads become busy again as the populace became blasé to the new world in which we lived. I saw posts on social media calling for older people to have to remain home allowing younger people to continue to live their lives.

It dawned on me that should a catastrophe happen worse than this, something utterly cataclysmic, society wouldn't survive, and I remember thinking, *what have we become?*
More personally, I saw my son struggle with his isolation despite my best efforts whilst my youngest daughter would against all odds, pass her second year, and progress into her final year.

I saw my friend; someone I'd known since we were 14 years old die of cancer. I attended a small service, only a few were allowed including the guard from the Royal Navy in which he'd served. I wasn't allowed to say goodbye as he died alone in the hospital while the selfish partied, still refusing to comply for the common good. I saw myself only leaving my home twice a week for food and medicines, and to shop for my elderly parents, both of whom are in their late seventies. (My father is a twice-surviving cancer patient.) I spoke to them through their kitchen window while I dropped off the shopping by their door. Each time I did it was lovely to see them, and also heartbreaking that this was the only way I could see them. It seemed to me now that this is how we live and will for a long time to come.

Finally, I've seen this year pass by quicker than any other, and yet at the same time, it's been the longest year of my life.

She thought for a while and then asked, "What haven't you seen this year?"

"That's easy," I replied. "Friends, family, and loved ones."